The Bones
of Garbo

The Bones of Garbo

A Collection of Short Stories by

TRUDY LEWIS

The Ohio State University Press
Columbus

Library of Congress Cataloging-in-Publication Data

Lewis, Trudy (Trudy L.)
The bones of Garbo, and other stories / Trudy Lewis
p. cm.
ISBN 0-8142-0930-0 (alk. paper) — ISBN 0-8142-5109-9 (pbk. : alk.
paper) — ISBN 0-8142-9007-8 (CD ROM)
1. United States—Social life and customs—Fiction. I. Title.
PS3562.E978 B66 2003
813'.54—dc21

2002154509

Cover design by Janna Thompson Chordas
Printed by Thomson-Shore, Inc.

The paper used in this publication meets the minimum requirements of the
American National Standard for Information Sciences—Permanance of Paper for
Printed Library Materials. Ansi Z39.48–1992.

9 8 7 6 5 4 3 2 1

Dedicated, with love and gratitude, to my grandmothers,
whose labor lives on in each generation:

THELMA BERTHA BATTLES, 1919–1999

OLLIE FLORENE LEWIS, 1918–1995

contents

preface

would like to thank the University of Missouri-Columbia for a good work environment, a flexible schedule, and two generous research grants. I thank the editors of all the literary magazines who have published my fiction, in particular: Hilda Raz at *Prairie Schooner* for choosing "Geographic Tongue" as the recipient of the Lawrence Foundation Award, C. Michael Curtis at *The Atlantic Monthly* for providing a thoroughly professional experience of the editing process, and Stephen Donadio at *The New England Review* for continuing to take a chance on my more experimental work. I thank my mother, Linda Lewis, for her unwavering encouragement and support, my father Frank Lewis for his unconditional love. My sister Terry Hall has been a constant source of inspiration. A number of colleagues have contributed to the thought process behind these stories: Ethan Bumas, Magdalena Garcia-Pinto, Kitty Holland, Elaine Lawless, Deborah Montuori, Mary Jo Neitz, Pat Okker, Karen Piper, Michael Pritchett, Trish Roberts, Gladys Swan, Marly Swick, and Nancy West. I also thank Amy Langen for being a good neighbor and Colleen Page for being a faithful correspondent and a longtime friend. I thank Toni Hoberecht, my first writing partner, for reappearing on my horizon. I thank Tina Hall for her intellectual engagement and unerring aesthetic instincts. But my greatest debt is to my husband and sometime collaborator, Mike Barrett, who has lived through the fire and ice of creation with me. And of course, I thank my sons, Eddie and Jude Barrett, for arriving to intensify my writing and my life.

acknowledgments

*T*he stories in this collection were originally published in the following journals: "A Diller, a Daughter" in *The Atlantic Monthly;* "Waiting Period" in *American Short Fiction;* "The Marijuana Tree" and "Geographic Tongue" in *Prairie Schooner;* "The Bones of Garbo" and "All Hallows' Leaves" in *New England Review;* "Astigmatic" in *PrivateArts;* "Goddess Love" in *Five Points;* "Galpal's Crib-notes to Pregnancy" in *Witness*; and "Evauation Route" in *Santa Monica Review.*

Waiting Period

t was one of those neighborhoods, in one of those times, when everyone is waiting for something. Some waited for government checks, some waited for wayward sweethearts, some waited for fame in one of its harlequin guises to give in and ask them to dance. Some waited by necessity and others waited by nature. There were people on the far end of the street who waited for the apocalypse; nearer to Main, they were just anticipating the depletion of the ozone, revolution, or population explosion, whichever came first. They waited for social change; in gardens planted in rubber tires and on wooden porches with open beers, in the street next to an idling pickup, around a picnic table passing a joint, under the bellies of their own ailing transportation, in a mixed game of horse or chance meeting of dogs. They waited for cures to diseases: in anxious pairs on the bumpers of cars, bare legs sticking to metal, in the back yard with a confused neighbor lady, in the bathroom with a sick child. They waited for the mail, which didn't come until nearly 3:30 in this part of town. They waited for free copies of the paper, to be delivered after the paying customers were served. They waited for the taxi and the bus. They waited for the new millennium with varying degrees of patience and frustration.

Meanwhile, the orange and blue moving vans appeared every summer in flocks. New crews of children patrolled the street with their bikes and balls and skateboards. The cars, usually of a dented and rusted vintage, with many bumper stickers but few vanity plates, assumed their places along the curb. The bushes filled in with trumpet creepers and wild potato vines.

The grass grew tall and thick, Queen Anne's lace, day lilies, and purple bull thistles cropping up where no one had requested them. And when the clay-colored street flooded every spring, since there was no drainage system to speak of, then the neighbors came out on their porches, one with a pillow, one with a series of colored candles purchased from an import store, one with a new lover whose body pressed up against a column and shape-shifted in the occasional lightening flash, one with a dirty book and a bottle of sweet wine, to wait out the storm.

And it was in this neighborhood and in this time, that Tom and Yvette served their own waiting period.

Yvette noticed the wreath first, lying on the sidewalk next to the house on the corner. It was about nine by eleven, heart shaped, and covered in red roses the size of brussels sprouts, with a purple band like a Miss American sash twisted underneath it so the writing was illegible. At the time, she thought it had been left out for the garbage men. But day after day, no one came to collect it, the petals began loosening and scattering over the neighborhood, along with the potato chip bags and fast food wrappers that landed like manna in the grass overnight. She walked out the back door in her nightgown and picked one up. It was smooth to the touch, smoother than the skin inside her own thighs that Tom had declared his favorite part of her body. And this too had started to make her nervous.

When Tom jogged past the wreath every day on his way to the bike trail, he'd tap a foot in the center, pretending it was one of the stations of his imaginary obstacle course. In fact, by the Tuesday it was part of his routine, by Wednesday he believed he'd suffer bad luck if he skipped this step in his ritual, and by Thursday he was going to the public library and checking back issues of the paper for suspicious entries on the obituary page.

"What makes you think someone died? It's roses, it's hearts, I'm thinking anniversaries and prom nights," Yvette said.

"Trust me, something irregular is going on over there."

The house belonged to a single black man in his early thirties. Yvette didn't know his name, but she recognized him from his front porch, where he was usually sitting in his bare feet, talking on a cell phone. His house was one of the biggest on the block, and the yard was one of the better kept—landscaped with railroad ties and planted with blazing star and evening primrose. He had a certain pride of place, threw parties on a regular basis and stood outside shaking his barbecue fork to 80's house music, washed his Jeep Cherokee in the driveway with a professional-looking chamois, wore striped shirts open over his tight and strangely appealing pot belly, entertained a number of women who wore slim slacks and gorgeous rayon dresses.

Tom said he hadn't seen him around lately. There was an empty dog dish on the front porch. He didn't have a dog, did he? There was a strange Buick in the driveway. There was a chesty lady in the back yard. Surely, the guy was too young to up and actually die?

"You're so morbid," she said, "Why do you always assume the worst?"

"I'll let you know after D-day."

That was Yvette's cue to go ahead and make the appointment, as they had discussed. She called it in exactly two years after they had moved in together, in fact. Two years, twenty-four months, seven hundred and thirty days, one cat, a sofa, a porch swing, and an automobile, probably two hundred fifty acts of copulation. They'd been talking about it for at least that long. But they could never decide how to arrange it. Would they make separate appointments, and spring the news on one another later on? Plan a big party and go in the next day with twin hangovers to pass the bottled water back and forth in the waiting room? There was just no established etiquette for the situation. Not to mention what they'd do once they actually found out. Yvette tried to make her long, twisting voice sound short and brisk. The woman on the phone assured her that the process was quick, safe, and completely anonymous.

But at the City Health Department, there were AIDS awareness posters with cartoon characters and smug messages all over the walls. Sure, there were some families with little kids who were obviously here for vaccinations. A Chinese couple bending over a five-year-old girl in a shrunken, striped cardigan and red pants so long they nearly hid her feet. An Indian family with a skinny wife, a bald husband, four big-eyed toddlers with their cunning shoes dangling in a row over the floor.

Beside Yvette, Tom filled out his form without comment and slid the clipboard down in between his metal folding chair and hers. Touching her knee on his way up, he felt it jump under the wasted-away cotton of her skirt and wondered how such a high-strung person would handle the real emergency, once it hit.

In the single-sex bathroom, he closed the door and looked in the mirror. Green splotches had appeared under his eyes, just like in that fucking commercial. He splashed some water on his face and wetted his comb. A horrible smell was coming off him too, like rotting cantaloupe. His gut was a rotten melon, cracked along a fetid seam. He washed his hands again, lifted his shirt and soaped his underarms. Then he looked behind him into the stall and saw what was really the matter. The toilet bowl was filled with a momentous turd, so long it circled the basin. He visualized the wreath on the sidewalk, the empty dog dish on the porch. His stomach lurched forward and jammed into his ribs. It would be funny, even, if it wasn't so gross. Then he wondered how it would be if he actually had it—would people think: "Poor Tom. He's losing weight, he can't keep his food up or down, his skin is covered in lesions like vampire hickeys. It would be gross, wouldn't it, if it wasn't so sad?"

Of course, the toilet wouldn't flush. He should've guessed by the way the water had turned brown around the edges of the vision. He turned and quickly left the bathroom, the soap already drying and caking under his arms.

"Seven days' waiting period," Yvette observed in the car on the way home. "Do you think you can make it all the way to Friday?"

"Let's make an agreement not to obsess about this, deal?" he said, wedging his hand under her leg. "So what did you put for question #9?"

That night, he came in and found her lying on the sofa in a greeny-blue caftan picking ticks off the cat. She looked up and flicked a tick at him. "I found out about that guy you're so worried over."

"Who?"

"The dead guy. His name is Lloyd."

"Who told you that?"

"I was out looking for Felicia and I saw the boomer next door, you know, single father, Oregon license plates, bicycle rack on the back of his car?"

Tom drew closer and stroked Felicia's orange tiger fur. "I know him," he said. "Tennis fan, right?"

"Well, this one says he's actually seen Lloyd. He says the wreath is from an old girlfriend, announcing the birth of Lloyd's child. Of course, Lloyd doesn't believe he's the father, so he's just signifying for the girlfriend's benefit."

"I heard that guy's wife left him for some lesbian sex ring that's run out of the Four-o'Clock Diner. He's hardly a reliable witness."

"What are you saying, you're standing up for Lloyd? Or just holding out for a real murder mystery?"

"I believe you're beginning to have a thing for Lloyd," he said, scratching another tick off Felicia's ear. He held it up and observed its tiny legs wriggling in the subdued light from the thrift store lamp Yvette had draped in a printed silk scarf, so that their living room was shadowed with the splotches of an outdated paisley. When he sliced his nail firmly into the tiny round body, it left a dull red smear on his thumb. "You've got to be careful about that."

On Saturday, Yvette made daiquiris in the blender and Tom fired up the barbecue grill. They stood at the table arranging chunks of green and yellow squash, red and green pepper, on shish kebab spears. In between, they'd stop for a modest bit of chicken marinating in cheap sherry in a leftover potato salad tub. It was fluorescent and gelid with fat, clammy to the touch, and Tom felt a grim satisfaction when he skewered each bite onto its appointed metal prong. He thought of all the women he'd gone through, how he'd felt himself moving through the initial friction and on to better things. And now it occurred to him for the first time that something in them could be getting to him. Not to mention Yvette and her own slimy past.

Yvette touched his arm, her hand slick with chicken grease. "Good news," she said. "Lloyd's back in action."

He looked up from his skewer, a chicken bit slipping out of his fingers.

"I talked to the neighbor lady down the street. You know, the one who works the late shift at the hospital."

That was the house where they had heard screams one night at 1:30. He and Yvette had been half dressed, arguing over whether the place was worth fixing while they repaired leaks in the bathroom, and he'd run out with a caulking brush in his hand. There was a man bleeding in her drive-way, a crowd of onlookers huddled around him in a circle. The man was rolling, egglike, on the gravel, cradling his head. Tom leveraged his way into the crowd, sent Yvette back to the house for a rag which turned to out to be a mangled gray pair of his old underwear. Only later, when he was standing on the porch, his ears ringing from the man's high, repeti-tive screams—Oh Jesus, oh mama, oh Jesus, oh lord—did he look at his bloody hand and think he should have protected himself.

"You remember Sharon," Yvette said. "Well, she told me that Lloyd's involved in some type of gang activity. No kidding, they keep a China-man in every precinct, it seems. Now Lloyd's on the phone all day, every day, with his operatives and finally he gets greedy and they tell him, watch out it's your funeral. They send over a wreath. Then Lloyd throws it out. But even the garbage men are in on the deal, they're afraid to pick it up, and so it sits there, moldering, terrorizing the whole community. Mean-while, Lloyd packs up and goes to Sun City. He sends his various ladies in to feed the dog. He sends a postcard to the mob boss and sits around the pool with a brandy snifter of Rémy Martin and his cell phone sit-ting on an inflatable raft in the off position."

"And you believe this?" he said.

"You're the one who wants a disaster," she said. "I'm only here to help you out."

It was true that Yvette had rescued him from one bad mistake after another. The fact checker at work, the divorced president of the neigh-borhood association, the bottle and the video games and the bong. Before, he'd had very little sense of time passing. But with Yvette, life assumed a kind of decadent domestic rhythm. Sundays, when the two of them walked out to the river or through the forest or the grasslands, made him particularly aware of this. Yvette picked a sprig of loosestrife. He leaned in and inspected a colony of mushrooms bubbling over the root of a tree.

He, on the other hand, had rescued Yvette from a lifetime of bore-dom with her long-term boyfriend, a pseudo-husband type who wore stiff, ironed jeans and pointed boots and liked to demonstrate Tae Kwan Do techniques at tense moments in dinner parties. When fixing meals or directing foreplay, Yvette often forgot which were his favorites and which were her ex's. He couldn't count the times he'd had to endure mustard in his potato salad or some highly unusual grace note in bed. It made him feel eerily gay, like he was sleeping with Tae Kwon Do by association.

Yvette pointed to a low field of rushes next to a sandbar. A group of birds had gathered there, some resting in the foreground, some fighting over a carcass. The wind rose and several of the birds—maybe turkey hawks—spread their wings and flew out over the road, over the phone lines, to the river beyond.

They'd been discussing the possibility of relocating.

"Well, we're going to have to move out sometime or other," he said. "As far as that's concerned."

Yvette kicked at a piece of driftwood with her mauve lace-up boot. "The only question is, will it be up and out or just on?"

While he was trying to think of an answer, she beat him to the car, and drove him back through the tall weeds and stunted trees, the cement subdivisions, the plush old town demi-mansions, into the dicier streets lined with crack houses and Quonset huts, past the public health clinic and on back home. There, they saw a couple from the two-story commune house walk by holding hands.

"We're aspecting Lloyd," the girl with the yeasty braids and the smiley face overalls said. "Do you want to join us?"

Tom rolled his eyes toward the truck garden with its psychedelic wheelbarrow, the front windows sprouting macramé God's eyes, the windowpanes shaking with drum vibrations, a homemade banner over the porch—"We support animal rights. Deal with it"—, and Yvette tried to cover, saying that they had some heavy processing to do.

In bed that night, Yvette explained that the members of the commune believed Lloyd had embarked on a spiritual journey. A victim of environmental disease, he had set off to find a more conducive spiritual home. And he'd sent himself a funeral wreath to mark his passage from one life into the next.

"Where do you get this stuff?" Tom said. "I never heard any of these bizarro stories before you moved in. I never even talked to any of the locals."

Meanwhile, the neighbors fought and fucked and drank and barbecued, celebrating high summer with metal anthems and spirituals, torch songs and reggae, Gregorian chant and rap. The temperature rose to nearly one hundred. The unemployed gathered in the streets over broken engines or came by to ask to mow the lawn. The employed took on double shifts. A hand-painted ice cream truck took to roving the neighborhood, "Marvin's Dairy," stenciled in sloppy black on a plain white ground. It didn't have the usual bright colors, fanciful posters, or the tinkling music box recording. Instead, the proprietor's wife sat on the passenger side and jangled a hand-held cow bell, calling out to the children: "Ice cream. Pure phat gladass ice cream. Go get your mom's lazy butt out of bed and tell her to give it up for the seventy-five cents." The drums grew louder in the commune house, often lasting until midnight. Yvette woke up at three A.M. to the sound of skateboards scrabbling over the rough pavement of the street. A cat called out like a baby. A baby called out like a cat. Little girls appeared peddling magazine subscriptions with bruised cheeks and big, burnished black eyes. Little boys, propped up on their bicycles, and steering without hands, rode in V-shaped formations after interesting strangers and stray dogs. The laundry snapped dry on the line. The sweat collected in a tree shape at the back of Tom's T-shirt. The air smelled of spice bushes and wild garlic, rotting fast food. And somewhere in the capitol city of their poor and isolated state, a lab technician juggled Yvette's blood sample and Tom's with those of hundreds of strangers, to arrive at their results.

Monday he met her on the street on his way home from work. She was poking down at the sidewalk. The wind blew her skirt against her legs, outlining their dancer's precision. Her fine, fair hair spread out in a fan, then fed down into a funnel. Felicia twisted around her feet.

"Can't you stay away from that thing?" he said, leaning over to unlock the passenger door.

"I'm checking for something."

On the sidewalk, the wreath had begun to molder. The bulb of each rose stood out separately, skinny in the neck, overblown in the head, the gray cardboard backing showing through between them like an unhealthy scalp. The petals were now more brown than red, a kind of umber, and a sweet and sour smell wafted off their matte surfaces.

"Today," she said. "I had an encounter with Mrs. Hecht."

"The old lady with the demon weedeater?"

Yvette nodded. "She needed someone to take her to the store. I guess that's what I get for trying to work at home. She said she needed more medicine, but it turned out to be plain old Metamucil and mineral water. You should have seen her wandering the aisles in her little flowered dress and her pocketbook out in front of her like an Uzi. It turns out, they don't carry the strawberry Metamucil anymore. So we had to settle for the cherry. But not, of course, without giving the manager the what for."

"I'll keep it in mind," Tom said.

"And guess what she told me."

"That she didn't approve of living in sin?"

"No, it seems our decadence has been eclipsed. Friend Lloyd's been stepping out on several ladies. And one of them is a particularly delicate type with a wasting-away disease. When she found a bottle of mousse in Lloyd's bathroom, she refused to believe it was his. And then, of course, maybe it was, maybe it wasn't, but we do know that Lloyd has multiple business partners."

"Hmm," Tom said. "We don't know that for sure."

Yvette raised her pale eyebrow. "So how many lovers do you think Lloyd has had?"

"In his lifetime, or just lately?"

"Let's take the past fifteen years. We can leave out the high school gropes and escapades."

"I'd say eight to ten, depending on your method of calculation. What's your guess?"

"I figure a guy like that had to do some browsing. I'd put it up to about eighteen.

"Not really," Tom said.

"Really. I don't think it's a very thorough life experience, do you, when you're dealing with a sample under a dozen?"

"So what ever happened with Lloyd's lady?"

"It was an ugly scene. She didn't have anyone to ask, she wasn't sure how much medication to take, so she was mixing, you know, very bad form. They found her in the bedroom in a skimpy nightgown with her lunch dribbling down the satin and a selection of assorted guts in her hand. The wreath was her suicide note, so to speak."

"So to speak," Tom said, reshuffling the available statistics.

He woke up the next day with a fever. His limbs floated in all directions like turkey hawks circling his body. Yvette touched his hot forehead, his sweating chest, that smelled of egg yolk and chives. She looked out the window onto the lawn that was now longer than the most negligent neighbor's and went to get a cold cloth for his head, but all she found was a fraying blue towel marked with a few grease stains. She wet the center and pressed it to his brow, letting the sides drape down on either side of his face. He looked regal, Arabic, laid out like that, and she remembered how she'd first loved him, his matte black hair with a pubic texture to it, big soulful eyelids in the shape of sea cowries, dark limbs vivid against the white sheets, where he'd collapsed after the tab of acid Tae Kwan Do had accidentally slipped into his hard cider. Proving that love, like disease, is based on a random series of chances. In fact, Tae Kwon Do had once set out to demonstrate this to her with a set of flow charts describing the sexual histories of their closest friends and the whole thing had dissolved into a major dispute, with Yvette moving out temporarily to sleep in the arms of an unrelated subset.

"Can I get you anything?" she asked Tom.

"Get me out of this place."

"I'm working on that," she said. "Shall I tell you about the last person to leave the area?"

"Let me guess."

"It was once upon a time in a side street of history when a young black man set out to make his fortune. I say he was young, which he was, in a relative way of speaking, because he'd kept himself free of any serious addictions or attachments. But the truth was, in chronological terms, Lloyd was nearing the midpoint of his existence."

"Does this get any better?" Tom said, "Because if it doesn't I'm going to go ahead and pass out for a while."

"Just hold on. This Lloyd had lived a full life. He'd had all the good times, bad music, recreational drugs and designer sex a man could desire. But there was still something missing."

"What?"

"Certainty," Yvette said. "The end of the story. That's something you never get until you die. So Lloyd went out in search of his death. He went from neighborhood to neighborhood and knocked on every door until he found the right temptation to do him in."

"And where'd you get this one?" Tom said.

Yvette rested her hand on his hot forehead. "From the postman, if it matters. He worked his way out to the burbs, and at the last house on the last block in the last slick subdivision of this benighted city, a beautiful woman answered the door. Her hair was braided with shells and precious stones. She had all the wealth of Africa in these heavy breasts jutting out like calabashes under an orange embroidered caftan. When she saw Lloyd, it was like she was waiting for him. She led him to a courtyard far too big for the house to contain. It was filled with orchids and coffee cans, rubber tires, rusted out car parts, parrots, pumpkins, fountains, and stray dogs. In the lushest part of the yard, a mattress was pushed into the foliage, covered in pillows and silks.

"'You can do me once and then it's over,' she said. 'We'll send a wreath to your family when we're done. Or did you change your mind?'

"'No, not yet honey. But how do I know you're worth it?'

"'Check out my references,' she said.

"And when he saw the skulls and bones embedded in the white shale of the courtyard walls, he stopped right there, his hand halfway up her caftan, and asked, 'What happens if I decide to settle for a little head instead?'"

But by this time, Tom was already asleep, his hand tucked inside the pillowcase, his cheeks flushed to an unearthly glow.

Wednesday, they just came home and hovered. Tom was too tired to go out to the coffee shop for his usual chess game; Yvette was too demoralized to go shopping or call a friend. They ate green grapes and tortilla chips in bed, with Felicia curled on top of Yvette's feet and an old folk rock documentary playing on the VCR. Tom let his fingers drift to the loose waistband of her sweatpants.

"Don't, just don't, I beg you, tell me what any of the neighbors say."

Yvette didn't even hint that the little boy who cruised the neighborhood on his beat-up Schwinn calling out code names and personal insults had dropped by to offer his dog poop conspiracy theory. She didn't indicate that she'd gone over to check out the situation, since she knew he'd been too sick to jog for two days, and found that the roses were rotting into an applesauce substance, with some kind of insect webs connecting the dissolving buds.

"What are we going to do?" she said.

Across the street from Lloyd's, a skinny white man in baggy clothes sat in front of the open door to a burnt-out house, the wood actually charred along the frame.

"Fuck ourselves into a better mood?" Tom said, but then got up and went to the kitchen, where he dropped something breakable and called out: "You do realize, don't you, that if this thing turns out badly I'm going to kill you before you start to experience any of the nastier symptoms."

In the middle of the night, Yvette felt her stomach roll over without her, and became convinced that she'd caught Tom's flu. The hot air was suffocating, she got up, drank a whole glass of water without stopping for a breath, and moved the fan so that its wind hit her more directly. When she woke up again, drugged, bedraggled, exhausted, at seven-thirty, Tom was already gone. All day at work, she kept counting down the hours until they went for their results. Twenty-four, twenty-one, seventeen. She wondered if he would call to say he was thinking along the same lines.

When he didn't, she came home at six and made yam stew. Her gut shifted gears again, into a sweet ache with a homey feel. The sharp and honeyed scent of cooking yam. Tom was over an hour late by now, but he'd never kept a regular schedule, it wasn't necessarily anything to worry about. She considered his comment the night before, started to tear up, then realized that she was getting her period. No matter how old and wise she got, she never remembered to count. But she had noticed that her flow, muddy and almost fecal when she was a girl, had now grown somehow astringent, smelling more like curry than the cheap Mexican food she'd favored in her first few relationships—even before Tae Kwon Do. She was turning a corner; she was moving on; but what was she moving toward? She went out on the front porch with her green Fiestaware bowl of stew and a dark, chilly beer. The fibers in the yams stuck between her teeth, the flavor melted behind her molars. The beer filled in where the emotion had left off. People began passing in the street: a gang of preteens dragging along a pit bull puppy, a woman in a loose dress and tennis shoes pushing a mixed-race baby in a dented green stroller, a guy in a long purple velvet cloak headed toward the commune, old Mrs. Hecht dropping in on the neighbors with an apron and a rake. A stray dog wandered into the yard, it was the one Yvette hated to look at, the slow black one, with an irregular tumor as big as a Frisbee high up on its back leg. An old man ambled after it, his long bald head spotted with sun, wearing both a sweater and a wind breaker in the heat. The dog was in the yard, peeing on the front bush, sniffing at an ice cream wrapper, nosing under the front steps.

The old man, struggling along right behind, shuffled to the porch railing and looked up at Yvette as if they knew one another. "Do you have a rope for him?" he asked.

She went out to the garage and found a bit of clothesline, watched the man loop it around the dog's neck, and lead him limping home.

After that, Yvette had to set the bowl down, she couldn't eat at all. Instead, she went into the house, slipped her sandals on and went down the street to Lloyd's. The wreath was reduced to a floral mush by now, sitting there on the sidewalk. Yvette got down on her knees, she didn't care who saw her, who would even be looking in a place like this? She touched the wreath, brought her finger to her nose and smelled the glop that came away in her hand. There was a desiccated aura of sachet, a sharp, sickening sulphur depth you thought you'd never get out of, a rotting apple decay. It was a smell you couldn't wait to get away from, and then couldn't resist trying again. She pulled handful after handful off the face of the wreath, trying to clear the surface. Her hands stained to the reddish brown of the clay streets; her nostrils reached saturation, so she entered the smell without smelling it; her fingernails filled up with the stuff. Felicia nuzzled at her hip, wandered over to sniff along, but then got distracted licking her own tiger-striped haunches. And Yvette just knelt there on the sidewalk raking the cardboard clean.

When she looked up, the sun was melting into the long vista of the street, bringing color down on the thick treetops and low, tiled roofs. Inside Lloyd's house, a light was on, the shades were open, and all the furniture was missing from the front room, except for an elaborate white light fixture drooping down like a lily of the valley, and there was Lloyd himself pacing the bare floorboards with his cell phone, wearing nothing but a very white pair of underwear, its elastic band worn high over the small of his back, low under his tight, buoyant belly. As he moved, he kept adjusting it, like even that was too much constriction for his body to bear. He poked his toe delicately into a warp in the floorboards; he reached up and pulled at his ear. A blank look passed over his face and he covered the receiver, walked over to the window, and flicked the blinds.

"Scat," he said.

Felicia arched her back. The crickets buzzed around them like an electric fence. Yvette felt her limbs fly out around her and she got up and ran, tripping over her long skirt as she went.

Tom finally arrived at 12:30, and Yvette was still lying there in the tub, goose bumps covering the parts of her body that weren't immersed in the hot water she'd replenished over and over. Parts on parts, needles on parts, needles on partners. With single, monogamous, multiple, bisexual, consensual, occasional, habitual. The variations made Yvette dizzy. No wonder Tom wouldn't come home.

"I know, I know," he said, outside the thin door. "I'm in violation of several treaties. But would you let me in to apologize anyway?"

Yvette touched the inside of the faucet with her toe.

"I know you're in there, I can hear the caulking creaking. Don't make me get the putty knife."

She stood up, leaned over to unlock the door, and stood dripping naked on the bath mat: her nipples two mismatched medallions, the long pear-shaped stomach, the surprising stretch of pubic fuzz.

He pressed the wet weight of her onto his shirtfront.

"I guess you wonder where I've been," he said. "Naturally, my first impulse was to go out and get laid again, before I find out anything for sure."

"Naturally," she said, slipping into her gown without drying off.

"Plus I wouldn't want to think that you'd outnumbered me with your prenuptial figures." Her nipples made dark blots in the pale cotton, he thought about a quarter of an inch down from the last time he'd seen her in that particular gown. "Just let's get comfortable now and I'll tell you what I did. Bedroom or living room?"

"Bedroom, please. I think I'd like to lie down."

Tom followed her into the room, with one hand on her shoulder. She arranged herself on some pillows and he curled around the other way, holding onto her ankle as he spoke.

"I wanted to go on an odyssey, somewhere I'd never been before. I considered the techno club, the gay bar, the jazz cabaret, even the lounge at the Holiday Inn. But they all seemed too predictable, probably packed with middle-aged guys trying to bag their last score."

"Very stock," Yvette said, and put her hand into his hair. "I expect more of you."

His scalp tingled, until he was ashamed of wanting to be touched so badly. But he went ahead and set her other hand on his thigh.

"So I just went around the corner to that little store. It's a beauty shop, bar, and convenience stop all in one. I come in and sit at the counter, watching some sister get her hair straightened. A teenage boy is playing pinball in the corner. An old guy is eating potato chips behind the bar. I thought I'd get a beer and just look around for a while. Then this woman comes up to me, she must have been about forty, gravity stopped dead in all the right places. 'You're from around here, aren't you? I'm Anita. I see you out with your lady sometimes. She's quite the Bella Donna, isn't she?'

"'What do you know about it?' I asked her, and she told me that she'd been dating a local hero, character named Lloyd.

"I didn't want to act too interested, ordered two more beers, and complimented her hair, which was bleached a dark maple blonde in four streaks in front and left dusky in the back. It's always been my fantasy to be seduced by an older woman like that and if I wait any longer, well, she'll be someone's grandma."

"I knew it," Yvette said. "You're probably still hoping your boss is going to give in and call you in her office to examine her desk top."

"We move onto the next draft, things get a little sloppy, she starts emptying her purse on the bar. 'This boyfriend of mine,' she says, 'he's a real scavenger. Take him about half a heartbeat to move in on the prey of some other sorry customer. You know, like a dog will get in there and roll around on something dead, wriggling his behind 'til you think he'd throw his back out. Nothing makes him happier. Anyway, it was a couple of months ago, my Zachariah passed on. That's him in the green suit there—good looking for a family man, I always thought. Lloyd shows up the next week, shine in his pants, grease in his hair, money in his clip, he wants to buy me an evening out of my misery, he says. Takes me to La Saggiotorre. Plays with my handbag under the table. Puts me to bed with a $25 bottle of champagne.'

"At this point, she picks a cork out of the pile on the bar, and starts running it over her wrist. Mine too, after a while. A couple of gangsta types by the pinball machine are giving me some hairy looks. And she just tells them to pop their bug-eyes back in their sunken skulls, this one's with her.

"'Of course,' she says, back to Lloyd again, 'that's when things begin to get strange—I mean, excuse me—white boy strange. Not just your usual skanking and dogging around. He starts to ask me about my husband—did it haint him or come on sudden, was he a good father, was he happy in his work? How did he feel about his brothers disappearing all around him? He even wanted me to show him Zachariah's love tricks, gets me right down in my own bed and begs me to tell him where it hurts.'

"'And then right when we're in the sweet of a long lap-up session, he looks up and asks me, what does it mean for a black man to die of natural causes? "I'm thirty-three, most of my friends are dead or in prison," he says. "What's left for me but to go around and try to satisfy their women? Come the judgement day, there's gonna be a whole lot of black ass waiting to devour those white devils. What am I gonna do but feed the fire? What do I have to do to set you free, sister? Tell me where to lay my burden down. Tell me where to set my stick in the fire." I mean to tell you, the man had been doing some heavy double-dipping in the Malcolm X.'

"'A lot of that going around,' I said. 'And how do you know I'm a white boy? I could be Asian, Native American, Italian, anything.'

"She snorted and blew a few sales slips and receipts right off the bar.

"'You've got white boy nerves. Any self-respecting brother would've had me half-way out the parking lot by now. The thing was, I have to tell you Lloyd's funny business was more attractive than you'd think. I fell flat out screaming and speaking-in-tongues in love with the boy. I'd drive by his place and check out the traffic. I'd lie to my kids about him, saying he was helping me with my taxes, that kind of thing. I'd do his laundry just to get the smell of his stink. I know it seems sluttish in a widow lady, it's not like I didn't love my husband, stayed faithful to that man most of my married life, with just one little lapse when my babies started to get grown. If I let loose now, it's on account of the grief.'"

"I take it you're not doing so well with your technique," Yvette said, moving her hand over his head to stroke the curls at the back of his neck.

"Just wait," Tom said. "I think you'll agree that I get my own back. Anyway, all this time, she's going over the stuff she's spilled out of her purse. She opens a makeup compact and starts tapping her nail against it, shaking the extra rouge powder off the mirror so she can see herself again. And let me tell you, she's nothing to sniff at, either. 'The thing about

Lloyd,' she says, 'once he sucked all the sweet stuff off me, he got restless. I catch him one day looking at the obituaries over grits and toast. And it's not just idle curiosity we're talking here. He's marking them up, like they're the want ads.

"'See anything you like?' I said. 'Teenage mistress of a gang-banger over Ruby and Vine? Pretty widow lady still nursing twins in the neighborhood of the Willow Baptist Church?'

"''I've got some things to take care of, might as well get started," he says, tucking his shirt in and walking out the door.

"'So I tailed the man for five days, and then I took action. I'm not the kind sits around waiting for the griddle to stick. Zachariah could've told you that. I squeeze into my funeral suit and march down to the newspaper office to do some fast talking. And here's where the black thing helps me out. Some white man, pillar of the community or garbageman or thief, they would have at least checked it out first. But they went ahead reprinted it, just like I wrote it. Come Sunday, Lloyd is looking at his paper, probably sitting at his genuine imitation redwood picnic table and picking up the stray piece of lawn litter with his barbecue fork. Then he folds over to the obituaries, rubs his nappy head, and sees his own spook.

"'When he comes in the door, I'm waiting for him, just sitting there on my brown velvet love seat in a low-cut teddy and silk hostess pants.

"''Zombie," I said. "You're dead."

"''What do you think you're doing, woman?"

"''Trying to help you out of your troubles."

"''You're an evil, destructive bitch, is what, trying to help me out of my mind. You've got your priorities in your panties. You got a missing dresser in your drawers."

"''Come on, Lloyd. You're not the only one has a little hobby. Tell it to my ass," I said, and then he did, for an hour or two, got to conversing good, before he gave up the farm and walked out on me and I haven't seen him since.'"

"So, did you ever check that obituary out?" Yvette asked Tom.

"I'm trying to tell you, there was no obituary, the lady's crazy."

"Think so?"

"After what she asked me to do, I think she's certifiable."

Yvette lifted her head off the pillow. "What?"

"She asked me to steal the wreath back."

Yvette looked at her hand on the back of Tom's neck, the red-brown residue caked in a miniature sunset over each pink unvarnished nail bed, and wondered if he could still smell the stink.

"The weirdest thing, though, when we drove by it wasn't on the sidewalk anymore. At first I thought it had been disappeared, that the city finally got disgusted and cleared the whole mess away. Then my friend, Anita, you remember, she says look there, and I saw that the petals were all gone, and the cardboard backing had been tacked up to the chain link fence, right by the gate, next to a morning glory vine. So it's just this gray, bare heart there, like the guy thinks it's a yard ornament or something."

"'Too late, I guess,' Denise said. 'But you're still welcome to take me home.'

"'Why don't I just give you a pale imitation of a kiss and drop you off?'

"'White boy nerves,' she said, and I drove her around the corner, just a couple of streets over, looked like a nice place, with a couple of good strong maples and a flagstone path up to the door."

"So you didn't get laid after all."

"Not yet, anyway. I guess by that time, I was more excited to come home and dish the dirt."

"That's devotion for you. So here we are."

"We are here," he said, pushing one hand further up her chilly leg. "At least for a couple more hours now."

Which was what Yvette would remember, driving to the clinic the next morning, the black plastic garbage bags out in droves along the driveways, Mrs. Hecht drinking coffee on her porch, her back turned to the road, a thin boy in a dashiki slipping out of the commune house, a little girl riding her bike and dragging a length of jump rope behind her, two men bent over a pile of yard waste, a woman in hospital scrubs sitting on the curb massaging her neck, a red bird, brighter than anything Yvette had seen that summer, zooming down toward the windshield with an actual twig in its beak, two green and black garter snakes entwined in a slippery knot on the sidewalk, a dog chasing a squirrel up a tree, and the gray cardboard heart nailed up to Lloyd's gatepost, here and here and here and here, to tell you where it all would end.

A Diller, A Daughter

A diller, a dollar
A ten o'clock scholar
What makes you come so soon?
You used to come at ten o'clock
And now you come at noon.

Your first word was "ma," and ever since then you've been using it against me. Even those early words were ten-dollar tongue-twisters out of the mouth of such a little two-penny sprout—or so your dad always said. But then, he favored you, being the youngest, and a girl at that. That's why it's so bold to get this bare engraved invitation in the mail, no note, no phone call, not even a photo of the prospective groom to give us some rough idea how our grandchildren might come out after all these years. Like you don't even want us involved. Don't want your mother planning a church-basement wedding shower or baking a chocolate groom's cake filled with the usual lucky family charms, don't want your father walking you down the aisle with his poor sense of rhythm and his accelerating gout. I guess that's not the thing, out there in L.A.

But no hard feelings, Ms. Pade, if that's what you're still calling yourself these days. See, I'm sending your letter album just like all the other kids, even though you must think it's a lame tradition, your old ma pasting up a scrapbook for every wedding in the family. When Nelson finally gave in and married the little Ames girl down the street, I put his old notes and doodles in a scrap metal binder that he keeps out in the shop for a conversation piece. Jim has his racing car album set up in a row of cookbooks on top of the microwave in that bachelor apartment where he's been living ever since the divorce. The fancy Korean dentist that Donnie hooked up with in Dallas is some crack housekeeper; she's got his cute cowboy organizer in the kiddie shelf along with the story books, to read to the kids when they get to be the right age. So you're the last, except for Aaron, who doesn't even have a fiancée yet, though to tell the truth, he's tested the wheels on two or three. You can stuff this tasteful valentine number in a eucalyptus tree for all I care. It includes all the words that ever got written between us, something to remind you where you come from on your wedding day. And if this one's a little lighter than the others, you'll understand why.

You were a quick child, I give you that much. Loved your brothers, rarely tattled, cleaned your plate. I seemed to be the only thing you carped about. From the time you were a measly little sprite: four freckles, three cowlicks I had to work your part around, the wind whistling through your missing teeth while you told some story with its kite tail dangling out the next county. Here's the first paper I have from you:

I go to the zoo. The animols yell. I like the bears. I pet them and my ma's voys gets big.

Patty Ballard

Notice how the letters lean forward, just falling on their face to get somewhere. That's your Aunt Nora all over. It was her who taught you to write, though I can't remember why, since I was the schoolteacher. Nora was never as good in school—not slow, just scatty—and always had her mind hopping onto the next prank she was going to pull. She was never afraid of anyone, not even our stepdad, with his lumpy shaved head and his fiddle collection shut up in the china cabinet like some hillbilly gun case while our grandmother's good silver spotted on the sideboard. He had a big cigar box with all his war souvenirs in it and when he was in a good mood he'd take out two yellow molars that looked like markers for a board game. They were Jap teeth, he told us. Inside each of them was a plug of gold. So yellow's good for something, he liked to say. He claimed he pulled them out of the mouths of dead Japanese soldiers and traded them for candy bars during the occupation.

"What's the occupation?" I said—that's how you'd know I'd be the schoolteacher.

"Sure you did," Nora told him. "Maybe I'll take them downtown and buy myself a beanstalk."

I didn't believe him either, but I had my own theory: these were my real father's teeth, all that was left of him after the hospital got done. I used to think that if I stole them and left them under my pillow at night, Papa would come back, like the tooth fairy in reverse. Only now I always pictured him as a Japanese, his eyes stretched so tight I could barely see the pupils flickering under the lids. I closed my eyes and smelled the smoky underarms of his winter coat. I was forgetting him already. Everything had been smeared over with the raw egg and catfish stench of my new stepdad instead.

Just be thankful, Patty, that you've got a mother and father, the original pair, no breaks or replacements. We may be a little chipped, but we're still something to come home to. Or that's what you thought in the summer of third grade, anyway, when you insisted on going to Blue Bird Camp and got all tangled up in the daisy chain. You were quick enough to pick up your Flintstone pencil then:

> Dear Ma,
>
> Camp is hot and dumb. They make you wear your undershirt all the time. They don't have any ice cream truck. I'm in the daisy cabin and my best friend Julie is a buttercup. Everyone knows the daisies are the dumbest.
>
> If you let me come home, I'll stay out of your hair. I won't say how summer is so boring and I don't have anything to do. I can play kickball and listen to my records. I can make a fort with Nelson and go to musyum day with Aunt Nora. I'll be still when you comb my hair. I promise. No one combs it here and just think how many nots I'll have if you make me stay.
>
> Love,
> Patty

Such a little charmer, you were. Nothing about I miss you, I love you, I don't like it here alone. But then you made a new friend, learned how to tie-dye your undershirt with sumac leaves, became a regular folk hero when you got stung by a dirt dauber and watched without making a sound while the hydrogen peroxide fizzed up on your arm like an exploding soda.

By the time you got my letter, you didn't even care:

Dear Patty:

It's three days since you left, and it's still noisy around here. All your brothers miss you. Cheeta growls when anyone tries to sit in your chair. Your dad says he gets sleepy so early because he doesn't have anyone to pull his leg at night.

Remember how you wanted to join the Bluebirds, even though your dad said you were still too little? You liked the camp uniform and the shiny canteen. Now you're a daisy and I'm proud of you. I'll call up on Wednesday to see how you're doing. Then you'll be halfway done. The cake will be half gone. When you eat the last crumb, I'll be right there to help you and you can save a little frosting for me.

Love,
Ma

Next comes this pile of postcards you sent when you went out west with Nora. She'd just broken up with that garage mechanic and had to drive clear across the country to clean out her lungs. So naturally, she settled on California, where she claimed she had spent the most spiritized years of her life, back there in her spinach salad days. I never had much faith in Nora's driving. She was too busy talking to see the road. I still believe she did it by vibrations, like a bat. That's what they mean, blind as a bat. The creatures are really just glorified rodents sailing around on sound waves in those big dark caves. They navigate the noise, like you used to do coming home after a late date, sensing your way up the stairs and through the hall, wafting past the bedrooms on one snore after the next, all of them off key at a slightly different kilter, until you got to the end of the landing and slid your handbag through the half-open door of your own room to plop down, fully clothed, on that unmade bed you called an office. Of course, this bat business is the kind of information you used to get from an education, not the stuff they teach now about social diseases and Native American rituals on crack. Back then, we wanted to learn something about the natural world. All except Nora, of course, who'd rather take her chances just feeling her way.

So Nora ditched the mechanic when he asked where she lost her virginity, was it a horse-back riding incident or a regular tractor pull?

Of course, I guess that's not the story she told you.

The men she got involved with—well—I don't know how she expected any better. Your dad never liked that mechanic; he couldn't believe your aunt would keep company with a man who couldn't even write his own kiss-and-make-up notes, but always asked me to help him on the sly.

This time, I could see it wasn't going to do any good. Nora got the idea she needed to get out of Windy Corners again, out of the county, out of the state, and explore the new world. The petrified forest, the trail of tears, the fountain of youth. Getting it all mixed up, in her usual jumble, like history was just a scrap box she could pick and choose her own quilt pieces from. She wanted you to be her spirit guide, she said. You were an old soul and she was a young one. She was only asking for two weeks. Your dad wasn't too keen on the idea. I had to promise him six steak nights in a row to manage it. And even then, he kept pestering me about what I thought my loopy, sluttish sister was exposing you to. "Don't pull my leg, M," he'd say. "Just what do you think goes on out there in the land of sky-blue nudies?"

Dear Ma,

This is the salt lake. People here have two wives and they can get baptized after they're dead. I waded in the water until my legs came out white. Then I licked my knee so I could taste it and it was just like a pretzel at home. Aunt Nora says she knows it feels good, but could I please stop. Right now. Just for her, pretty please.

> *Love,*
> *Patty*

Ma,

Yesterday we saw a dead turtle in the desert where we had our picnic. I couldn't eat my peanut butter and marshmellow sandwich. But Nora took it back to the motel and soaked the shell out in the sink. It smells funny. She says she's going to keep it in her apartment for a moment of Morty. I think she feels bad about him. I miss you too. Say hi to Dad.

> *Love,*
> *Patty*

Ma,

We're at Las Vegas and there are all these places kids can't go in. We have to play the little slot machines outside. They roll their eyes at you till you come up with a cherry. I wonder why they pick that fruit, Nora said. We won $17.75 and went out and bought ourself a bead purse and a moon pie.

Love,
Patty

Dear Ma,

Now it's finally California. All the trees are funny shapes, like in Dr. Suess. Or else they're bigger than me and Nora put together. They can build a tunnel through the big red ones. I get a headache when I look up at them. Nora wants to write now.
Maisy—Your little girl is a good coconut. She never litters and she washes her hands after every meal. Maybe she washes them too much, if you know what I mean. They say that can be an indication of something or other.
We're in the land of giants. It makes my little man troubles look like small potatoes. Keep peeling, sister. And take care.
Don't forget to check under those fingernails.

Love,
Nora Patty

Nora never could keep her eyes off my papers. At home, she kept sidling over to my side of the room, shaking out my schoolbooks or groping through the trash basket. She used to claim she was doing an art project and needed a kleenex box or a toilet paper roll. But I was wise to her, even though she was three years older. She wanted to know my secrets, just because she was too free and easy to have any of her own.

Dear Maisy,

Patty doesn't know I'm writing. I wonder what you'd think about letting her live with me for awhile and getting her out of the corral with all those brothers. From what I've seen of the situation I think it would be safer and cleaner, all around. We get along super, and I have the time to take her places and tell her the things a girl needs to know. I remember

what it was like for us, and I think how sad it must be for Patty, not hav-
ing a sister to keep her honest.

Love,
Nora

Well, I sat there with my scissors still in my hand and cried so hard the tears dripped onto the construction paper on my lap, bleaching out little islands in the blue. I'd been cutting out a bulletin board for my summer school class while your dad watched a baseball game on the TV. It was a beach scene with striped umbrellas and fat men in old-fashioned swimsuits. There was going to be real sandpaper for the background, and for each book the kids read they got to put another sea creature—dolphin, jellyfish, octopus—in the water. I wondered if you and Nora were sighting any whales yet. I wondered if you'd stop when you got to the ocean, or just keep traipsing over to the Orient and give the Japanese an eye-opener. That was something I still thought about, maybe for a twenty-year wedding anniversary. But I'd never get to go with my own girl.

Anyway, I'd wanted to go in to school that day so I could get the corners right, put the whole thing together before the kids got in on Monday morning. The administration had been onto us about teacher accountability, and bulletin boards were about as far as their observations ever developed. But your dad told me that if I couldn't get my work done on the weekdays, I'd just have to do it at home. He needed company while he watched his games. That was your dad: he liked to have someone minding him even when he was sunk up to his eyeballs in a deep dark sports funk.

I looked at Nora's letter and I wanted to cut it in half. But what I did instead was cut a paper fish out of it, saving all the print. I knew no one would ever believe she had the gall to ask a thing like that from me. I wanted to preserve the evidence for arguments later on.

"What are you sniffing about over there, M?" your dad said. "Are you finally missing the baby as much as me?"

"I just can't bear to see your team get beat so badly," I told him, and he left it at that. Your dad would never understand anything as complicated as your aunt.

But you just might, so I'm sending this letter too. Maybe it'll untangle some of the knots you've got tucked up in your hat about Nora and me.

After California, you two hurried home pretty fast, no souvenir stops along the way, and you stayed stick still in Windy Corners for a good long time. Nora never mentioned the letter, like she'd forgotten all about it. She got a job at the courthouse, transcribing trials, which was about the only gainful employment fast enough to keep her busy at her rate of speed. She started seeing the bailiff; you started in on junior high.

That was your great period of scented stationery, five colors of ink in a single pen, a leather diary under the radiator in your room, a compact with four cakes of neon perfume, all of them sickly fruit flavors that reminded me of teenage sweat. It was the same smell I used to leave in your aunt's party dresses when she was out on a date and I tried them on, wanting to do something to make myself feel special. I wasn't prying. I just wanted to be pretty, was all.

Those days, I was running across the same smell in your laundry, and it made me nervous. The boys' stuff I could handle, the sour T-shirts, the cheese rind socks, the smears from soggy cereal dreams. It was all regulation. But the other was something I wasn't prepared for. It just came out of nowhere and whapped me upside the head: spring fever, lemon chiffon, sticky fingers, key lime pie. I remembered squirreling my stained panties under my mattress. I remembered a girl who stood in front of me in the lunch line—how the static electricity in her glittery brown Rapunzel hair made it fizz out and tickle my face, and I thought that was the sweetest feeling, what people sang about, and that it had nothing in common with the things I had to do for my stepfather at home.

Sorting the laundry one day, I shook a note out of your hand-embroidered jeans. It was written in green ink on a pink rectangle torn out of your autograph book. Your handwriting had changed by then—rounder curves, more curlicues, whole circles dotting the "i"s—just what you'd expect from a thirteen-year-old. We don't let them get away with this kind of thing down in the lower grades:

Dear Jill,

Salut, oh foxy one. We've got a butt-kicker sub in French class. He's making us conjugate verbs: Je fuck, tu fuck, il fuck, we all fuck for good luck. It sucks. This guy is sick. He keeps touching his chest like he's trying to feel himself up. Wait—I had to stop because he came over here and wanted to "check out my homework." These guys'll do anything to look down your shirt. But I surprised him, huh, 'cuz there's nada in there.

Let's go down to wrestling practice after school. I'm going to take Jerry today, and you can give old Craig a workout. That'll keep them going. À bientôt, ma chérie.

Luv,
Pade

P.S. : I got a new pen—snotgreen—what do you think?
P.P.S.: You look fab in your push-up B-cup. I wish I could borrow them sometime.

I slammed the lid of the wash machine and slapped the note down on top. Then I reread it, with the wash cycle quaking and rumbling underneath my elbows. That's a trick my stepdad taught me, and not the only one either. If you've got to blubber, he said, you best hop up the hoover and run it on full throttle. Otherwise, your mother will get suspicious and send you off to live with the crude side of the family.

It was a bumpy ride, that note. You didn't sound any better the second time. I didn't recognize you, but who else could it be? There was only one teenage girl in the house, that I knew of. One set of dirty electric curlers in the bathroom, one size and style of training bra in the wash, one pair of saddle shoes at the front door.

But I'd never get used to this "Pade" who came in and swallowed up my baby. It isn't even a name, as far as I can see. Just a long, lazy syllable waiting for someplace to lay its money down.

I went up to your room where I knew I'd find you, snuggled up to the radiator in your Hawaiian T-shirt and tie–dye knee socks, staring at a magazine. The air ticked around you, thick with some amazing insect song inaudible to the adult ear. I watched you through the half-closed door. You shifted and stretched one leg out, pushed your toes into the sweet space between the mattress and the box springs, so I could see you had on the mod polka-dot panties you'd bought at the mall, a grainy yellow bruise disappearing under the red elastic. The leg was long, its shin sleek and bare as the blade of a threshing machine, its thigh still covered in fine blonde down, and I couldn't believe, after all I'd done, you could turn out so perfect.

Then I remembered. I had to punish you. I pushed your door open so hard it bounced off the wall and hit me on the ankle on my way in. That only made me madder, like my own house was turned against me, and I grabbed the first thing I could find—a soft, sponge curler matted with strands of butter blonde hair—and stuffed it into your half-open mouth. Then I pulled the magazine out of your hand and slapped your smart leg down with it.

You didn't know what was happening at first. Your face went soft, then hard, and you spit the curler out on the floor.

I picked it up again, dustballs and all, and pushed it back into your mouth.

That's when I saw your dad look in at the door. He was carrying a plate of leftovers and a newspaper, and he stopped for a second, rolled his round head around the corner, blinked at me, then bulldozed off into the other direction.

I picked up the magazine and started hitting you again. I'm not proud of it, Patty, but it was all I could think to do at the moment.

You just sat there and took it. Until something turned in you—I could almost feel your cylinders grinding over—and you slapped back. Not hard, but enough to let me know you were waking up.

It was a sharp sting. The only person who'd ever slapped me like that was my own mother, and even that took her a good long time. I dropped the magazine and sat down on the bed.

"We have to do some talking, girl," I said.

By the time Nora came over for cards that night, you were sitting at the kitchen table in your robe and pimple cream drinking hot chocolate and copying out sentences:

I will not speak or write obscenities.
I will not refer to implied sexual activities.
I will not pass notes in school.

"What's this?" Nora said. "The Girl Scout Code?"

You looked up, squinted your eyes at me, and went back to your writing.

Then your dad passed through the kitchen with a newspaper and smacked Nora on the bottom with the rolled up sports section. She gave a jump, whacked the paper out of his hand, and landed practically in my lap while he retrieved his property and strolled on into the living-room where the boys already had the TV tuned to the proper game.

"This is a little home remedy for wandering penmanship," I said. "Patty—or rather—Pade—has been writing dirty notes at school."

"Hmm." Nora straightened up and eased off a bit, swinging her car coat over the back of a chair. "Maybe she's bored. They don't even get up to calculus in this two-horse town."

"Somehow, I don't think that's the problem. What about you? I suppose you would've been valedictorian if things had just been a little more upscale?"

Nora took out her lipstick and tested it on a paper napkin. "You never know." She kept marking the napkin, reshaping the lipstick till it had the stiletto edge she liked. "I bet Pat just needs a little intellectual stimulation." She touched up her fuss button lips and then started in on you. "How's that, doll? Looks stellar. That's what we say in the law 'biz now."

You stared. "I'm not talking, if you didn't notice."

Nora gave me the look. "That's OK, sweetie. Then you'll keep your lipstick fresh."

"That's not all," I said.

Then Nora pulled another napkin out of the dispenser and scrawled on it in lipstick:

I will keep my mouth shut.
I will be a good daughter.
I will not talk back to the teacher.

The kitchen was quiet and we could hear Jim and your dad in the next room. The crowd at whatever game it was worked up to a long, frantic cheer, with your dad and brother barking along: old point and counterpoint senior and junior.

I pushed the napkin away.

Nora put her hand on your shoulder. "I'll teach you shorthand, next time, Pade honey."

For a while there we didn't speak, just communicated in refrigerator notes. When I went off to school in the mornings, you were still asleep, and by the time I came home, you'd be off shopping or flirting in another time zone. I told you what chores needed to be done; you wrote back and said what we needed from the grocery store, how much money you wanted and why, what your father felt like for dinner. You might as well be living with Nora. I finally gave in and left a note behind your radio, where you'd be sure to find it:

> Dear Patty:
>   This has got to stop. I'm your mother. I'm on your side. Now go look in the lint compartment of the dryer.
>
> > Love,
> > Ma

In the dryer, another note told you to go to the side pantry, and so on, until you found the fancy white garter belt set settled in the nest of tangled pantyhose in the top drawer of your bureau.

"Well, I know you're growing up," I said, when you came in the bedroom and kissed my cheek. Your skin was so elastic that garter belt would never put a dent in it. Your breath was sharp and minty over a whorl of pheromones, so that I wondered whether you were still covering something up.

Probably so, because not six months later, you were acting out in school, getting reports from the principal:

> Dear Mrs. Ballard:
>   I am sorry to inform you that Patricia has three unexcused absences from school. In addition, there are reports of smoking, back talk, and illegal activities. Patty is one step away from complete suspension.
>   Sorry to have been the bearer of bad news.
>
> > Sincerely,
> > Arnold Loftis,
> > Ed.D.

Don't let that fool you, Arnold loved dictating that letter to his secretary, sitting there in his swank oak office in the new junior high. Arnold had had it out for me ever since I shamed him in the school board meeting. He'd blamed his problems on incompetence in the lower grades one too many times. So I pulled up the stats and set them out in primary colors for the whole blessed assembly.

"Actually, there's a significant drop in student performance once they get to your fine institution," I said. "Maybe you need to do a little teacher accountability up there instead of spending all the cash on that fancy indoor/outdoor carpeting and a new swimming pool."

Arnold bit his pen. He started with the cap but then moved on to the nub end, and teasing at the plastic stopper with his yellow teeth. He finally extracted it completely and spit it out into the aluminum ashtray on the desk in front of him. Meanwhile, the ink had spilled on his hands—blue and gray speckles—the leper showing his spots. He went to wipe his face and came up with a blue beard. I'd always suspected as much from him.

And now here he was salivating over your discipline problems. I could just see him casing through your files, rubbing the grade reports and aptitude examinations over his puny crotch, eyeing your third-place speech awards in the new plate glass trophy case, contemplating suspensions, home conferences, and psychological examinations.

Dear Dr. Loftis :

I'm sorry if Patricia has been making a nuisance of herself. She's in that difficult phase between detachable mittens and handcuffs. I'm doing my best.

Sincerely,
Mrs. John J. Ballard

Dear Mrs. Ballard:

I take it you are beginning to realize the behavioral difficulties inherent in this developmental phase. My guess is that Patty's acting out her frustrations and anxieties. I suggest you take the time to sit down and write a case history of your daughter. We can proceed from there. This should give us some documentation to work with.

Best Wishes,
Arnold K. Loftis,
Ed.D.

I didn't like his implications, but I figured I'd have to come up with something, just to keep the man in paperwork. I even took a sick day to contemplate the subject. After the whole crew cleared out that Wednesday morning, I made a pot of my special brew, got out your baby book and a set of notecards and did some long, tall thinking. Jim was the wise one, Aaron was the sweetheart, Don was the bully. Nelson was the kid you catch with the lights on and some important household appliance spread out over the floor in pieces at 2:00 A.M. You were just the girl. You talked at ten months, walked at fourteen. You sat at the kitchen table and waited for the dust to clear so I could go over and sharpen your crayons. You told me stories about trolls and princesses. You went out for ice cream cones with your aunt Nora, loved tall boots and orange slushes. You got gum stuck in your hair.

It's not much to go on, but it's all that was there.

All five times, I'd hoped that I wouldn't have a girl. I would sit in the bathtub and baste my big gut with scalding water, soothing the back pains and trying to shift the position of the groceries. Low-lying meant a boy, supposedly. "Puppy dog tails," I'd say. "Axle grease. pigskin, foreskin, Indian chief." It worked too, all but the last try, when I must've slacked off in my method. Then I came out with you. Surprise. Like I'd never had a kid before. It was back when they still did breech, so I didn't have to put up with a C-section. But what happened was even worse: nineteen hours of hard labor. Then you came into the world sitting down.

Which should've prepared me for your teenage years, I guess. Not that I wanted you any different. I just didn't know what to do with a girl. I only know the facts, Patty.

When I was just a girl myself, I used to sit down at bedtime and try to figure out the pertinent facts on my own family. I'd found a big black ledger in my real dad's property, and I kept it hidden in my bottom drawer, under a layer of bobby socks rolled up fat as snowballs. It kept company with my dingy garter belt, my savings stuffed into the toe of a ripped nylon stocking, my reversible douche-and-hot-water-bottle, my costume jewelry and Girl Scout awards. That old ledger was huge, a real dinosaur of book-keeping, with gold-rimmed pages, red and green lines cutting across the bias, and the musty rainy day smell of back rooms. Papa was a restaurant supplier, and he sometimes took me out on follow-up visits to the regular customers. Our favorite was the old ice house behind the Squires Hotel. You know the one—it's been a junk store, a disco, an electronics wholesaler and I don't know what all in the past twenty years. But back then it was still a family operation, and they'd always give me a free snow cone. I loved to squeeze Papa's hand while I watched the syrup soak color into the pale shaved ice. I thought it was magic, I guess, and that if I let go the red or blue juice would seep back out again, leaving me standing there with a cone full of the nasty saltwater your old ma pours out of the bottom of a barrel of homemade ice cream. Once, the man behind the counter ran out of ice chips, and he took a scoop and bucket out from behind the counter. Then he opened a huge, heavy door, like the door to a vault. Inside, I saw more ice than I could believe—tall totem poles of it standing up in the middle of the room, long skinny coffins on the floor, stubby blocks stacked one on top of the other. All gleaming and glistering like the river in winter.

"Look there, Maisy," Papa said. "Think that'll make enough snow cones to keep you in business?"

I could feel the cold from the other room, and a shiver brushed across the back of my neck in a long, drawn-out wave that I still get when I pick up a new piece of information. I focused on the gleam on one tower of ice until I could make it bend and buckle in the light. I felt my father's rough palm against mine. It was the first time I knew there was a number you couldn't count to, and that it could feel so good to be confused.

Then, after he died, every time I picked up the ledger I saw that cold room again. Sometimes, I imagined that's where he'd gone. Our papa was a practical man. He wouldn't have had much use for a heaven made out of puffs and lace and cotton wads. I was sure it was a land of solid assets, where he was at. I pushed my finger down the column of figures:

industrial strength mixer	$ 4.95
cast iron frying pan	$1.50
Dutch oven	$7.75.

Over the years, the columns had changed some. I recorded, in stages, the number of times I brushed my hair at night, the boys I liked and in what order, the clothes I intended to buy myself whenever I won the American Legion speech-writing prize. Now keep in mind, this wasn't a diary like you or your Aunt Nora. I never went for anything as girly as that. I would just keep track of things. I had read all about Ben Franklin, and I wanted an almanac of my own, where I could show how much I'd progressed, and what I'd made of myself. That way, when I finally left home, no one would be able to tell any lies about me. Ben Franklin had all sorts of sayings like that. I wrote some of them down.

Then, one day, I noticed that someone else had been sneaking their way into my book. Under "*A stitch in time saves nine,*" they'd written: "*Stitch your wagon to a star.*" Beside "*A penny saved is a penny earned,*" they'd added: "*A Diller, a dollar, a Saturday night scholar.*" Someone. It was obviously Nora, with that sprawling hand that looked just like her taste in clothes. I was furious. It was like I couldn't keep anything for myself in that house. I went right over to her side of the closet and pulled out her new red formal. It was low-cut, and it had a band of accordion pleats stitched close together at the cleavage, then wafting out in big chiffon wings over the shoulders. She was so skinny she looked like a dragonfly in the thing. I touched the chiffon and its angel-hair texture only made me angrier. I snatched down the zipper, hoping I'd rip it accidentally. But no such luck. So I took off my clothes and tried the dress on. In the mirror, I looked just like my name: mazy, lazy, lackluster, plump. It was no wonder I was the one staying home.

I saw the nail clippers on the nightstand, and I started clipping into the collar. Opening and opening, like I was shucking an ear of corn, and I was the poor country cob inside. When I finished, I threw the dress over a hanger and picked at the tiny cuts on my shoulders. They looked like bug bites, was all. I'd seen worse, in my time.

For days, I waited for her to corner me. But a formal is a tricky thing: you can never tell when it will turn up. Meanwhile, I got more notes in my ledger:

> *He doesn't like perfume.*
> *He can't handle whiskey.*
> *The library's open 'til nine on Friday nights.*

They were done in pencil, and I erased them as quickly as they came. But I could still see their spidery shadows whenever I went to make an entry. Smoky patches on the starched yellow pages. Nora was always out by then, dating sometimes, but mostly just stretching her allowance on slow sodas at the diner, becoming a professional busybody and french fry thief:

Mama isn't asleep when she says she is.
He was never in the war.
Rinsing out with vinegar won't do a thing.

Then Mama came in one night and shook me awake. I was a heavy sleeper; the first thing I knew, I felt a weight on the bed, lighter than usual. Then there was something flimsy over my face, a sleeve, a hand, the smell of menthol mixed with linseed oil. I looked up expecting the old bald buzzard head and the hawk nose that got sharper as it moved in close, and saw her face instead—its flesh slicked down to the bone. That's when it hit me like a tether ball to the solar plexus that she knew what had been going on.

"Where's Nora?" she said, still shaking me. "Where's your sister?"

"I didn't want to," I said.

"It's after three in the morning. Where is Nora? Where has she got to, girl?"

"I was just asleep and I didn't know."

"Maisy. Nora. Where's Nora?"

I looked over to her bed, slipping out of its white chenille spread. On top, the stuffed sock monkey lay with its face pressed against a satin bolster. There was a book on one corner, and a single house slipper on the other, the way you try to hold down a picnic blanket on a windy day. Nora. Out in the middle of the night. Alone.

Then, when I finally understood, that's when Mama backed up and slapped me. The tears clenched tight behind my eyes. No matter how many times he touched me, it was only Mama who could make me cry. "That's for your smart tongue," she said. "I'm not going to ask you again. Where is she?"

She pulled a note out of the pocket of her robe and handed it to me:

Dear Mama:
    I'm off to tackle the world. You can give my other clothes to Maisy. I won't need them where I'm going. Don't ever let them tell you I don't love you. But then, I wouldn't expect me back anytime soon.
                                              Love,
                                              Nora

My mother's hands wove together in front of her, just aching to get the letter back. Her fingers were short and arthritic, speckled with sunspots, swollen at the joints. The right thumb had been sewn over at least three times in the blue jeans factory where she was working to save up for our college tuition. Its nail was split like a cracked peanut—and all for another girl who wouldn't even finish high school.

"Give it here," she said. "If you won't talk to me, I'm going to wake up your father."

I wish I could tell you I was sad, or worried, or even guilty. But what I really felt was mad. Madder than slapping mad, madder than punching. Madder than my stepfather when he got down to the last layer of clothes under the covers and found out that the Redcoats had landed before him and he wasn't going to be occupying anything that night. After all, it was me who was saving, it was me who was planning, it was me who deserved to go. But Nora had beat me to it, without ever giving me any idea. She never even noticed the dress that I'd cut up for her. Just as usual, she had her mind wandering on to other things.

Mama's voice shrank up quiet, then stretched out tight again.

"Sugar, isn't there anything you can tell me? Didn't she leave you anything?"

And then I remembered. I got up, went over to my bureau, and started tossing socks. I dragged out the ledger and skimmed through the pages, slowing down toward the last ones that I'd used. Everything gone, every curl of her handwriting erased. Every bit of Nora brushed away.

I dumped her drawers out on the rag rug.

I tore her dresses off the hangers

I pulled back the covers and lay down in her bed, listening to the ruckus already starting in the next room. The sheet was cool under my legs, and I rubbed my heels against it, burrowing in, settling down for the long haul. Because this was going to be even tougher, from now on.

Now that I could never leave my mother, like the two of you have done.

So Patty, that's why I couldn't find a word to write about you on that last Wednesday. I knew I couldn't do much without the facts, and the facts were just what I could never say. I slammed the baby book shut on my finger. Someone had been playing games with me. I drove to the junior high in a flurry, pulled into the faculty lot in my old gray sweatpants, my hair still set in orange juice cans, and dove through the lobby with the crushed green carpet and the skylights and dying yellow trees. In his office, Arnold K. Loftis was shooting a golf ball into a dixie cup. His desk was covered in fast food wrappers and gag gifts. On the oak-paneled walls were posters and calendars of international cheesecake in educational poses in front of tourist landmarks.

"Come out and say it like a man, Arnie."

"Well, Mrs. Ballard, I didn't expect to see you today."

"I just thought I'd drop by to pick up my daughter. We've got some shopping to do."

"I'm sorry, that's not possible. I've just released her to her aunt."

"And why would that be?"

"Oh, just say there are some suspicious factors in the case. Your sister thought Patty might be better off at her home, for the time being."

"So you think she's better off living in a one-bedroom apartment over a liquor store?"

"Well, frankly, that decision's not up to me. But Ms. Cooper brought some interesting facts to light, which Patricia corroborated."

I stood looking at the bright body of an Australian teenager on her bike, pinned to the scene on a long spike of sunlight. "And you believed them?" I said.

He pretended to poke around at some papers on his desk.

"Really, Maisy, I saw the marks."

So I know why you didn't write me all those years, and why this book is so empty, and why you don't want your dad to give you away. But I wonder if you think about your own daughter: what you'll keep from her, what you'll save for her, what you'll just never be able to explain to her. Because, frankly, this engraved invitation doesn't look much like your handwriting, and I've got so much more to say.

The Marijuana Tree

*D*enise got the inspiration at her local Trust & Loan. She was off work for the afternoon, due to an untimely trip to the gynecologist, and when she dropped by to make another deposit toward retirement, she noticed the unusual Christmas display they'd set up in the foyer. Bells and bobsleds she could stomach, and yes, even a few sly-faced elves who looked like they might be contemplating a career hike to upper management. But there was no tree, or none to mention, only three fat dollops of tree shrub, no trunk in sight, as if the Republican's famous trickle-down policy had finally dripped into the heart of Christmas and eroded it into pint-sized portions. The treelets looked attractive enough in their white flocking and tasteful bulbs and bows, but she didn't see a lot of evergreen underneath. In fact, she realized, scraping off some of the flocking with a Kleenex, the trees were downright brown, not even needled, but shriveled into the rope-like texture of an ivy vine in winter. She slipped the Kleenex back into the pocket of her beige wool cape—the centerpiece of her new gracefully aging lady wardrobe—and twirled around the display slowly, the way she would at an art gallery if she couldn't quite make a piece out.

A man in a gray striped vest and yellow power tie nodded in her direction. "Afternoon, Miz Crane," he said. Only in Wheeler would this be an abbreviation of "Mrs." rather than an out and out concession to the changing times. Denise bit her tongue and smiled.

"Afternoon, Larry. Management down-scaling? Holding a Christmas benefit for dwarves?"

The banker blushed in a delicate filigree around his male balding pattern. How maudlin, Denise thought, when she noticed herself waxing sentimental about some receding hairline in a crowd. Carl, her husband, had a lovely one, a curling blond flame over each ear, and a pink cervical cap of scalp at the top. More and more, it was this bit of exposed flesh which she called up when she felt obligated to remind herself of her love for him.

"This is your new ecological style Christmas ensemble, ma'am. No harm to the environment, no shedding pine needles, minimal cleanup." He laughed into his handkerchief. "We just roll them away."

"Artificial?" she said, raising an eyebrow. She'd staved off her craving for artificial greenery for years, regarding it as an embarrassing half measure. When she finally gave in, it would be for a wooden crèche, a pinecone wreath and a gallon carton of unspiked eggnog.

"No, ma'am," Larry paused, dramatically, for a banker. "Tumbleweed."

Tumbleweed. They didn't stock them at the supermarket, or heap them up in bundles on the uneven asphalt lot of the volunteer fire station. But you could go chasing them out on Highway 66, as they went rolling out from under your tires like wild turkeys. Which is exactly what Denise did, since she'd lost the afternoon anyway, and had some considerable thinking to do.

She pulled off the road at an observation point and just watched them run for a while, pretending to be a state policeman clocking their speeding violations: 75, 69, a whopping 97. What wonderful power men must feel, rushing through the world at car chase velocities. Denise never speeded. It was bad for her heart, which murmured at any disorderly conduct. She had a number of minor health conditions: heart murmur, insomnia, dysmenorrhea, with which Carl was unsympathetic. He hated any mention of her fragility, and would turn to some pressing project and hum a country ballad every time she had any new development to report.

Not that Denise was frail. She'd raised three children, saved two businesses, jogged through the fitness craze, and mellowed into aerobic walking. But she needed to pace herself. Carl, on the other hand, was a sprinter. He'd work himself into a frenzy with every major law case, discarding first social engagements, then formal meals, sleep, and any unnecessary contact hours with herself and the children. Afterwards, he'd simmer off at a slow boil, sleeping ten hours at a stretch, preparing extravagant meals, family outings, and demanding athletic sex at all hours. Denise regarded it as a sign of health, a hunter-and-gatherer instinct. She loved feeling the fever break at each one of these pressure points, his body too hot to touch all night, then, in the morning, magically cooled by a fresh sweat smelling of lemon and newly mown grass.

But it was hard on her. There was no denying it was hard to keep up, she thought, as she changed into her tennis shoes, slammed the car door, and went after her Christmas tumbleweed.

By the time she got the thing home she was more enthusiastic. At some point in the quarter-mile chase, her adrenaline had kicked in and infused her with the Christmas spirit. Or maybe it was just Christmas panic. Since her children left home, she'd been leaving preparations later and later, until she was practically buying her gear on the very eve of the blessed event, just in time for their annual bed-and-breakfast in the country. Carl didn't notice anyway, and the kids wouldn't show up until late afternoon on Christmas Day.

At least there was no struggle up the stairs, no mechanical difficulty with the tree stand, no chopping and hacking to the proportions of the room. Denise pushed up her sleeve and shook the can of flocking spray, then delivered the blasts with all the energy of the street vandal, her own winter storm. As she worked, she fantasized about being pricked with a pine needle and falling asleep for a hundred years. When she woke up, she'd be a truly old woman, past all the quandaries and embarrassments of transition. Her lawn would be overgrown with mysterious vines, her great-grandchildren would be hosting their golden anniversaries, her retirement fund would have blossomed with interest.

The tumbleweed looked delicious now, like a huge ball of Christmas candy rolled in powdered sugar. Denise went to the kitchen, poured herself a vermouth and dumped in some candied fruit, for color, then climbed up onto a kitchen chair and went digging for ornaments in the cabinet above the refrigerator. Over the years, they'd collected every kind of decoration: glazed gingerbread, styrofoam snowballs, stuffed and embroidered rocking horses and Santas, pipe-cleaner sugar plum fairies with glitter matted in the pink netting of their skirts. At some point, Denise got in the habit of buying each child an ornament every Christmas, and there was a

fuss if everyone's favorites didn't make the tree. Then the children started earning their own incomes and bought her ornaments in return. As
her collection got bigger, her trees got smaller. And now that she was
reduced to this tree nublet, she didn't know how she'd manage.

She pulled out a snaky strand of red glitter, some glass bulbs, and
selected one novelty ornament for each member of the family, including
a baby in swaddling clothes for Sally's newborn, her first grandchild.
Denise had always wanted to simplify, to plan a color-coordinated Christmas, but the children panicked at any mention of restraint, preferring the
usual jumble of unmatched wrapping paper, family memorabilia, and
clashing motifs. Maybe she could get to like this new era, she thought,
pouring herself another drink, garnished with a sprig of mint this time.

When Carl came in at six-thirty, his camel coat half- unbuttoned and
his scarf tangled over his arm, Denise knew he'd started another one of
his manic jags. He sat down to beef stew and Caesar salad without even
loosening his tie. Denise pleated her napkin in her lap. If she didn't make
her move soon, she would lose the advantage of attacking while his
mouth was full. She forced herself to eat a carrot or two, but she didn't
have much of an appetite for what would follow. Then, with his last sip
of iced tea, Carl began a long explanation of his latest frustration: the
plaintiff in a libel suit wouldn't settle out of court because he was so interested in the glamour of courtroom procedure. He wanted to edit all the
briefs. He wanted to choose Carl's tie for the court date.

"This would never happen in Chicago. I can't believe I'm out here
in the provinces doing nickel-and-dime melodrama. We didn't need to
raise the legal consciousness of your average small town citizen. We need
to lower it. Take the goddamn soap operas off the air."

Denise turned her wrist over and looked at her watch under the table.
This could go on for twenty minutes without interruption. She knew.
She'd timed it before. Carl's favorite subject these days was the inadvis-
ability of his move to Wheeler, three years ago, to take over his father's
law practice. Anything could lead to his long-running, fast-moving dis-
quisition on the woes of small town life.

"The choice of health care providers in Wheeler isn't too tempting
either," she said, throwing her napkin onto her plate.

Carl looked down at his salad hopefully, searching for any bits of
roughage that he'd missed.

"You've been home for half an hour and you still haven't asked about my day."

He slapped his hands on his knees and pushed away from the table. "My God, what's that?" he said.

He was staring into the living-room, at the tumbleweed balanced among the throw pillows on the window seat.

It did look strange, Denise thought, like some kind of alien space pod masquerading as an igloo. Well, it would do him good to try and figure it out, look at the holidays from a different angle.

He was already at it with his key chain by the time she cleared the plates.

"Don't scrape off all the flocking. I spent all afternoon decorating."

"But decorating what? Where'd you get this thing, Denny? Do you know what it is?"

Denise brushed some hairs off the back of his suit coat and resisted the impulse to tell him it was a plant from the Pentagon, a New Age herb remedy, a bonsai tree imported for Western converts to the Buddhist faith.

"I'm serious, Den. Do you know what it is?"

"Why, you must remember Christmas trees. Very popular among Christians and non-practicing atheists in the late twentieth century."

"Jesus Christ. Where do you get this stuff? Some guy's going to come in here and sell you a rainbow some day and charge you extra for the fucking cloud cover. Come here. Come here, you."

He cut off a sprig with the nail clipper on his key chain and held it up to her nose. Denise was smelling very little but vermouth at this point.

"Mistletoe?" she said.

"Well, there won't be any at my office party. It's cannabis, sweetheart. Herb, hemp, weed."

Denise's nose itched. She was going to laugh, and there wasn't a thing she could do about it. "Where do you get that from, a *Dragnet* rerun?"

"Very funny, Den. Do you remember that I'm a representative of the law? How do you think it looks for me to have illegal substances displayed in my picture window? Not to mention fines and penalties. The real possibility of being disbarred."

"For what? Illegal importation of holiday cheer? Hunting down shrubbery without a license?"

"Possession. That's a lot of reefer, love. Ignorance is no excuse in the mind of the law. It doesn't matter if I'm blindfolded in the bedroom and you're out here passing out quarter baggies. I'm still responsible."

"So, now you suspect me of dealing weed? Sure, that's what I'm planning on giving as Christmas gifts. Little bags of marijuana dolled up as party favors. I hide them in the Christmas ornaments. Want to see?"

"Never mind. I'll take care of it for you. Just let me get on my work clothes."

"This is not a marijuana plant. This is a tumbleweed I picked up out on the highway."

"So you just picked it up somewhere. How do you know what it is? You're not a botanist."

"No, but believe me, I recognize our friend Mary Jane. I'm the veteran of three teenagers, remember?"

Carl pushed her arm away and gave her his wrinkled forehead glare. The man was all concern, and the waves broke further and further up his forehead as he aged. "Just what are you trying to tell me?" he said.

"Oh nothing that you'll pay any attention to, dear. Why don't you run upstairs and put on your play clothes. Then you can go putter in your study."

"I'm not the one who's going senile."

"Humor me," she said. "Or if you can't do that, muster a little fear. You're not going to ruin Christmas again for me."

Carl touched the oversized art brooch on her blouse. "You want to come upstairs and help me change?"

Marijuana, the kids used to sing. *L-S-D. All the teachers have it. Why can't we?* This before they had any idea what they were talking about. *Marriage-you-wanna? Meet me in Tijuana. You can bring your own iguana. Where the air is like a sauna. And the honeymoon is sweet.* A jump-rope chant she'd heard Sally and Darla yelling in the street, before she got them in their father's study and explained. Tim was worse. At fifteen, he used to come home with his pupils dilated like chocolate chips expanding in the oven and sit down to eat all the cereal in the house. When she brought her magazines and her cup of tea into the kitchen and tried to engage him in conversation, he'd laugh at all the wrong spots, as if he was listening to the seedy underside of what she said. She was afraid for him, but she was also embarrassed for herself, trapped in a frame of mind where she couldn't understand her own son.

So when she found a couple of joints in his jeans pocket, she looked around the laundry room and decided to give it a try. She turned into a suffragette out there sneaking a smoke. At first, she didn't feel anything, just a prickly irritation in her throat. The stuff sure smelled good, like the tea shop in Marshall Field's. She certainly preferred it to beer. Then, when she was ironing one of the girls' church dresses, it dawned on her: the peachy glow of illumination. Her fingertips were transparent on the handle of the iron. The knot on the back of her neck unwound, nerve by nerve, until she worried it was the only thing holding her together. The more she ironed one side of the frilly dress, the more wrinkled the other one became. And this suggested some kind of truth to her, as if the smooth, well-tailored self she'd made up over the years of her marriage was just one half of the garment: the fresh face she put on all the irregularities of body and soul. If I were standing on the other side of the ironing board, she wondered, would I be the same person? The light bulb stuttered and a strobe kept beating a consistent rhythm in her head. Who am I? Who am I? Who am I? it said, like one of the riddles they told to the children.

A three-legged stool. A teapot. Twenty white horses stomping on a red hill.

I'm just Timmy's mother, and I'm here to take him home.

That's when Tim barged in the laundry room, looked toward the washer, and spotted the joint in a canning lid on the end of the ironing board. He gave a small, embarrassed smile and held up his hands, arrested. Denise will always remember the rip under the arm of his blue work shirt, the sparse blond hairs poking out underneath. and the change that started somewhere behind his eyes and swept up toward his father's forehead when she began to giggle.

"You thought I was going to be mad, didn't you?"

"What are you doing with this stuff?"

"Oh, I ran across it in your dirty clothes and I thought it was some kind of tip. I didn't want to look a gift-horse in the mouth."

"Geez, Mom. You're stoned as a fish."

"Oh, is that what this is? Hmm, it's pretty zippy, huh?"

"Oh, yeah, it's real be-bop material."

"So I'm stoned. You've been stoned for the last six months now, haven't you? You've been stonewalling me."

"Well, off and on. You know, that's what kids do now." He leaned back against the dryer, prepared to settle for a while.

"So, how do you like it?"

"What?"

"Being stoned as a fish?"

"It's OK. OK, Mom, could you just go ahead and ground me or something?"

"Here, why don't you come over here and smoke a peace-pipe so we can make it up."

He edged up to the ironing board, reached over and rubbed the back of her neck with a deep, muscle-drenching kindness, the way he'd done when he was small. But by now, he was so strong that the force reconnected her bone by bone. "Hey, I'm sorry. It doesn't mean I'm going to turn out to be an axe murderer or anything."

He still smelled of baking soda, something she remembered from his first days of life. As if he was always meant to grow up this sweet and expansive, extended beyond her ken. Denise felt her tear glands squeeze open. She figured the drug made her more susceptible, and dismissed it as an allergic reaction. She pushed the half-smoked joint toward Tim. "Shut up and take your medicine, boy."

Tim inhaled in an audible and expert manner that made her heart complain. But in the middle of the second drag, his handsome face turned red and he started choking. "We're not going to tell the D.A.D. about this, are we?"

Lying in bed with her leg crossed over Carl's, she realized that her loyalties must have shifted long before that point. Once she's completed her family, what use does a woman have for a man? she asked herself, reversing the doctor's rhetorical question. Even money wasn't a consideration, since she'd been nourishing her own nest egg at the Trust & Loan. But tonight, just as she'd almost given up on him, she felt a physical twinge toward her husband, as if someone was wringing out a dishtowel in the general location of her womb. Her legs were still good, but when he lifted and twisted them in love-making, she noticed new licks of cellulite at the tops of her thighs. In certain lights, her breasts looked similar. And now fibroids were proliferating in her uterus.

Carl touched her eyes and closed them as if she were dead already. "Relax," he said. "If you could have anything you want for Christmas, what would it be?"

Possibly, her life wasn't even two-thirds over yet. She might need all her remaining organs for the long nights ahead.

"Anything?"

"*Carte blanche* for a white Christmas."

Denise ran her hand over his chest, and felt the hairs springing up under her fingers, thicker than she remembered. When she married him, there was just a trickle of gold running down in a gully toward his groin, but now it looked like he'd be a hairy man, before he was done. "A marijuana tree," she said.

Later, when Carl wandered off to his study as she'd predicted, she went down to the kitchen and called Tim in Chicago. They let it ring four times before picking up. Then Miranda answered. The two of them weren't formally married, but they had both voices on the answering machine in a kind of electronic prose poem, and Denise assumed that amounted to almost the same thing, these days. She wondered if she'd interrupted something.

"Hi, Mother Crane. He's just coming in from the lab. It's your mom, Mr. T."

Denise supposed Miranda was a good choice: a girl with a crisp mind and farmer's market beauty, the kind that would wear well. Tim was too wise, even at twenty-five, to be running after the flashier models. But Denise worried about the proprietary note in her voice, as if she had to cajole the boy into talking to his own mother. Denise would never take that maternal tone with her son. But maybe that's what Tim was looking for. Maybe he'd been missing it all along.

"Hey, Mom. Did you get my message?"

"Seven o'clock Christmas day? I guess that gives me time to come across with the goodies."

"We'll bring the wine. There's something I want you to try."

"Tim, I have to tell you that this Christmas might be different."

"Did you forget the mistletoe again?"

"Worse, the tree."

"Well, we'll bring Miranda's rhododendron. That ought to do her."

"And I went to the doctor's today, and got, not really bad news. But he's trying to convince me to yank out the spare room."

Tim paused. "Hysterectomy?"

"What do you think?"

"Just a minute," he said. "Let me switch to the other phone."

While she waited, Denise scraped at the coagulated stew stuck to the counter. It was Carl's night for the dishes, though he hadn't gotten around to it yet. Perhaps he thought the sex would act, miraculously, as a substitute. When the children were home and he was in an amorous mood, he'd say: "Your mother and I are going upstairs now . . . " and the kids groaned, knowing he was about to put half-an-hour of soapy water between them and their evening's play. Denise sometimes pretended they were still down there, little blonde elves clattering away at the china and cutlery while he did the inventory of her body. Who would ever notice if a cup or plate turned up missing some day?

"Did you get a second opinion?" Tim said. "Is there any particular reason the guy's harping on it now?"

"'Tis the season, like they say. No, I've been having some pains, nothing serious. But he thinks it'll improve family existence for your father and me. His wife did it last year and he's never been happier."

"I'll bet. You've got to come up here and talk to someone else, someone who's read a little literature in the past twenty years."

"Well, the good doctor is quite the bedside companion. 'Think of it as an orange,' he says. 'Once you eat the fruit, you can throw the peel away.'"

"Mom, he didn't say that."

"I wish I'd had a tape recorder."

"Why don't you fly up here and see your old doctor, then we'll take you back for Christmas?"

"Well, that might not be a bad idea. You're always the practical one. You know, I suppose it would make more sense to call your sisters, but Sally's so taken up with the baby and Darla is just discovering her sexuality and all. I don't want to put a damper on the process."

"What about Dad?"

"Lost in space. He's more worried about my drug consumption."

"You've got to tell him sometime."

Denise heard a creak on the stairs. "There's the old Clause now. I'll get back to you. Thanks a lot, Timmy."

"At least give the guy a chance to screw up first," he said, and Denise wondered if his loyalties weren't shifting too.

Every morning for almost a week, Carl offered to throw the Christmas tree out on his way to the garage, and every night, Denise talked him down again, took him upstairs for consultation. She pulled out gowns and camisoles she hadn't worn in years, brought dessert to bed, lit scented candles all around the room, narrated him through the erotic scenarios of a lifetime. By now, she knew all the springs and catches to his libido and she built her stories accordingly, with the levers and false leads of a mousetrap: her imaginary love affair with the schoolgirl vampire haunting the old hotel in Charleston, the commuter train ride where she'd put his hand up her skirt, then carry on a conversation about the shocking stuff they were showing on television with the woman next to her. The time they'd pretended to be brother and sister on a trip to Spain, not touching until their shadows tickled on one another's skin.

Carl started leaving his shoes at the door, his tie draped over the mantle of the fireplace.

Denise stopped spending her usual half hour in the bathroom each morning and put her makeup on in the car instead, the way she'd done in her twenties, rushing from bed to board and back again.

Her flesh hummed as she drove. Her breasts responded when she lifted a coffee cup or picked up the phone. It was like the desire to have a child, only in reverse. She craved everything burnt and bitter: coffee grounds, popcorn kernels from the bottom of the pan, rhubarb crisp. She walked around in a fever of feeling, her skin worn thin as an old Victorian gown, so all the light came through.

She didn't tell him about the doctor.

He didn't insist about the tumbleweed.

They arranged their usual Christmas Eve outing to a little Swedish town devoted to tourism—the closest thing to a resort within a hundred-mile radius of Wheeler. There, they'd stay at a bed-and-breakfast with hand-carved furniture, eat cinnamon rolls served to them by air-brushed blondes in embroidered aprons, and shop for hand crafts and more extraneous Christmas decorations, then hear the *Messiah* sung by a choir of

Lutherans who descended like Mayflies from all over the country. It was usually a treat, but this year, Denise was reluctant to go, nervous that any alien element would upset their rare equilibrium.

Carl, who took his leisure seriously, packed a cooler full of champagne and told her she was faking.

"You know you'll be fine once we're there. You did this with New Orleans and Europe too. The minute we're up in the air you think you left something burning in the oven."

"I left the coffee pot on that once."

"And who called the Delaharts to come in and turn it off? When will you learn that details are just details? Whatever it is, I can expedite it, Den."

Denise untied the scarf around her throat and rearranged it over her head. She was practicing posing as an old peasant woman. She only hoped he could get to like that too. "You think everything's just logistics. Some situations are real, well, situations. You can't just write a memo and make it go away."

Carl shifted behind the wheel, his long legs jammed up against the steering column. "What are we talking about here?"

She set her purse in her lap and started going through the contents: Kleenex, Tampax, nasal spray. "Famine, for one thing. And then there are plagues, like AIDS. World wars. The greenhouse effect. Old age."

"Oh, not that again. I thought we already did the middle-age crisis routine."

Denise snapped the purse shut: you could tell the old lady models because they made a more resounding cackle as they closed. "Excuse me. You went through the middle-age crisis routine. I sat home with bated breath waiting for you to renounce your racquet-ball partner."

Carl blushed, then blanched, so that she could see the long, double-branched vein standing out in his temple and then glanced back to check his blind spot, pretending that he wanted to change lanes. "I kept my marriage vows, that's something not many men can say."

"I kept my mouth shut, but then a whole gaggle of women have that to brag about."

"Let's continue the trend, shall we?" Carl turned into the left lane, a little recklessly.

"Well, you sure wanted to go on about it at the time."

"I was being open and honest, like all your self-help books are always preaching."

"You were trying to negotiate your position."

"Maybe you really don't want to take this trip?"

"What about you? Do you want to go back to Chicago? You can drop me off at the nearest rest home."

He put his hand on her knee and her nerves flinched all the way up to her armpits. "Denny. it's been three years. Have some mercy. Haven't I been a good husband to you?"

She untied the scarf again, and wiped at her eyes with one corner, then unwadded the silk to see how much damage her mascara had done. She had no idea what it meant anymore, to be a good husband. Someone who tilled the womb well, didn't overgraze or sew wild seed, grafted his rag-taggle genetic material into sturdier stock? At this point, she'd rather have a houseplant.

"Don't worry," she said. "No one can ever tell you that you haven't done your job."

The hotel wasn't as crowded this year, and as Carl unwound his butter twist, Denise sipped the strong, fennel-scented coffee and surveyed the other patrons: a young couple with identical sweatshirts and tawny collar-length hair who couldn't afford a more exotic honeymoon, a pudgy man and wife badgered by two pre-teenagers playing war games across the tablecloth, a thirtyish grade-school teacher type with an older woman, perhaps her mother, in tow. The mother woman kept going on in a squeaky leather voice, like bare skin peeling off a car seat: "They're clean, they're decent, they're trustworthy, but they like their coffee breaks, these Swedes. From ten to eleven, then from two to three in the afternoon. Makes you wonder how they find time for lunch in between. Could be we'd have a lighter skin population right now if the Vikings weren't always off on some meadfest killing time."

The younger woman held her coffee cup in both hands and looked into its depths. Then she tipped the cup toward her, spilling it, deliberately, Denise thought, from the tick flickering in the dimple of her pretty cheek.

"Goodness, Lucy. Your table manners haven't improved much since the harvest banquet in seventh grade. What do you ever do when men take you out for dinner? Or is that still happening much these days?"

Carl wiped his fingers on his napkin and touched his knee to Denise's. She strained to catch Lucy's reply.

"No, nowadays we usually cut straight to the cappuccino," Lucy said. "That's actually more difficult for them, since they have the extra added problem of keeping the cream off their mustaches."

Denise made an effort not to laugh and felt the caffeine hit her capillaries in grand style, producing more space in her head than she thought possible. She hoped she wasn't this way with her daughters, especially Darla, who was so sensitive she'd turn white and start pinching the backs of her calves when anything remotely squirmy turned up in conversation. Denise gave Carl's knee a nudge. The skin behind her ears burned, and there was a little preliminary gnawing in her personal forest of fibroid tumors. The doctor told her that coffee only exacerbated her condition, but she couldn't give up the feeling of expansion, her consciousness doubled and trebled.

"Don't you ever hear chords?" she asked Carl.

"Only when I'm with you."

"I mean, do you think it's possible to read someone's mind?"

He looked right into her eyes, the way he'd done when they were dating and they held long staring contests in her dorm room, in his Plymouth, in the First Methodist parking lot, where the first one to look away had to give in and say what they were thinking. His milk-blue irises iced over and the sunburst wrinkles around his eyes flexed. "After all this time, why would you want to?" he said.

During the afternoon of Christmas Eve, Carl bought an antique end table and a pipe stand; Denise found a pair of hand-carved candlesticks and a brooch made out of pheasant feathers. No more Christmas ornaments, to her relief, though the little town seemed to be on permanent Yule time with its festive blue and yellow tiles, potted pines, and the red Swedish rocking horses painted on every possible surface. This was even odder, Carl pointed out, because the snows here were so sparse. The early settlers must have missed their native climate, and built this town as an island of winter on the plains. Denise liked the idea. She'd just as soon live here as in Wheeler, as long as they were off in semi-retirement repenting of their sins.

They came back to the hotel room and took off their clothes for a nap before dinner; just as Denise suspected, now that they were on actual vacation, Carl wasn't interested anymore. He lay on top of the bedspread with his hands crossed over his stomach. Denise listened to his wispy breath deepening into a long, uncanny snore. She had the covers stripped off her side of the bed and had to keep adjusting them to the changes in her body temperature: the whole bedspread combination, twisted-back blanket, bare cotton sheet. Her torso was a low-lying plain subject to the slightest atmospheric shift, with cold fronts coming in from the north, unexpected heat waves flashing up from the stippled mountains of her thighs. She smelled of green tornadoes and thunderstorms. She rolled over and bit the corner of one pillow, pulled another down between her legs.

When she finally fell asleep, she heard Carl rustling on the other side of the bed, getting up and running the shower. In her dream, this was the noise of the locker room behind her. A woman in a white shorts set came out of the steam, her sandy hair frizzed up in a halo around her face, her low-cut sweater revealing freckles sifted deep into the snowdrift of her cleavage. She took a balloon out of her pocket and proceeded to fill it at the sink. As she did, her breasts wobbled, and her lips moved. Denise's abdomen pulsated in response, its walls pushed and polished to the texture of chewing gum. Then the woman held the balloon up to the fluorescent light, a warm red water bottle, with a round belly and a long turkey's neck stretched out with the water's weight.

"Do you know the ceremony?" she said.

"I'm not paying for anything," Denise told her. "Just remember that."

"Hold out your hands."

The woman let the bottom of the balloon rest on Denise's cupped hands, and Denise felt suddenly dirty, as if she was touching herself in a way she hadn't done since she was twelve, and spent all those hours in the bathtub letting the water run between her legs, opening the secret panels of her labia to find the second belly button inside.

"Tell the truth, do you really want to go?"

In those days, the nursery song about Alice kept running through her head, and she was convinced that she'd be another one to go slipping down the drain if she didn't stop just in time, before she fell into a trance and forgot her milk money, before her mother called out for her to stop primping and come set the table, before she turned into a grown woman who had to cross her knees in public, even in slacks, and sleep on her back to avoid squashing her bosoms.

"I want to stay," Denise said. "It's not even dinnertime yet."

The woman lifted the balloon above her head and swallowed it, like a circus seal swallowing a fish. Then she followed it with a steak knife, a thermometer, a syringe.

Denise felt herself getting warmer. "Why are you punishing me? You're the one going around stealing husbands. You're the one who has to go."

The woman pointed to her full cheek, and Denise saw the dimple winking in its hollow.

"OK, just this once, you can talk with your mouth full."

Then the racquet ball partner pulled something off her tongue, like a hair that had gotten caught there during love-making. She held it out to Denise.

It was a whole branch of evergreen, a shred of shriveled red balloon caught in its needles.

"One for the road," she said.

Denise woke with a strain in her belly, as if she was in labor again and a fourth child had set about unraveling her intestines like a pretty strand of glitter. She was marinated in sweat, and the sheets were wet underneath her. Everything smelled acidic, like her urine in asparagus season, and she was convinced she was going to die.

Carl sat at the foot of the bed fiddling with his cufflinks. When he saw her eyes open, he gave the springs a couple of bounces and grabbed her around the ankle.

"My God, Den. You're soaked. What, did you have a little private work-out session without me?"

"I think I'm having a miscarriage," she said. "You better take me home."

In the car, Denise lay in the back seat and grasped onto her purse. She felt the pain build and burst in fever blisters underneath her. At the moment of the fiercest pressure, she bore down hard, knowing she was about to get the payoff of a couple seconds of relief. It took all her concentration just to ride the contractions, which she imagined as a series of men far too young for her. If she let down her guard, they would notice her gray roots and kill her off right away. But Carl kept calling to her over the seat, wanting reassurance that she was still conscious. She couldn't really talk, but she managed the single syllable: "Hi." Even at this late date, he was getting her signals crossed.

"Do you want me to turn the heat up? Are you OK back there?"

"No."

"Denny, we've got this thing under control. The hospital's only three miles away. Den, you just hold on there. Remember, you can do this. You've done it before."

"No." Denise knew there was something else, outside the rhythm of her pain, that she had to think about. Did she want to die without having it out with Carl, letting him off the hook for eternity?

"There's something," she said.

"Something important?"

"Something to say."

"Denny, love, you should just maintain back there."

"Got a bank account."

"Money's not a problem. We don't need to talk about money now."

Denise lifted her head off the seat so she could speak louder. "Saving up to leave."

"Leave where?"

"Back to Chicago." She waited for the downbeat of the contraction to make sure, then added: "I'm not dead yet."

"What? What are you talking about?"

"Give it to Darla. She'll need it now."

"Denny, don't you know how much I love you? How much I need you to stay?"

Denise dropped back down to the seat. She didn't doubt him, but it seemed too late, and beside the point somehow. He couldn't help her now, she was riding out beyond his reach, where she was probably headed all along. The highway was spun glass beneath her, and she felt herself hydroplaning up off the surface of her pain. It was like the moment when the aircraft tipped up off the runway, her Darvon kicked in, and the question of elevation didn't matter anymore. She was finally speeding, tumbling faster than any spin cycle or rambling weed, and she didn't want to stop.

∾

They did the operation on an out-patient basis, so Denise was scheduled to be home for Christmas after all. Her doctor wasn't too enthusiastic about being consulted at ten o'clock on Christmas Eve.

"This is going to keep haunting you until you have the surgery," he said. "You need more R-and-R after every D-and-C."

"Thanks for the tip. Don't call me, I'll call you."

"You really can't take care of it soon enough. What does your husband say?"

"If you don't mind, I'm in pain. Merry X-mas, doctor."

"Suit yourself, but I'm going on the record recommending surgery."

"And I'm bloody exhibit one."

The nurse took the phone away from her and handed it back to the intern-on-call.

"All over, Miz Crane." she said, "We can get you ready to go home now."

Denise looked into the nurse's unlined face and grimaced. Was she going to have to go through the rest of her life hating younger women for an ignorance they couldn't conceal? Her breath curdled in her mouth, and she remembered a year when her mother wouldn't go shopping for clothes with her anymore, when she stayed in her bedroom wearing a mottled green housecoat and transferring photos from one album to another, sorting out items for Good Will. Was that the year it had happened to her? Did she have to separate herself from Denise to make the change? And then—Denise felt her heart burn, thinking of it—she met Carl and started confiding her problems with Mother in him. Her sadness shaded into a deep, warm melancholy where some new feeling could begin.

The nurse touched Denise's forehead and looked at her chart. "Now, we need you to take it easy for a while. Let that cute husband of yours baste the turkey for a change."

When Denise woke up, it wasn't morning anymore, and she was lying on the couch staring at the daguerreotypes of the three children on the wall: a cowlick, a headband, a ponytail. They were period pieces by now, with no particular resemblance to anyone in the family. But she kept them on because they reminded her of a black-and-white segment of her life when she was too busy to bother much with the color details. Strange smells were coming from the kitchen. She got up and dragged the grate away from the fireplace, poked around the fire until she felt a stitch in her gut. Then she went over to the marijuana tree. Lucky it was so light, she told herself, not much to weigh her down here.

The tumbleweed bristled against her robe, and a couple of ornaments rolled off onto the floor, knocking against the furniture and tinkling like icicles breaking on the pavement. It was difficult to get a handle on the thing. It had no shape, no stem, no bottom and no top. Denise ended up holding it in her arms as if it were a fat baby, picking stars and ballerinas out of its hair. She gave it a final dusting, tweaked one of its branches, and rolled it into the fire. The flame flapped against her face, lighting up her whole nervous system with the hot pipes and blown fuses it was specializing in lately. But the weed didn't catch fire right away. It rolled toward the flue, resettled, crackled and crinkled. There was an industrial smell from the flocking that wafted up and stung her eyes.

Then a spark jumped from a yule log to one spiny strand of the tumbleweed and followed it all the way around the maze of curves. Another licked up next to it, lit out on a second circuit of branches. A different scent rose from the fireplace now, something spicy and woodsy and too close to the earth for perfume, like a black-eyed cow flower, or Denise's own sour sweat. She stood back and admired the tree. She could see the whole thing now, its broad girth and delicate filigree of embers. She could remember what had mattered in her life.

She sat back down on the sofa to enjoy the show, and as she did, Carl came running into the living-room, the tail of his work shirt flapping behind him, and the curls over his ears flying like a winged Mercury.

"Don't panic. Don't panic. I'll get it," he said. He reached into the fireplace and lifted the tree by its top branches, those that hadn't been touched yet. The sparks shot into the living room, blind fireflies nose-diving into the carpet and the drapes. And just for once, as he stood there holding the burning bush up over the hearth, unable to admit he couldn't save anything, Denise was glad of his speed.

Astigmatic

*L*auren always had more grace than that. It's the kind of grace, I maintain, that comes from seeing poorly, so that she gave each person, each object, that much more time, came up close, seemed to trip toward you, then caught herself with breathtaking nonchalance on the margin of your breathing space. That's always the effect it had on me. When she came over to the studio to see the still lifes, I was afraid she'd fall right into them, spilling the brandy, scattering the cogs and gears, squashing the carefully arranged seal-like corpses of seaweed. Or maybe that's what I was waiting for, the *coup de grâce* of photo-realism, the apotheosis of friendship. Imagine my surprise when I discovered it was the other way around.

Lauren lived in a renovated apartment downtown with a menagerie of stray art objects and an underemployed roommate, Ellie Gilliam, who was always lounging about in the sauna room of my health club and offering her services as a model. When I folded my *Interview* and explained my exclusive and obsessional interest in the *nature morte*, she rolled over onto her stomach, her paisley towel twisted inadequately around her waist, and assured me that she could look as dead as anyone. Her muscular hip was cocked at a dancer's isosceles angle, and her slightly barrel chest was beaded with sweat. I had no doubt that she could hold a pose for hours, if that's what was required of her. But I had given up on the human body years before.

That was only one indication that there was trouble with the rent. Lauren's grant was about to run out. She had to proofread in the daytime in order to keep up with the furious materialism of the alternative culture scene. Her act suffered. Her eyes suffered. Her boyfriend, a reggae musician and a part-time bartender in my local jazz bar, suffered too. He told me so while he poured my champagne and waited for the bubbles to dissipate and the conversation to break into a more improvisational style. I gathered the neck of my dress closer to my throat and sipped without comment, until he gave up and abandoned the bottle to its silver ice bucket with a treble clef on the side. One advantage of my peculiar situation is that I no longer feel obligated to listen to men complain about their wives, girlfriends, romantic and/or financial entanglements. But I reserve the right to eavesdrop for purposes of my own.

So, no doubt to save money toward some prop or other, Lauren settled for a seedy optometrist in a storefront office. Eyeless frames tipped up against the glass in a blind multitude. Thin wood paneling covered in charts and diplomas, perhaps a badly reproduced Renoir or Gauguin to cut the general atmosphere of utilitarianism.

There, after some embarrassing fuss over her hair, which was sure to have gotten caught in the frames with every adjustment, the doctor explained her difficulty in lurid detail. Apparently, Lauren's eyeball was shaped like a football, whereas the normal, healthy eye is closer in form to a round and buoyant beach ball. At this point, Lauren, I'm sure, is eyeing the bare-chested Gauguin to the side of the man and contemplating the advice of sex manuals, *Our Bodies, Ourselves*, and various women's magazines as to size, shape, and alignment. These works, of course, assure us that variations in our anatomies are normal, and that, to exploit an analogy, it makes no more difference than what sort of fruit we choose to highlight in a still life—the forthright apple, the rich and irregular mango, the freighted melon half. Actually, Lauren's breasts were more plum-like than anything: small but soft, their cleft barely indicated, their weight elastic with love and decay. Though I have known women whose breasts might be described as footballs, by the way.

But this was not the doctor's point at all. The eye, psycho-fantasia aside, is not the breast, and its shape is to be, if not prescribed, then at least corrected. Did Lauren ever see double? he wanted to know.

That's been a question in my mind during out entire acquaintance. When we were out having dinner together, Lauren often squinted at other tables. "She's giving him a royal flush," she'd say, or, "It's their first date. I can tell by the proportion of laughter to conversation." Then she'd add: "That always turns me on."

But when I glanced over, I'd see an attractive man or woman sitting alone.

I never said anything, though I did toy with interpreting it as a hint of some kind.

However, back at the optometrist, Lauren wasn't paying the slightest attention. "I guess so," she said. "Maybe." Instead, she was picturing the doctor's wife, since she'd noticed a wedding ring as it brushed her cheek on the third pass at her obstructing bangs. Did the doctor's wife have perfectly round eyeballs, she wondered, was that what attracted him to her? And how did this supposed wife feel about her darling looking into other women's eyes all day? More dangerous than gynecology for my money, any night of the work week.

Lauren was already putting together her performance piece on the subject when the doctor interrupted her again. When, for example, did she see double? When she'd been drinking? When she was tired? The tone of his thin voice was wheedling, suggestive, and if Lauren was offended, as she most probably was, we can hardly blame her.

After all, the man was staring into her dilated pupils the entire time, though he had specifically instructed her not to look at him, but rather at the poster—Gauguin, we agreed—to his right. An inequity which puts me in mind of the *Déjeuner sur l'herbe* dilemma—a woman framed naked in a forest of stuffed suits. And now that I think of it, this painting may be a better choice than Gauguin, especially given the perpetrator of our story.

Again, it could be that Lauren was offended, or, in the worst case scenario, only bored. But I'm convinced that her response resulted in a particularly virulent, if not punitive prescription.

"I always see double," she said. "That is, if I really look at something." Here she finally pushed her hair back, to give the doctor a good glimpse at her ear lobe, shy and prominent at the same time, like a piece of newly minted money stuck in the mouth of a child's piggy bank. "Don't you?"

The man, you can be sure, avoided the question and went on to perform a series of bizarre optic experiments in which he forcibly and repeatedly split apart Lauren's field of vision, only to bring it back together again.

"See how that works?" he said. "People like you, people with an astig-matism, have two different focal points. Corrective lenses can help reuni-fy the picture."

Lauren twisted in the headgear covering her face in a Halloween hockey mask. "Like Protestant and Catholic Ireland," she said. "East and West Berlin? Is this civil surgery? Foreign or domestic?"

"You can pick out your frames and pay at the door," he told her. "Lenses should be in by next Wednesday."

We had lunch the day she finally got them—not until that Friday, as it turned out. She showed up at the studio twenty minutes late, after I'd already given up and gone back to the massacre of spaghetti squash wait-ing for me on the credenza, junk jewelry scattered at random through its orangey pulp.

Lauren stopped at the threshold, held onto the door jamb, and took off her glasses. "Sorry I'm late. I had some pretty horrible hallucinations on the way over."

"Such as?" I said, still lingering over a sticky strand caught in the intri-cate prongs of a rhinestone brooch,

"Such as workmen falling off buildings and earthquakes opening at my feet. Such as cats mating with mailboxes. Such as the white cliffs of Dover showing up on my front stoop."

"Ah." I lifted the brush for another go at the rhinestone. "You must be in love."

"Blinded by it," she said. "That's not lunch, I hope. You can't imagine what it's like. It's like someone lifting up the drafting board that your whole life is plotted on. Or when you're at school and the teacher dumps out your desk. You look at your crayons and your doodles and your bar-rettes and you don't even recognize them. When they're lying on the floor, they look like they belong to someone else."

I set down my paintbrush and went to take her coat. "So do you," I said.

"I thought we weren't going to talk about that."

"I heard you put it into your act. That means you've talked about it with thirty people a night for a whole week now."

She shrugged and one of the buttonholes of her lace jacket caught on the silver lipstick case she wore on a ribbon around her neck.

"Let me," I told her. The ribbon was as slick as the single stretch mark on her thigh, or the stubborn strand of spaghetti squash I'd been trying to pin down for the last ten minutes. I thought of Ellie Gilliam's blank thighs tight and athletic beneath her exotic underwear, the endless fuss over the striptease, each layer to be torn off as delicately as a leaf of romaine lettuce. Then the heart prickly and acidic as an artichoke.

"I heard you said it was like a social astigmatism," I said.

"What?"

"The act. The urge. The revolving Rolodex. And I was just wondering whether you meant the feeling in general or only when it happened with me."

Lauren put her glasses back on and tugged at my hand on the ribbon. If it hadn't been for that sadistic doctor, I might have never known.

Geographic Tongue

y nephew came into this country with five words of Korean, a blue terrycloth playsuit that didn't cover his midriff, and fine black hair shooting up in a geyser. When the woman from the adoption agency carried him off the plane, he was blinking—surprised to have to do this all over again. Or at least, that's how it looks in the video tape that my sister plays over and over when I come home to crash after my last rough landing with Peirce. I pay close attention to the action, notice the dark shell-shaped indentations on the side of the baby's face, a stain on the woman's shoulder, and Nettie's confident smile smug as the open-and-shut handbag she doesn't even bother to slide off her shoulder before she picks him up. He twists in her arms and says something unrecognizable; the film shakes, then veers into a long free fall of color while the cameraman bends to retrieve the purse which has, by now, fallen out of the frame. I think if I can just get the hang of this, I'll be able to get up and go back to my life.

Nettie, who has a romantic view of adoption, tells the story as if it's a fairy tale version of childbirth, the international airplane a streamlined stork, the flight attendants angels, the adoption agent a holy midwife delivering Jesse from the smooth loins of the 747. She makes her hand into a bird to show her daughter, who had a similar landing, how the plane looks insignificant on the horizon, then gets bigger and bigger as it blocks out the golden prairie sun in a cultural eclipse, a symbolic meeting of sperm and egg, east and west, nature and nurture, before dropping, like Newton's apple, with a palpable thud on the coffee table in front of us.

"Then what does Mommy say?" she asks.

Tina pretends to peer beneath her mother's hand. She sets down her plastic milk cup and waves her tiny almond paw like she's fanning herself. "Come on out, Jesse," she yells, in a surprisingly deep voice.

Beside her, Jesse slaps his hands against the table and wobbles, since he still needs the leverage to stay standing. His hands are bigger and darker than Tina's, fat rye-colored pads thick as dinner rolls bulging in the oven, and I wonder whether, once he learns to speak again, he'll grow to agree with her story.

Me, I'm not so sure it's all that easy. I know something about displacement, having lived in five states in the twelve years since I graduated from high school. In Colorado, I was Val, a smart college girl with my shirt-tail tied in a determined knot over my navel, signifying the difficulty of undoing my virginity. In Newark, I turned, without warning, into Miss Baines, a bad translation, pale and rumpled, walking too quickly through the halls of the educational rehabilitation center, so that one of my more petite students pulled me aside and offered her personal protection if I'd just chill on those skeezers and work up an attitude. In Maine, I was a cold young researcher; in Virginia, a hot older scholar, approaching the meridian of my sexuality, and willing to take out every book in the library. In Kentucky, they call me Valerie, stretching my name out like an embroidered tablecloth, at the I.R.S. office parties where Peirce, my live-in lover, refuses to explain anything about this wheaty white woman holding his car keys whom I barely recognize as myself.

Meanwhile, my sister stayed home. I mean, almost literally. When I visit the frame house that she and her husband bought the last time the market dropped, I see the floor plan of our childhood: the stunted front stoop, like the missing thumb of someone's veranda, the lozenge-shaped living room with the kitchen wandering off one love handle, the hallway off the other, and the hallway itself with the three bedrooms arranged as deftly as alternating blossoms on its stem. And this makes me nauseous and jealous at the same time, like the sweet, chalky taste of the hot jello our mother used to give us when we had the flu.

In fact, Nettie and I usually managed to have the flu together, I remember, as I stare at her new motherly haircut, the clipped, permed, and dyed Easter bonnet that throws her round baby face, with its nutmeg freckles and sensitive nose, into a whole new gestalt of respectability. She used to lie with her head at the foot of our bed and crochet cat's cradles for us, then, when she got bored with that, fold up finger-puppet oracles, that started out with easy instructions like choosing your favorite color off the five crayoned panels to complicated questions such as, "Would you ever let a boy touch you on top? On bottom? Would you wear a string bikini?" When you answered, she'd weave the mouth of the pentagram open and closed a certain number of times, flip up a tab and underneath, there'd be your destiny, printed in the clean, astringent blocks of her handwriting.

Sometimes, I think I got the answers wrong, or Nettie just didn't know what she was doing. How did she learn how to make those contraptions, whose origami construction of diagonal folds was too confusing for me to comprehend? How did she decide what to write in the different compartments, since, as far as I'm concerned, she left out the more pertinent questions? And most of all, how did I end up so far off from the preordained pattern, when we both started out in the same place?

Nettie picks Jesse up and slides him along the table, far away from his sister and the precarious milk cup. "Come on down, Jesse," she says. "Just don't knock over any stewardesses on your way out. So what do you hear from this Peirce?"

She slips it in like it's just part of her play-talk to the babies.

"Not knocking over stewardesses." I say. "Knock on wood." I tap the walnut table, harder than Jesse does, and look at the sharp beveled edges that catch the fluorescent lighting of the room. Tina did that, when she was teething, and Nettie decided just to leave it 'til she stopped adopting infants, a kind of communal teething ring. I like the effect. It reminds me of the folk art in our apartment in Louisville—Peirce's apartment—depending on how you look at it. He may pay the rent, but at least three quarters of the furniture's mine, from a collection I started in Virginia when I was working on American Folk Traditions and earning my living as a social worker for the county. I admit I wasn't very successful as a rehabilitator of dysfunctional families, but I certainly found a lot of art—icons on unfinished slabs of wood with hoary gray bark clinging to the sides, gaudy red and yellow footstools with depressions for your feet painted to look like canoes and water babies, wind vanes guarded by wildebeests, a rocking chair with long-bodied hunting hounds carved on its arms, their mouths open to provide convenient handles of teeth and snout, a grip to seize for emphasis during the pressure point of an argument. When I moved in, I explained to Peirce that these objects, each steeped in the vernacular lived-life of the people, gave some sense of connectedness in a culture coming loose from its moorings, and he didn't contradict me, although he eventually let on that he preferred glassy geometrics and regarded my hobby as middle-class slumming. I wish he could see my sister's living room.

Now Tina's spilt her milk after all, and Nettie rushes over to deal with it, setting my hand on Jesse's back before she does. I came home to talk to my sister, but now I doubt this will ever happen.

"He wants me to marry him," I say, aspirating my vowels to sound exasperated, and rubbing Jesse's shoulder for emphasis.

"Are you going to be careful this time?" I almost hope she's scolding me, but no such luck. She's holding the cup high above Tina, who stands on her tip-toes and lifts her hands up into the air.

"Mommy, thirsty," she says, a whirr of a temper stirring up the underside of the words. I've been here long enough to recognize that, anyway.

In the books, they say ignore it, so I do: "He thinks we'll have better arguments without an escape clause. You know, the ultimate solution. You just break up and everything's settled. But I'm a little suspicious about his motives. I think he just wants to claim me on his income taxes."

Nettie lowers the milk, a level look of concentration between her thin, blonde eyebrows. "OK, but no more. You do it again and there's no more milk for you until the cows come home."

"Cow come home," Tina says, giggling into her milk so that bubbles break on the surface, blue in the reflection from her black hair.

I've always liked that shade. I remember Peirce telling me I was so white I was blue, a milk bottle in the cold, a pigeon's wing, the vein o'er the Madonna's breast, the glimmer in an oyster shell. By this I thought he was trying to say that the edges of one race curl back to reveal the other, like the silver-sided leaves of a birch tree. I get it, I said: Blue-black, black-and-blue, blue-grass, bluebeard, blue-blood, blue-stocking, blue-white, bluing. Peirce, who was from the flip side of Richmond, didn't appreciate this interpretation. He said it was whitewash, not to mention hogwash. His eyes are the color of good, imported beer, and the tips of his fingers are pink underneath their nails. His palms are chalky, with deep, indented lines of pink and brown, and I wonder if this means he'll live his life more intensely than I will. He has carnal caramel nipples, large for a man, a briefcase full of tax forms by day, a satchel full of law books by night, a grainy cat's tongue that catches like adhesive tape on my skin, and an elaborate moral code as intricate as his love-making. It was actually me who wanted to marry him, but he didn't believe my people understood his people. "But I don't have any people," I told him. "I've got at least six different nationalities fighting it out in my bloodstream and I haven't phoned home in four months." He licked my hairline from the nape of my neck up to my ear. "You just don't get it, lady, do you?" he asked, repeatedly, before he left.

"Well, are you going to?" Nettie says.

"What?"

"Get serious about someone."

"Oh, it's just you take so long on the comeback I forget I'm talking to you. Or is that what we're doing? I can never tell anymore."

Jesse starts to cry, a sliver of panic pinched out of nowhere. Nettie picks him up and pats his back without looking. "I guess you can see I've got nothing better to do than sit around eating bridge mix and discussing your love life. At least you've got one. Anyway, what does it matter? You always want to know whether I think you ought to marry someone or other just so you can ignore my advice."

"This is different," I say. I want to see the placid surface of her face break, to set the freckles out to sea. "I didn't tell you, but he's black."

Her nose doesn't even move. "Oh. Some people are, I guess. With your rate of exchange you're bound to hit one sometime or other."

"Well I'm happy you're oh-so-enlightened out here in the suburbs. Let's see, then, miscegenation's OK; it's serial monogamy that's the problem."

"The longest-running serial in America," she says. "If you really want to give us some entertainment, you could at least go through the divorce courts."

Tina finishes her drink, hands the cup to me, and I hand it back again. "So you think I should marry him then."

"Whatever. Then maybe my kids would have some cousins to play with."

I catch my breath, and it bobs up in my chest, as if someone's hit me in the stomach. "What makes you think I'd let my kids play with yours?" I say.

But by the next day, she has me baby-sitting while she goes out to make arrangements for finalizing Jesse's adoption. I sit on the couch in my stir-rup pants, antique batiste gown, and fleecy sweatshirt with my feet under the sofa cushion and count shampoo commercials: I wonder how many I'll be up to by the time she gets home. Jesse sits on the floor beside me playing with a little people's fire station while Tina rushes around the house banging cabinets and toy chests, then dumps a pile of dolls, place mats, toiletries, and dishware on the living-room floor.

"On sale," she says. "Tina shopping. All on sale."

"Oh, I thought you were doing a collage installation. I was going to offer to use my influence to get you in a show."

She smiles, then does a little skip over to the TV and flips to the shop-ping channel. "Show."

"Hey, I'm counting commercials. You messed up my score."

She shrugs, and her long hair rides up on her shoulders. "All gone. All gone, Aunt Val."

I wonder, once more, how much she understands about who I am and why I'm here. "Quick, what's an aunt?" I ask her.

"Aunt Val," she says, so they've already trained her in tautology.

"You worry me, babe. You're already inducted into the capitalist con-spiracy and you haven't even gotten your first allowance yet. For Christ's sake, you don't even have a social security number."

She arranges her purchases, ignoring me, like her mother. "You know, your mom thinks I move around too much. She thinks it's anti-social. But I can't think of any society I really want to be a part of. Can you? Sure, the way of the Tao sounds tempting, but what about foot-binding? Hey, what about that? Or you could be a vegetarian animal rights activist if it wasn't for the tofu. Can you say tofu?"

"Achoo."

"Achoo yourself. OK, I know it's confusing, but playing dumb doesn't help. You're not helping me at all here."

Then Jesse starts to talk too. As he picks up the round peg people, he names them: "Mama, Dada," he says, holding each one in the glow of language for a moment, his face round, triumphant, and greenish in the television's light. Then he pushes them down the fire pole and shouts: "To-whee."

"To-whee," I repeat after him. "Is that Korean, do you think? Is he talking Korean now, Tina? "

But what am I saying? There's no way she can answer my question. They got her before she accumulated the first word of her native language, felt its sting and slap on her taste buds, its slippery lisp wriggling out from between her teeth. Maybe that's why it's so easy for her to assimilate, I think, looking at the blonde baby dolls laid out in a cannibal casserole dish: Winken, Blinken, and Nod, out on a shopping spree.

"Bad," Tina says. "Jesse eat something."

"What?"

"Toy."

I touch his face, which is smooth as mother-of-pearl, but with padding underneath. The color and texture of the dark meat on a turkey. I put one hand under his chin and my finger into his mouth, trying to jack it open. This is all I need, for the baby to choke on something while Nettie's away. Inside, I find a red plastic fireman's hat sitting on his tongue like a cherry.

"All right, give it up boy," I say. "Come on out with your ear-flaps up."

"To-whee," Jesse says, and sticks his tongue out, as if it's just another gadget in his arsenal.

But when I pull the hat out, there's still something left on his tongue. Raised bumps, like braille, the way our carpet looks after I haven't moved the furniture for a long time. As if something's been sitting there and left its mark. I try to make out the pattern, which is a collection of amoeba-like pods resembling the squashed balloons left for dialogue in the funny papers. I'm making progress too, just about to crack their fishy code, which seems specially directed at me, when the phone rings and scatters my concentration.

I take it in the kitchen, sprawling over the breakfast bar to reach the receiver.

"Hey, Valerie there?" someone says on the other end. Valerie. They only call me that in Kentucky. But the voice reminds me of my students in Newark, with their deep, quick articulation, the buffed affricatives and whiskey alveolars.

"This is me."

"Hey Valerie, girl, I got your boyfriend over here and I'm giving him a blow job. 'Course, his big old black dick's gonna pay me back. He say my pussy's even sweeter than my fine molasses ass. He don't want no more of your scrawny skeezing onion. Don't like that oatmeal grit no more."

My chest empties out, till there's just a thin glass shell between me and my ribs. Or my rib cage is the glass—a cracked crystal-white chandelier, an upside-down wedding cake, a bouquet of icicles hanging precariously from a porch railing in the snow. I can hear a toothpaste commercial on the television, saying come a little closer, get a little closer to this moment of your life, and Tina telling Jesse how the garage door of his fire station is supposed to work, and Jesse screaming for her to go away.

"I'm sorry you feel that way," I say. "But please don't call me at this number again."

How very white, I think, as I hang up the phone. This is only proving her point. Peirce's point. I'm too refined to fight for a man, too damn granulated to take or make an impression. Too speculative to recognize, much less protect, what I love.

The dog starts to bark and the front door crackles open in the cold. Tina and Jesse yell "Mama" and Nettie says, "Hey mush-kins, did you drive your cranky old aunt off already?"

"I'm here," I yell from the kitchen, because I'm not up to looking at anyone yet. "I'm on the phone. Peirce called and he wants to know when I'm coming home."

"I'm not playing Mother, May I," she yells back. "Make up your own fickle mind."

I pick up the receiver again, holding down the clear plastic nubbins to muffle the dial tone, de-fanging the beast. "Little Nell is back," I say. "We'll talk about it later. See you, lover." Then I hang the phone up again, loudly this time.

In the living room, Nettie's sitting in my spot on the sofa, holding both kids in her lap at once, and pressing her cold, pink cheeks to their warm dark ones.

"Mommy cold," Tina says.

"Mommy met Uncle Sam and he pinched at her nose," Nettie explains, grabbing at the middle of Tina's flat face, where there's not much of a target. "Why's Peirce calling in the middle of the day?"

"Things must be slow down at the tax mines. I thought you weren't interested in my love life."

"No, just phone rates. You know me, Miss Totally-Consumed-with-Insignificant-Details. Like how to keep the government from taking my children away."

"Why? What happened?"

"They think I need one more home study to determine whether I'm a fit mother. You think they investigate birth mothers to see if they're fit? Or sober? Or conscious, even? You think they expect them to shoot their schedules and fumigate their houses at twenty-four hours' notice? Oh, maybe they start to get the idea a little home quiz might be in order when the kid shows up with third-degree burns in the emergency room. But not fucking likely. If the poor slobs've got your genes, they're yours for life. Like a brand or something."

I think of the marks on Jesse's tongue, but this doesn't seem like the right time to bring it up. "Relax," I say. "It's no big deal. I used to do this in Virginia. They just want to make sure you have running water and a little milk money."

"Then why are they coming again? They've already been here three times. Three times, that's all it's supposed to take."

"Like magic, huh? Three trots around the track and then they're yours, they've always belonged to you. You've got the film to prove it."

Her face seems to get broader, her eyes straining away from one another and her chapped pink lips stretched out tight. Her freckles finally flicker: the first time I've seen it this trip. Then I finally feel as if I'm back.

After a static-filled lunch of crackers, peanut butter, and cling canned peaches, Nettie decides we need to go to the mall to get supplies for the social worker's visit, and I'm surprised at my relief. I hate shopping, especially at malls, where the angles and alleys, the repetition of shoddy merchandise, and the mirror fetishes give me headaches of overstimulation. I hate to see my own reflection dogging me like a bad spy, her pale gaze the color of a raincoat in any weather, her fine hair as shapeless and undefined as the yard waste raked up in little piles all over Nettie's neighborhood.

But I've been sitting in the same spot for three days. Everything in this house happens within a five-yard radius of the sofa. In the morning,

I have my coffee here while Nettie chases the children with their clothes in her hands. At noon, we take our lunch on TV trays, while the kids crumble crackers onto the floor, munching on bare hot dogs as they roam from toy to toy. And all day long, we watch television—singing elephants, puppets with nasal conditions, aging New Agers explaining ecology and personal hygiene; talk shows about women whose men have left them for transvestites, communes, causes, celibacy, and other men; soap operas where everyone has a glamorous job with a flexible work schedule and not a soul is ever certain of the father of their child—while she knits and I rub at coffee stains on my clothes and on the beige corduroy sofa, trying not to think about Peirce. At night, the husband—Dave—will come home and sit on one end for a few hours, flexing his fingers and plying the remote control, occasionally inspired by the evening's programming to shake his big silky head and erupt in a song or rhyme about Jesse or Tina. Then they put the children to bed, a long process of delicate timing, split-second decisions, unexpected setbacks, fake anger, real anger, hilarity, caution, exhaustion. Finally, Nettie brings out an afghan crocheted with yellow rosettes and I fall asleep in the same spot where I've been sitting all day, my suitcase behind my head, under the far arm of my sofa.

It's no wonder these people like their malls, their trick mirrors, giving them the illusion of space.

Sure, I'd like to go shopping. I'd love to go shopping. Just let me get my pocketbook, as our mother used to say.

In it, I have forty-six dollars, a prayer wheel of birth control pills, a half-used lip gloss in Peaches-n-Persuasion, a catalogue from a friend's show at the gallery where I work part-time, and Peirce's going-away letter in a long legal envelope, the kind that's lined with blue honey-combing to prevent visibility through the paper. Who is he trying to fool? Who else going to want to read his lurid legal prose? Just in case, I zip open my suitcase and slide it in while Nettie works the children into their snow suits limb by squirming limb.

It's not that I have the letter memorized, I think, as the babies doze and Nettie hums along with the car engine in nervous 2/2 time. It's just that certain phrases tend to linger around unconnected, like objects hanging from a child's mobile over the crib. "Unreconcilable differences," "ethnic slumming," "cultural lesion," "tongue-lashing, pussy lynching," "*quid pro* Jim Crow."

I string them together in a song along the road, each telephone pole holding another hard knot of twisted truth, the slack line between them the distance I have to travel to see his point of view. But travel is good for that, even if it's only the ten miles out to the mall. After a while, I begin to hear his voice, that Yankee rhythm over the Southern swell of vowel sounds, the scat rapping with the legalese.

Cross over the road, he says.

And what if I do?

What happened when the white girl crossed the road?

I don't know, what?

She got her onion peeled.

Onion, I always wonder why they call it that. There's nothing whiter than an onion; in fact, every layer's whiter than the last. Even though it may be yellowish on the outside. Each tissue the texture of damp skin after a swim in chlorine. So that you can peel down your cuticles and it doesn't even hurt.

Your scrawny, skeezing onion.

But when they said it, they usually meant a black person's. A black ass. It was a different shape, supposedly. Rounder and more palpable. With the stubborn heft of a tuber, something that grew in the ground. I used to think Peirce loved my body because it was grounded, with muscular legs and significant hips. But now I wonder if he loved it as a fluke, a delicacy, an oddity: one prize vegetable that grew miraculously and defiantly in the shape of another. The way certain small natural wonders—a potato with the face of Jesus spelled out in its warts, a two-hearted tomato—got enshrined in folk art. Was it because I was a white woman or in spite of it, and which was really worse after all?

At the mall, Tina recognizes all the trademarks and brand-names, even though she can't read yet. "Nickels! Boytano! Shop Ink! Denim Minimum! C-Mart!"

Nettie repeats after her every time she gets one right. "Yes, that's Shop Inc., Tina. That's where we bought . . . ," and I try not to think about how long this has been going on. But it also gives me an idea about the marks on Jesse's tongue: what if I'd been reading them wrong, trying to make out pictures when they were actually symbols like trademarks? I have to get him alone, maybe in a dressing room, so I can check out the situation without making Nettie suspicious.

Meanwhile, I might as well look for something to buy. Something outrageous and comforting, like a pair of purple elbow gloves or a set of zebra-striped tumblers. I start to feel good, pushing Jesse along in the stroller, making my muscles pulse to the subdued bubble-gum snapping of the muzak, working the cramps out of my soul. Then I notice that people are staring at us. I can't tell whether it's Tina's loud voice or the sight of two blonde women with these beautiful oriental urchins. I should be used to this by now, but I'm not. Alone, I'm a ghost, a cipher; people walk into me without knowing that I'm there, and I don't bother to disguise the emotions in my face, or my eyes wandering in and out of focus. But when I'm with Pierce, everyone looks. It's as if his colors throw me into relief: in his wake, I'm suddenly a person with recognizable features, a profile that can cast a shadow over a crowd.

I relish this attention and fear it at the same time, and I suspect that Nettie feels the same way.

In one of the more prestigious cut-rate department stores, a woman with waxy hair and stylized wrinkles—just a few, to add authenticity—comes up and asks if she can help us.

"No-we're-just-looking," I say, panicking already. But I know Nettie won't let me get away with this.

"Do you have any jumpers?" she says. "Maybe a jumper is the right thing for the social worker, sporty yet ladylike. What do you say, Val?"

I just grip the handle of the stroller.

While Nettie sorts through the rack with professional ease, the saleslady makes eyes at Tina, who bats her eyelashes back like a star hitter, smiling as if she knows there's going to be trouble.

I touch her shoulder, and brace her against my legs. Her body is relaxed; she knocks back against me in a regular rhythm, as if she's swinging. She smells of baby shampoo and peanut butter, and I wonder who I think I'm protecting.

Then the woman begins. "What a pretty little girl. Japanese isn't she? Just like a doll. Or is it Chinese? They sure make them dainty over there." She touches a flyaway strand of Tina's hair, which looks reddish in this light.

"My doll," Tina says.

The saleslady draws her hand back, stiff inside her ruffled sleeve. "And smart too."

Then Nettie looks up from a handful of denim and paisley. "Actually, she's Korean. It's really different from Chinese or Japanese, if you look close enough."

"Oh. And the little man too?" Are they brother and sister?"

Nettie's had this question before. "They are now," she says.

I can hear her voice lifting, tickling under the edges; she's about to give her public service announcement on adoption.

"I think I'll go try this on," I say, grabbing a polka-dotted babydoll dress I wouldn't even wear as a makeup smock. "Don't worry, I'll take Jesse with me."

I leave them somewhere in the briar patch of U.S. adoption policy.

In the cubicle, Jesse starts to cry, the same dizzy whine as the alarm on his fire station. I pick him up and check his diaper. Nothing. Then I look into his mouth. The minute I do, he stops, as if he's been waiting for me to get there. Now the shapes on his tongue have changed. They're shifting like the crop circles in England, where you can fly over an abandoned field and see a pair of them one day, and a whole Olympic diagram the next. But it's only been a few hours, and they've parted and melded, forming bigger constituencies, irregular townships of pink tadpoles and red amoeba, some climbing on top of one another, some dormant and covered by a gray ash of dried skin. I wonder, for the first time, if this hurts. Is it part of teething, an unavoidable phase like a childhood disease? I make a note to ask Nettie; maybe it'll distract her from her home visitation.

Then I hear something happening in the next cubicle. A hanger scraping on a hook, a zipper grating open, the pock mark of bare flesh meeting fresh elastic.

"Did you really think you'd get away with it, bitch?"

I set the baby back in the stroller. "Don't worry, Jesse." I say out loud, as if my voice will ward away the other one. "We'll get somebody professional to take a look at that later."

"Don't give me professional, girlfriend. I seen more professionals than Wilt Chamberlain, and you ain't nothing but a whore."

She's still after me, no matter where I take my clothes off.

"I didn't know about it," I say, slipping my peasant blouse up over my head.

"You know shit. A man's got tooth marks on his shoulder, he's engaged. Got hair on his chest, he's a married man. Got calluses on his hands, he be somebody's daddy. Ain't no other reason for a brother to raise a finger."

"Fine with me. I didn't make the rules. I don't fuck with my eyes open. I don't ask any man to take care of me."

I look under the partition and watch a red and orange flowered slip slink, slither, slip down on top of a high-heeled patent leather boot. The pointed toe catches in the folds of polyester, then kicks the slip off into my booth. There is no leg that I can see. Chicory? Indigo? The high yellow of a well-worn butter churn? I've never been able to tell.

"You fucking well better fuck with your fucking eyes open. It was a story about that once. Said anybody messes with a messer's mister better keep her onions peeled."

"Yeah, I heard," I say. "When we talked on the phone, I definitely got that impression."

Now I'm undressed too. I reach down for the slip and feel its glossy texture. I was right, it's polyester and not silk. But it's a good blend, thicker than I thought, with a patina like polished wood. I pinch it between my fingers. Just to know it's there. The electricity left over from her body snaps and curls, clings to the fabric clinging to my skin.

Then the boot steps down on the back of my hand. Its high stiletto heel wobbles, unbalanced, and sinks between two bones where there's not enough room for it. I feel a sharp pain, then a dull one, spreading out over my whole horizon.

But then I see the broken spoke on the wheel of Jesse's stroller and I know what to do.

I pull the front bar toward me with my free hand and position the spoke to batter into her leg, or the place where I think her leg should be. Something falls off its hanger in the next booth. A saleslady rings back a curtain on a curtain rod down the hall. Jesse gives a surprised hiccup. My hand shoots a stingray of adrenaline to my spine.

So that I jab the stroller spoke into her five times without stopping. There is no scream, no curse, just the resistance and give of breaking skin. Then the pressure lifts and both my hands are shaking so hard I can't tell which one's been injured.

It's Jesse's cry that finally brings me back, with its fine ridges and deep inclines of passion, like the fierce and delicate pattern of teeth marks around Nettie's coffee table. His face is mottled, pink and tan, and distorted as a plastic squeeze toy in its rage. His hands fight in front of him, as if he's pushing someone away. She wouldn't hurt him, would she? I can't believe she'd take it out on him.

I stand up, lift him out of the stroller, and push the sweaty bangs off his forehead, hold him against my bare chest so I can feel his heart thrumming in the back beat of mine. His face is wet too, and his cowlicks flare with electricity at my throat. I rock him until he opens his eyes again, at least as wide as they'll go, and I'm staring into a brown that there's no good way out of, since his eyes are folded so gradually into his head, paper-sharp ridges under the lashes, racing car turns in the inner corners by his nose.

"Are you done hiding in there?" Nettie says, from the other side of the curtain. "I'm just about to crash the limit on my credit card. You might want to put on your skinny pants and come rescue me."

Afterwards, we clean house—Dave in the kitchen, me in the bathroom, Nettie in the bedrooms and living room, with the babies corralled into their playpen, wailing along to the tune of the vacuum cleaner. Green cleaning powder cakes under my fingernails, in the cracks in my skin. Ammonia dithers in my nose, aches onion-sharp in my eyeballs. It seems like we haven't seen the surface of anything for days.

Nettie looks in at the door and throws a rubber glove at me, then sprays a shot of woodsy air freshener into my hair. "Don't try taking any short cuts either. I know all your tricks, Miss Sweep-it-under-the-carpet. Scrubbing the floor doesn't count unless you get down there on your hands and knees."

I pitch a wet washcloth in her direction. "Oh yeah, what's in it for me?"

"I'll do the hustle at your wedding, duckie. I'll refrain from casting the first stone."

Her hair is caught up in a sweatband, yellow tassels sprouting over the sides. It makes her look more like her old self, and I wonder how I could ever lie to her.

"I'm not really getting married," I say.

"You're kidding," she tells me. "What about the flower arrangements? What about the lounge band? Isn't my Tina ever going to get to fulfill her destiny as a flower girl?"

Then she walks away before I can explain.

At bedtime, Tina insists that Dave set up her new tent in the clean living-room. "I sleep Aunt Val," she says. "Jesse sleep bad."

Nettie pulls the panda sweatshirt off the little girl's head and drags on a polka-dotted nightgown. Tina keeps talking the whole time, though neither of us can understand what she says.

"The kid's got her own ideas. Lucky for Auntie. Are you OK with that, Val?"

I'm already settled on the sofa with my book, a monograph on the work of a Georgia folk artist who's recreated the travails of the Children of Israel in a clearing in his back yard. The plagues are individually represented, static in time; the Southern pines and rushes shelter the baby Moses on one end of the natural spring, while, a little further on, the shellac gleams on the faces of Pharaoh's drowning horseman, and a white rock dam approximates the parting of the Red Sea. The artist appears in a panel on the page opposite: he stands with one hand on the golden calf, as if he's about to swat her off to pasture. His white hair and black face make him look like a negative, reversed. "I never made any figures before. There wasn't any call to. Then the Big Man comes to me in the toolshed and says, 'I got some business for you, Theo. I'll give you three thousand more days of good fiddling to make me 364 of these prayer people.'"

I turn the page and Tina slaps her hand down on my book. "Story," she says. "Tina bed story."

"OK, you win. So what do I have to do?"

"Just get her to sleep," Nettie says. "If there's a crisis, I'll be in my room, planning loopholes for the social worker."

"Once upon a time," I begin. "There was an old man who got tired of shopping. Every time he got home with his goodies, there was something wrong with them. The candy cane was broken, the horse had a twisted leg, the doll baby cried too much. So he said, 'I think I'll make up my own world.' And so he did."

"Froggie," Tina says, pointing to a close-up detail of the plagues.

"That's right. What do we do with frogs? We kiss them." I bend down and plant one on the glossy swollen throat.

"Yucky."

"Hey, it's not so bad. You try it."

She pushes her hair back in a lush gesture that could foretell her whole life, leans toward the page, then backs away again. Her nose makes a squiggle, a barely perceptible rearrangement of her face. It's just like Nettie, I think, and something in my chest follows suit.

"Come on, you can do it babe."

She touches her face to the page, then jumps back, as if its surface is buoyant, elastic. "Yucky, yucky, yucky," she yells, as she runs around the living room in a circle.

"Hey, hold it down," I say, and go back to my book. The plagues move into tighter and tighter focus, until I'm staring at the boil on the neck of a cow. There's even a fly on the rim of its crater—the detail is that fine. The wings are dotted with impressionistic points of color. I count at least five different pigments. By the time I get to the page with the plague of locusts, I realize I'm sleepier than I thought. But Tina's still moving, emptying out Nettie's knitting basket over by the stairs. I want to watch her, but I can hardly keep my head propped up that far. It droops off my neck like an overripe tomato bending on a stalk. I can't fall asleep. Nettie will just have more to blame me for. Tina's up alone, she's tipping over the piano bench, she's pulling on the lamp cord, she's working her supple shoulders through the bars of the railing and toppling over the stairs.

"Ow," I scream, and wake up again. "Tina, are you OK?"

She laughs. "Aunt Val cry."

"I'm not crying, I'm laughing. Sleeping's just so much fun. You ought to try it sometime."

"Funny Aunt Val."

I pick up the book again. I've made it all the way to the last plague in my sleep. A woman in a long striped beach robe holds a bucket while a man—her husband?—paints a jagged red rainbow over the door of their house. Above, a figure in glitter and sequins touches one bare, pointed toe to the rooftop, and springs out to a full wingspan of almost oriental design, two interlocking screens with the fleshpots of Egypt depicted in graphic detail on their scales. Men in transparent loincloths lounging at a feast, cattle collapsing in the field, sheaves of wheat consumed by fire and hail, women beating out the family clothes on the rocks by streams and rivers of blood.

I close my eyes and go on reading. The Angel trips off the roof and Peirce appears behind her, as if he's just going to parachute along. He's wearing a thin linen shift, like a muslin curtain, and through it I see the haloes of his nipples, the loose bud of his penis lapping at his leg. My mouth is dry. My nose closes up, and the pressure shifts inside my head, so the air I need to breathe is in my ears instead. Bubbles snap over my eardrums, then break, spilling his speech in a wet glaze through my ears.

"Legally, it's a trick bag," he says. "You can't really call it the first-born. Because Keisha's kid came before. Also because it never got born. But you're one ass-backward assassin, Valerie. How could I marry a lady who'd do that to her own baby? A sister would never do it. Keisha never could. You people are so evil you even smell bad to your own selves."

"Then just jump," I tell him, from where I'm standing on the ground in my nightgown and hip-boots, holding my pocketbook flat against my chest. "Go ahead and try it."

He puts a toe out, testing the air waves.

"You'll never be a lawyer," I say. "You don't have the vocabulary for it."

"You'll never be a woman," he says. "You don't have the balls."

He jumps, and a loose shingle falls into the bucket by my feet. I bend down, retrieve a kitten-sized crawdad, its legs bent under it like broken hairpins, its eyes protruding like the warts on a potato stored for too long in the dark. As I look at it, they start to grow, and the thin legs wriggle in the spidery scrawl of Pierce's handwriting. What's he trying to tell me? Do I really want to know? The eyes are distended now, and glowing, growing like the ash on a cigarette, then dropping off into the lengthening pools of their own shadows. I bring the crawdad closer to my body. One long antenna lashes out at my chest, and I try to hold on. But it keeps striking, something beads up in my breast and I open my arms and let the baby fall through—it wants so badly to be set free. But once I let go, I find it's me that's falling, not him.

I wake up to Tina's scream.

I stumble against the coffee table and drag over to the tent, where she's lying stretched out sideways in front of the opening, her eyes closed, her face pillowed on a stack of fashion magazines, her eyelashes shuddering. She's bracing her body to break out of sleep, stuck fast in its elastic gum.

I touch her hair, sweaty and coarse against her silkscreen face. She smells of clean laundry hot from the dryer. "Wake up, Tina. Tina, it's all right."

She pushes me away, opens her eyes, then grabs me close again. Her pupils are still dreaming.

"Water," she says. "Get water. Thirsty, Aunt Val."

She takes my hand and leads me down the familiar hallway of my sister's house. Her hand is damp, her grip is steady; she moves at a determined pace, so I'm convinced she's not sleepwalking. But then she passes the bathroom and turns into the nursery, where the door is slightly ajar and the light is on.

I push at the door with the flat of my hand and see the shape in the rocking chair before I'm ready for it. Maybe if I'd knocked, I think, maybe if I made a noise. But she doesn't seem startled at all, just keeps on rocking, sitting there with her dreadlocks falling down through the cane curlicues of the chair, some heroic figure with her hair caught in the spokes of a chariot. She's wearing a silver fox fur, its tails darkened in stripes, brushed out through the nap like heavy eyebrows seen sideways. And she's holding Jesse in her lap.

I look down at Tina, to catch her reaction. She starts to hum. It's the song about the alphabet, though she can't get the words right yet. I recognize its hesitations, the wheedling toothpick construction of its tune. I move toward Jesse, and Tina follows me, never loosening her grip on my hand.

"Morning, Valerie," the woman in the rocker says. "Bitch that you be. Cunt-plugger. Kid-killer. Whitey whore."

"What are you doing with the baby?" I say.

Her coat is open over her silky yellow blouse, and she's holding him to her breast. But his mouth is filled with something else, a piece of flannel, just a rag, really, in a pastel nursery pattern. She's going to suffocate him, I think, but he looks healthy, half asleep, and he's sucking on the rag with satisfaction, little zips of suction zigzagging through the night.

"Not as you'd notice, but this child has a sore in his mouth. Big as a cockroach and raunchy as a roach-clip. Are you trying to exterminate this one too?"

"What do you care? It's one less paleface for you to scalp."

"Look here, Valerie. I don't love your flaky filet-o-fish ass. I don't even like you. I just got to bother you like you bother me."

"I didn't know," I say. "I swear to God. I just picked him up at a gallery opening. He never looked like he belonged anywhere in particular. In a way, that made me believe that he could belong with me."

"Belong. This long, that long, too long. Girl, you don't even know the beginning of belong. Do you comprehend black man? Nigger? Big black buck? Why do you think he even want to shove his piece into your old double whammy?"

"Please," Tina says. "Thirsty, Aunt Val."

"Does that satisfy you, Keisha?" I say. "It is Keisha, isn't it? Do you want to get the kids involved in this, too?"

"Girlfriend, they're involved already. They fucking always been involved." Jesse's quiet now, asleep, from the looks of it. She takes the rag from his mouth.

"What is it? What are you feeding him, anyway?"

"Something my people known for a long time. A long time medicine from my man's mama."

"Give it to me. I want to check it out. My sister will kill me if it's anything weird."

I reach down and pull at the rag in her hand. I feel her thick fingers close on mine, the glossy skin and dolphin-smooth muscles, like Peirce's. But I throw my weight behind me, and grab the rag away from her. Then she rocks back, and the chair bobs up, its long haunch spilling forward, its front claw landing on my bare foot.

"Ow," I say, but it doesn't stop me from bringing the rag to my mouth, smelling its bitter bouquet of camphor and mustard greens, tasting the alkaline shiver on my tongue. Then the chair goes on rocking, though there's no one in it anymore, and I am rocking with it, tossing on the billows of my inner ear, spilling over my own feet.

"Where'd you go, Keisha?" I say. "You bitch. You hypocrite. I wouldn't marry you either. Why do you pick now to disappear?"

But when I come to, I'm looking at Nettie instead. She's standing over the crib, patting Jesse's back. Tina is sitting on the floor beside her, playing with the torn fringe on the bottom of her mother's nightgown. The overhead light is out now, the room illuminated with a greenish glow from the gingerbread house lamp. And it's me sitting in the rocking chair, wrapped in this ratty yellow afghan again.

"OK," I say. "Just tell me what happened to Jesse's tongue."

"Oh that." Nettie turns, and her face is washed clean of makeup, transparent in the dusky light. Her freckles are even more pronounced now, forming whole constellations, where I think I can read twins and bears and scorpions, a nursery full of night sky in reverse. "The doctor said it's nothing. It's called geographic tongue. The taste buds make these patterns, circles usually, but they change all the time. There aren't any other symptoms, really. It doesn't even hurt. And it's supposed to go away by itself by the time he's six."

"I don't know if I can wait that long," I say.

"I hate to point it out, but you're not the one who has to. In fact, I never noticed you were very good at that."

"Well, I waited to get married, didn't I? I waited to have kids. I waited this long for you to talk to me."

She kneels down, works the tail of her nightgown out of Tina's hand and looks up at me. "What am I supposed to say? That you can't remember how to be happy? That you make yourself miserable just for fun? That I've got my own family to worry about now?"

My foot throbs the rocking chair fell on it, and I lift it up and tuck it under my leg. "Family," I say. "I don't even know what that means. What makes you think you're more related to them than you are to me? After all, you just acquired them, but you came with me. All your life, all you've done is buy things, accumulate people and junk and ideas, and all I do is give them up."

"It's not my fault. What's wrong with you, anyway? Did you take some kind of Buddhist vow?"

"I had an abortion," I say. "My whole life is one fantastic D & C."

Her hand wavers on Tina's gown, and she tries several times to refasten the hook at the neck. She doesn't speak until she gets it. Then she just asks, "Why?"

"I know you hate me because you couldn't. But I wanted to get to bottom of everything. Scrape it all clean. I couldn't stand to have Peirce marry me because I was pregnant. So I did it and then I told him and he left because I did. Turns out he also knocked up a home girl who was willing to germinate his precious seed. Not that he's planning to marry her either, even though her kid must be about two by now."

She looks at me as if I hadn't answered anything.

"All right, don't tell me. You don't want to talk about it, do you? Let's discuss the kids' vaccinations, or the new knitting patterns for the fall."

"How do you get involved with these people?" she says.

"What people? Why does everyone want to tell me about their people, our people, you people. These are the people that are out there. That's all I know."

She walks over to the rocker and puts her hand on my shoulder, then starts to knead it through my sweatshirt and gown. Tina gets the idea and starts to pat my knee. Her touch is tentative at first, working itself into a heavy beat, and she looks up at me and bats her eyes, like she did for the saleslady.

Now my sister moves her fingers down my arm, lifts my hand and holds it to her belly. She gathers up the gauzy folds of her nightgown, so I can see her waist-high underpants with the nylon torn away from the elastic on one side. Then she pulls them down to reveal a long, pearly scar on her abdomen, like driblets of semen or mother-of-pearl, and I touch my finger to its ridges.

"From my operation. To have kids," she says. Then she laughs.

"So it's a scar one way or another, no matter how you look at it. Do you know, I've been seeing her, Nettie,"

"Who?

"The woman with Peirce's kid."

"Jesse's father died in a car crash. Did I tell you that? He was just about to marry the mother. But since he died first, that means that Jesse didn't even exist legally. If the mother kept him, he wouldn't have even been able to go to school. Or join a club, drive a car, vote, or get married. But they still make them do military service," she says. "I think about that sometimes."

"No, I mean I see her. We talk on the phone. We go shopping together. We get into these cat fights."

The air shivers over by the crib, and Keisha reaches over Jesse to adjust the spinning mobile gathering speed above his head. Her fur coat bunches over her hips, and bristles out like a field of dandelions gone to seed behind her. One of her dreadlocks drops into the crib. She ties the rag around a red toy horse and sets the mobile in motion again.

"You better stop it then," Nettie says. "Before it gets to you."

The bitter herbs resurface in my mouth; they re-map my tongue, the place-names for love and lust and anger. And I don't know how to tell her, but it's too late for me to stop now, and we're both at home here in the dark.

The Bones of Garbo

I am a seagull—no that's not it. I am an actress. CHEKHOV

I want to be alone. GARBO

I. HOW NOT TO DRESS

A pair of brown velvet slacks, one leg cut against the bias so that it shone a deeper hue and slenderized the left hip without diminishing the right, but looked great under strobe light. Brown strappy sandals with a spiked, wood-look heel purchased on discount from the Pump Room, where my best friend had worked up a great sales record by caressing the ankles of middle-aged women as he slipped on their pricey loafers and spectator pumps. A *Chorus Line* T-shirt, brown on cream, with a string of dancers stretched across my chest, the leggy star's posture distorted by one newly developed breast, the married couple's hands clenched tightly over the other and knotted at the nipple. At my neck, a homemade brown velvet choker with one of my mother's prize ivory earrings stabbed into its bow. All topped off with my own dishwater blonde hair caught up in an asymmetrical bun and tied with a coarse brown shoestring.

⁖

She wants to be an actress, my mother explained to her friends, when I crossed their path in the entryway. They were not sympathetic.

"Why not just go the whole hog and study up to be a wood nymph?" one said.

"You know, Sandy, you'll get enough of that later on when you start dating."

84

They were sturdy, ironic women—schoolteachers with distinctive laughs and all-purpose wardrobes: the volleyball coach with the potty mouth and the perpetual pair of culottes; the history buff with her unfiltered cigarettes and shag cut, crates of movie stills and sixties albums stacked up in her homeroom; the English teacher sporting classic tailored blouses, gap teeth, and tennis elbow. My mother was their queen, the first divorcee in the school system. Every Friday they'd pack their apples and cream cheese sandwiches and take off for the matinee.

"But you all love the movies," I'd say, as they tramped out the door, my mother's glossy raincoat brushing my bare calf and a script of illegible smoke signals trailing behind them.

∞

Alone in the mod condo we'd bought when my dad went through his life change, I examined all the makeup in the medicine cabinet. But I longed for more exotic thrills than my mother's sensible collection would allow: blue mascara, purple lipstick, metallic eggplant eye shadow. She'd told me I shouldn't wear makeup at all, that I had a beautiful skin to begin with, and I'd only ruin it with all that extra. She claimed she only indulged because of the Pill, which had marked her face with a fine mask of sunspots—nothing more sinister than a healthy cover of freckles, if you hadn't known better. When she was a girl, in fact, her face had been completely open sierra, pride-of-the-prairie, like mine.

But then I looked in the mirror and remembered the single freckle on the slope of my nose. Oddly enough, my mother loved that one, and had raised a stink when a photographer tried to airbrush it away in a close-up we'd done for my junior high graduation. I turned my head so that it didn't show. I had a face that should only be looked at from the side, never straight on. I had to remind myself. Her face is her fortune. Her fortunate fate. The face that launched a thousand ships. Sentences from books I'd read over and over. I turned my eyes up, then down. I ran a finger along the outline of my cheek. I tried to tell the future.

∞

They say that Greta Garbo's face had no bad angles, but she looked like a different woman in every shot. A barely insinuated cleft in the chin. A needle-fine, but sizable nose. Wide, expressive lips. A gap between several of the front teeth, narrowed in Hollywood. Eyes. Eyelids. Cheekbones. Eyes.

But then, Garbo never spent much time looking in the mirror.

She was born in Stockholm in 1905, Greta Gustafsson, the flower of seven generations of rural peasant stock. Her father was a street sweeper and gifted amateur singer who died of kidney trouble when Greta was fourteen. Erratic financial support came from Uncle Jack, a taxi driver. Her first shorts were promotional films for Bergstrom's, the department store where she began her working life at age fifteen. A supervisor, recognizing her talent, promoted Greta from the millinery department to women's ready-to-wear, where she prospered.

൭

"Miss Gustafsson . . . always looks clean and well groomed and has such a good face."

൭

The face wasn't divine at first. In early photos, it looks alternately: too round, too crowded, too broad in the chin. The kinky hair clouds the outlines. The crooked teeth give the smile a comic cast and Miss Gustafsson looks every syllable her name—a parody of a strong Swedish milkmaid—sturdy, willing, but of dubious intelligence. She will surprise us later on, by becoming one of the most sophisticated actresses of a generation.

In *How Not to Dress,* Greta loses herself in the logistics of a reversible riding habit. She fumbles with the buttons. She flashes on and off in her goofy gap-toothed smile. An earlier version is more plot-oriented. In *Top to Toe,* the family home has been razed by a fire. Instead of despairing, mama, papa, and *childer* descend on Bergstrom's in a carnival spirit. They will get themselves a new wardrobe out of the ordeal. Miss Gustafsson shows her legs and smile. Everyone buys. Everything is delivered.

൭

I want to come out of the divorce like that, dressed in a wardrobe my father has never seen, one that my mother wouldn't be caught dead in. I reach down and pull the bottom of my T-shirt up through the neck to make a halter. I paint some rouge onto the mirror, then rub my face in it, keeping my promise never to mar my features with a makeup brush.

II. FLESH AND THE DEVIL

To get the part, I have to do somersaults on stage. Really. Then a dash up and down the orchestra pit, a reading of a clean limerick, and an improvisation based on Hansel and Gretel. It's not until callbacks that I get my hands on the script, which turns out to be an early play by Woody Allen. I'm reading for the part of the *ingénue,* a tourist from New Jersey who can't quite figure out what she wants in a man until she meets up with a befuddled diplomat in an Eastern Bloc American embassy. She makes a lot of long speeches filled with ellipses and run-ons. I fill the gaps with gestures I've learned from watching the Matinee Club imitate the home ec teacher.

My best friend, Kerry, gets the part of my father—a coincidence that fills me with mystic 8-ball awe. He reads the lines in an exaggerated, campy style and takes great pleasure in finding an Ugly American wardrobe from thrift stores downtown, where we spend most Saturday afternoons scoping the racks for dinner jackets and tuxedos to wear with our designer jeans.

But the real sleeper is the male lead—a blond wrestler who shows up with a motorcycle helmet and plays dumb so convincingly that he fascinates the whole crowd. He blinks his long, rabbity eyelashes in the spotlight. He acts with his arms, bare even in the heart of February, so I can see the muscles flinch with every lurch of the plot. He has trouble with the lines. I can't believe no one's noticed that Todd's too beautiful to play Woody Allen.

Meanwhile, Mr. Morris the director tells my mother and all her friends he thinks *I'm* beautiful. But, when we're blocking at the early rehearsals, he lets me know, in front of the whole cast, that I walk like a duck, my dark roots are showing, and I don't know how to kiss.

"Melt," he says. "You're in the throes of passion, you've been through a string of bad relationships, you've just been woken up in the middle of the night out of an erotic dream, and you're supposed to let your torso melt into his. Sandy, what's the matter, hon? Haven't you ever been kissed before? You look like you're playing the little teapot, not a healthy American girl."

೦৺

Backstage, Kerry teaches me how to walk with my heels farther apart, how to apply Sun-In with more precision and substitute a powerful hair dryer for the sun's rays. He demonstrates a ball change, for quick moves on stage. He mimics my lines so that they jostle and jiggle, sloshed over with emphasis and implication. When he shows me how to melt, his face goes slack, his hipbone digs into mine, and I smell the jade green *frisson* of his cologne.

∾

It was Max Stiller, a prominent Swedish director, who created Garbo as we know her today. He was a former actor himself, a handsome man fond of jewelry, displays of temperament, and risky business negotiations. He cultivated a collection of elaborate antique waistcoats and an obsession with beautiful women with whom he was never known to become romantically involved. While Greta was still attending the Royal Dramatic Theatre Academy, Stiller cast her in The *Saga of Gosta Berling*, warning that she would have to lose twenty pounds for the role. He conducted long arguments with the camera man over Greta's best angles and made her repeat scenes until she cried. He then escorted her into high society, told her what to say and how not to dress. She called him Moje. He called her Garbo. That is to say grace in Spanish. Wood nymph in Norwegian. Divine on any tongue.

∾

"Tell Miss Gustafsson that in America, men don't like fat women," the American movie mogul commented to Stiller, as they planned the break to Hollywood.

∾

The somersault turned out to be more than a whim. At one point, I had to maneuver out of a half nelson in the arms of the hero to tumble over a hard sofa arm. Lucky me. Todd had to actually dive over the back. Every time we did it, I had a moment of panic, as if I was going to roll off the stage. It was similar to the moment of the stage kiss. In both cases, I went into a dark place where I lost all sense of orientation. There was the earthy smell of Todd's sweat, like my father's old running shorts in the bottom of the laundry hamper, his hand on my lower back, the crick in my neck, the furball in the pit of my stomach. Then he'd pat me further down and I'd jump, leap, catapult back into the clutch of my own skin. Later, Todd started a rumor that I was a little too aggressive with my tongue, and Kerry said I'd finally get to start dating after all.

∞

"You know that when you blow out the match . . . that's an invitation to kiss you?"

It was a revolutionary love scene, Greta Garbo and John Gilbert in *Flesh and the Devil*, close up, for at least five minutes and illuminated only by the match they hold between them. They were flesh-and-blood lovers by that time, or so MGM would have its audiences believe. Gilbert was a film idol, a frustrated director whose education had halted at the edge of eighth grade. Garbo was a rising star, traumatized by her loss of Stiller, who failed in Hollywood and returned to Sweden alone to die six months later of tuberculosis. Gilbert taught Garbo to play tennis and took her out on long jaunts with his roommate, all of them dressed alike as handsome bachelors. Greta repeatedly refused to marry him and called herself a bachelor for the rest of her life.

∞

"Wife is such an ugly word."

∞

After rehearsals, Kerry and I would go to my house where he'd hint around that he wanted to go sit on the sun porch and drink out of the ornamental, fish-shaped whiskey bottle my father had left behind. After-wards, we'd supplement what we'd drunk with water from the tap, as if we really believed that the old man would come back some day to rep-rimand us, and as the spring wore away at the alcohol content, our evenings got longer, our highs more expansive, and our conversations more philosophical.

Kerry told me what he thought was gross:

French kissing

Marijuana joints

Waking up in the same clothes you went to bed in.

I told him the things I'd never do:

Take the Pill

Really dye my hair

Sleep with someone unless I wanted to.

"Oh, you already do, girl. You're just frigid as hell."

I kicked at his ribs with my spike heel. "No, I'm not. Besides, that's a contradiction in terms. If I want to sleep with someone I'm not frigid. And vice versa."

He grabbed my ankle and started stroking it with the bottom of his glass. It was so cold it made my teeth ache and the blades of my shins sting, but it felt good too, and I concentrated on not pulling my leg away. "Not necessarily. Everyone wants to. It just means you might want to, but you can't enjoy yourself."

"I always enjoy myself just fine, thanks," I said. The glass was soaking into me, was becoming part of my leg, part of the slope of conversation, part of Kerry's lap. Maybe this was what Mr. Morris meant by melting.

"That wrestler chump really bothers you, doesn't he?"

"I'm just worried he's going to forget his lines in the middle of a performance. What would you do?"

"I don't know, San. A diva's only as good as her last leading man."

"Thanks a lot," I said, and we heard the front door jostle on its hinges.

"She should've hired a woman detective."

"She should've bounced him out on his balls."

"She should've skipped the face lift and gone for the ski lift."

Then I heard my mother's voice, scraped dry with tears and cigarettes. "It's just so sad," she said, and I felt the budding hangover beneath my hairdo blossom like a cabbage rose.

III. GARBO TALKS

Then there was the problem of delivery. I couldn't project past the twelfth row. Mr. Morris had his assistant testing it for me. Whenever I heard my voice on the tape recorder, I thought it was someone else—the time and temperature lady, the mouse on my favorite cartoon, the timid female voice on the phone that used to shed excuses down to its very last fiber then ask for my father during the middle of the afternoon. It wasn't an ugly voice; in fact, there was something attractive in its timbre: a twist, a curving inward, a verbal blush. But I felt embarrassed by the sound of my own lines, especially when Kimber caught them on tape, fast forwarding and reversing, flashing her elbows and pressing her lips together, isolating the words like guppies in plastic baggies.

"You think you know what you want."

"You think you know."

"You think you want."

Kimber stopped the tape again. "What?" she said, so that the word echoed on both ends. Her hands pulled at her long rumpled hair and her thin nostrils dilated. The tail of her men's dress shirt rode up over her hips as she squared her knobby shoulders and tried to track my career.

∞

It was a convention by then: Garbo made her appearance almost a quarter of the way into the film, just as the viewer's anticipation was paling. Then it reasserted itself at the moment of impact, a raw craving for some essential beauty, like the yen for raw beets and carrots the actress exhibits in *Ninotchka,* and which she was known to share in her off-screen life.

∞

"What? I can't hear her. Is she trying to be an actress or a seagull? I don't hear the gravel in her gullet, Moje." Kimber ran the tape backwards again without dimming the sound. There was a blip and gush, a shriek and caw of cellophane that made my eardrums quiver.

"Yakablom. Yakablom to you too," she said, and I laughed along. "There's your doppelganger, your demon voice, you ought to try it sometime, kid. What did you read for try-outs? I did *The Seagull* but Aaron— Mr. Morris—thinks it's maudlin. His taste is more Neil Simon-y. Mistaken identities, harebrained schemes, light romantic comedy. It makes me want to weep. I can really weep, you know, real professional tear-jerker quality. Anytime I want."

And she started in, her whimpers bleeding imperceptibly into actual moans. Real tears manifested in the corners of her eyes. Pencil rimmed her eyelids, looking like Cleopatra kohl.

I'd made a point of teaching myself to cry without making any noise at all, sitting stock still on the sun porch, staring out the window and clutching a sofa pillow. I'd hold the sound in until I felt the shallows of my face solidifying, the look congealed at last. But now it turned out that wasn't the way to be an actress after all.

෧෨

When it comes to *Anna Christie* the effect is doubled: Garbo has made her name in silent pictures filled with long close-ups and placard ellipses: "You are . . . so beautiful" "You are . . . so young." Galloping horse hooves kick her name up out of the sand; trains spark its syllables through the rails; she has no need to speak up for herself. But now Garbo must raise her voice in the service of technology. The posters for the movie concentrate on this singular fact: "Garbo Talks."

෧෨

"Are you all right?" I asked.

"Gimme a whiskey, ginger ale on the side . . . and don't be stingy, baby," she said, in a coarse, spiky accent, her face suddenly drawn tight, her eyes dilated and focused somewhere behind my shoulder. "Who's that? Who's that?"

I thought she was hallucinating, her eyelids flickering in a REM tattoo. Then I realized she was asking me something—a quiz, a joke, a riddle.

"Who?"

"Don't you know? She doesn't remember, Moje. It's her, Sandy. It's the Divine Garbo. Those are the first lines she ever said on film. They say I look like her. I'm supposed to have her cheekbones, no?"

෧෨

The effect was fabulous: throaty, chocolate, erotic, deep-salted, divine. John Gilbert's career plummeted when his high-pitched whine shattered his screen image. But Garbo's voice veiled her face, coated and saturated the picture, safe-sealed the mystery.

෧෨

I'd never talked to Kimber much before. The people in the cast called her the Kook, the Kook-umber, or the Kook-Under, and avoided her at all costs. She seemed older than the rest of us, her features deeper, her odors darker, her vocabulary more pronounced. She showed up at rehearsals with movie magazines and paper bags full of odd snacks—a pickled green tomato, a sardine sandwich, a butcher's package of smoked herring. Her curly reddish hair looked oily under a series of hats and berets. In conversation, she salted her speech with allusions to movies and actors no one had ever heard of before. The men's dress shirts she wore over jeans or dark trousers were thin enough that you could tell she didn't have a bra on, and underneath, her baseball breasts stood wide-set and stolid on her chest. Once when she rolled up a sleeve, I looked up its huge arm hole and saw a thick spiral of light red hair, like a sea sponge waiting to expand.

"She's a narc," Todd told me, after the lights went out on our kiss and he patted me on the backside, as he did more and more often now that he was beginning to memorize his lines. "No one our age would wear a hat like that."

"She's Mr. Morris's love interest," the plump girl who played my mother confided.

"No, she's just a fashion disaster," Kerry said. "Come on, Sandy. Let me fix your hair."

෬ഄ

In Garbo's first scene, she stares across the table at an old woman in men's clothes. Both characters are ragged, exhausted, well on their way to being drunk. Garbo's beauty is shaded by a hat and a hangover. She wears a string tied around her neck, a ruffled blouse, a frown plaited into her forehead.

Marthe, the wharf rat, meets her gaze.

"I know who you are," Anna Christie says. "You're me in forty years."

IV. GRAND HOTEL

The story came out soon enough: Kimber was a transfer student who had lost her parents in transit. Just after she got settled in our school, the Air Force shot her father off on Temporary Duty Elsewhere and her mother spiraled into some personal crisis that sent her through a series of institutions and rehab centers. That left Kimber alone in her senior year of high school, three months to graduation. Mr. Morris had figured out she was flying solo when he pulled into his driveway one January night and saw the open door of the house next door. A girl was swinging on the newel post on the front porch, dressed in a sheet with a man's tie knotted around her waist. Her body was illuminated in the porch light, its peaks and ridges as defined as if she were nude. He remembered thinking she looked like the Columbia Studio muse, the unreconstructed one, before the fat censors took an eraser to it, and then he wondered whether he'd really done it this time, he'd stayed too late at Marly's, and gone into one of those sex-infused hallucinations. He parked and picked up his gym bag, and went in for a closer look.

৩৩

"The Grand Hotel. People come, people go, nothing ever happens."

The movie opens with wide shot of a switchboard, showing us the potential for crossed wires and missed connections. We can find its analogue in the spiral stairwell of the Grand Hotel, a huge cutaway wedding cake of plot.

"I wonder if anyone ever jumps?" the Baron says, leaning in toward Joan Crawford.

"I don't know. Why don't you try it and see?"

৩৩

When Mr. Morris got closer, the girl stooped, as if suddenly exhausted, sat down on the porch, and shucked off her ballet slipper. Then she rubbed its toe against her cheek, so Aaron—Mr. Morris—could almost feel the texture of the waxed ballroom floor against his ten o'clock shadow. He watched her kiss the slipper's underside, then take off the other shoe and sit it on the porch railing. She paused for a moment, watching it balance. He saw his breath move.

৩৩

Across town, my father is holding a business meeting in the lounge of the Plaza Suite. His drink is dry and the potential buyer has offered to refill it, but the guy's not being aggressive enough at the bar, standing there chatting up a woman in a black studded halter instead of concentrating on getting the bartender's attention. Once again, Dad has the opportunity to regret the intrusion of disco into the more respectable hotels.

He rolls the ice around in the glass like the dice in a crap game. His video lottery franchise is flourishing, buckets full of silver every afternoon. The flash color of rainbow trout he'd be hauling into his early retirement. But only if he can manage this merger. The woman shifts so that he can see up the hollow of her armpit. Jackpot. A nickel shot of nipple. Without even trying, as usual.

∽

That's why Kerry thought I was frigid. When we took our *Private Lives* duet acting entry to the state forensics tournament, we stayed overnight in the Capitol Holiday Inn. After Mr. Morris gave us the mutual respect speech and locked himself in his room with his gym bag, we went for a late night swim with some of the competition, then padded around the halls on bare feet, no cover-ups, feeling like the exhibitionists we were trying to become. The hotel was a theme park of adulthood. A bird cage took up one entire wall of the lobby, showcasing parrots and toucans, some of whom actually called "Toss the crackers, cookie" and "Sock it to me, sailor" at us as we passed. When an indoor cafe appeared at the end of the atrium, umbrellas and tables set up on astro turf, we landed at an abandoned table and rehearsed our roles, adlibbing to suit the situation, and there was a sharp chlorine smell in my nostrils, a sticky glow over Kerry's rough-complected winter tan that made me imagine being ten years older, my fame made or broken, and remembering this night. Then we went back to one of the rooms and sat against a wall, watching two of our friends make out on the tacky brown and orange queen-size bedspread.

"An eight for poise and presentation," I said.

"A ten for expressiveness. Did you see the size of that boner?"

"Ow, what are you doing?"

"Checking your qualifications, San."

∽

Just as Mr. Morris became convinced the girl was going to expose herself, he power-walked up the front steps, holding both hands over his head, then realized that he'd watched too many movies and let them sink back into his pockets. His gym bag still sat like a penitent dog in the driveway: who's to know what's inside?

"Are you all right?" he said. "I'm Aaron Morris, from next door. I teach over at the high school, I think I've seen your face over there."

Kimber threw her head back and tucked her bare feet under the sheet. But she didn't get up off the porch. "Strange man, strange man don't look at me."

"I, ah, I don't want to intrude, but are the folks around? You know, the administrators, the producers, the payroll department, the sponsors?"

"I won't lie to you. I'm here alone. I'm depending on the kindness of strangers. You can do whatever you want to me." Her voice was strange: hoarse, fatalistic, demanding, like no teenage girl he'd heard after ten years in the business. He felt his own throat close.

"Right now I just want to get you in out of the cold."

꩜

Garbo's role opposite Baron Barrymore looks like deliberate typecasting. By this point, she's reached that dangerous curve in her career where she's suddenly able to parody herself: a rich tragedienne who can't bear to wear her pearls or cast them off either. Once she steps out of the tutu and slips back into the adoring men's dressing gown, she's herself again, vamping from one hotel room to another, uniquely anonymous. You might say Garbo lived her life as if it were a series of movie flats and hotel rooms. She didn't take the time to accumulate furniture or husbands, never entertained, rarely answered the phone. Her apartment in the Campanile Building was marked with a simple "G," the doormen neither affirmed nor denied her presence, and three of her seven rooms were permanently blocked off. At actual hotels, she registered under an alias:

Miss Karin Lind
Miss Jane Emerson
Miss Emily Clark
Miss Mary Holmquist
Miss Gussie Berger
and the favorite: Miss Harriet Brown.

꩜

I was the only kid in my group who lived in an apartment, as I called it, since I couldn't pronounce "condominium" without stumbling over the "condom" part, and this seemed either lower-class or urbane, depending on how you looked at it. I tried to see myself as a New Yorker in one of Woody Allen's movies, although our furniture was far too plump and crowded for that, and I suspected he'd never approve of the white plastic dinette set with sunflower cushions or the farmer's market still life in the hall. For my mother, the condominium was the fulfillment of a girlhood fantasy of living like a bachelorette. The minute they got the separation, she went out and bought it, said she wasn't going to give the old bluffer the chance to back out now. The compact dishwasher, the laundry chute under the bathroom sink, the fold-out ironing board were amazing to her: I often caught her opening and closing them rhythmically, her mahogany wedge haircut bobbing in the draft, and I only wished he could see how she looked then.

But our new living quarters did mean that I heard everything that went on, whether I wanted to or not. And one night while I was applying another coat of Sun-In, breathing in its nasty nail polish zest, I switched off my blow dryer to listen to Mr. Morris describing the scene in Kimber's house once he finally got her inside. Candy wrappers and movie magazines all over the floor, male and female clothing draped over the chairs and sofas, a strong odor of sauerkraut in the air. When he went back into the kitchen, he found that the gas stove was on, though all the pots in the house seemed to be stacked up on the counter and the refrigerator contained only a bottle of cheap vodka, a package of radio batteries, a few stalks of celery and a half-empty jar of jalapeño jelly.

"The girl was trying to off herself," he told my mother—Marlene, let's call her.

"Don't be dramatic, Aaron. If she was really serious, then why was the door open?"

"Maybe she ran out of nerve. Anyway, I've been keeping an eye on her. But I think it would be even better if you'd take her. It's more kosher, don't you think?"

"It's always more kosher for the woman to carry the extra weight. That's why we've got the stretch marks."

"Marlene, did I ever tell you you're a living doll?"

∽

When her last lover, George Schlee, died of a heart attack in the Crillon Hotel in Paris, Garbo panicked, packed, and left without notifying the authorities. His wife, who bore a striking resemblance to the film star and had tolerated the affair in a dignified manner up to a certain point, never spoke to Garbo again. She had her New York apartment exorcised of "the vampire's" presence. That's why it's not surprising to see Greta sweep out the door in her fur, without even accounting for the Baron's corpse.

∽

So Kimber moved her movie posters in with us. She packed her car with three paper bags of clothes, a milk crate of books and magazines, a suitcase full of jalepeño jelly and peanut butter cups which she hoarded under my bed, and brought out for special occasions. The vodka she left at home, but we made commando trips in whenever we needed fortifications. She slept on the daybed in my room and I watched her twist in the sheets, throw a leg over a pillow, wind the covers over her head, mutter into the Hollywood headboard, get up and bring a sardine sandwich back to bed. My mother, who had her own mysterious bouts of insomnia, would look in at the door, bobbing her tea bag in a cup of hot water, and wink at something over my head.

∽

"There's always another Grand Hotel."

V. GARBO DIES

It happens in an opera box at the theatre. But it could be anywhere: two girls sitting in a bedroom, a beauty parlor, a carriage. One must be darker than the other. One must be leaner. One must have intuited the vast black and white archives of the human heart, while the other is just beginning to suspect a few things. They peer down at the chorus girls kicking their legs on stage, measure the distance from there to here. Then, after surveying the prospects in tails, they finally get down to business and place wagers on which men will make it up the stairs.

∽

"There's a revival downtown, kid." Kimber told me one night, when we were stretched out on the floor eating peanut butter cups and looking at magazines. She had my *Glamour* draped over her knee and I was leaning on my elbows over her yellowed copy of *Photoplay.* The strong smell of must gave the chocolate a fishy taste, but I still let it melt in my mouth as long as possible, while I mulled over old gossip—would Garbo ever marry John Gilbert, were her feet and her salary really as huge as they claimed?

"I don't know how you can read this rubbish." Kimber said. One side of her surprising face was lit by the floor lamp, since she insisted on reading in semi-darkness, and I wondered whether it was true, as one photographer swore, that Garbo had such a fine sense of the camera that she could actually feel light and shadow on her skin.

"What? Do we need to know the winter blues of skin tone or seven ways to stump a man? Anyway, over at the *Bijou* they're showing two for the price of one Garbo. Let's shake rehearsal and take my car down there, just us two bachelors. My treat. All you have to do is think of something to tell that strange man."

I had two feelings about Kimber: one was embarrassment, and the other admiration. When she dropped me off to meet my friends at the disco where I'd flash the fake I.D. Kerry had made for me, join the boys drinking gin and tonic, the girls drinking sloe gin fizzes, and practice couples dancing until we dropped away, one by one, reclaimed by our various curfews, I felt guilty that I didn't ask her to come along. I looked down at my black fishnet hose, the black patent leather spikes, the orange satin Mata Hari dress slit up both legs and tied at the waist with my gold honor cord and I hated what I saw. I wanted to be as committed as Kimber, not just a schoolgirl mouthing lines.

"Sandy, I don't know how you can pretend to be an actress when you don't know anything about the greats. Quick, what's Marlene Dietrich mean to you?"

"My mother's named after her." I was losing interest in Todd anyway, ever since Kerry told me that he'd been writing crib notes on the undersides of his voluminous arms. Besides, I got to kiss him every night. "I'll pack the sandwiches," I said.

∽

"But why Garbo?" Kerry asked, when I begged him to cover for us at rehearsal. "I looked her up. She has no tits. She looks like a linebacker in a sweater and she's got boney knees to boot. I like someone like a Jean Harlowe or a Marilyn Monroe. Someone with a little oomph to them. I hate to say it, but this Garbo must've really stunk in bed."

"You're saying she was frigid, I guess."

"Wasn't she the one who was always ragging on how she just wanted to do it alone?"

∽

It's 1937, and Garbo, at thirty-two, has earned her most adult face, a gaunt heart pinned under picture hats and sausage curls, ragged white camellias. "I always look well when I'm near death," her character claims. But in real life, she only says she's tired of playing "evil womens" who do nothing but make stupid love.

∽

The marquee read: "Garbo Dies: *Camille* and *Anna Karenina.*"

I pulled the hood of my Red Riding Hood cloak up around my head and scrunched my boot heel in the snow. We'd done *Anna Karenina* in junior English, which Kerry called "Adultery Lit" making me think of my father and his goings-on. In that book, it was hard to decide which one you wanted to be: Dolly was old, Kitty was stupid, Anna was doomed. It was like looking at my mother and her friends. Maybe that was why I could never imagine myself as a woman, only an actress or a girl.

"Isn't it terrific?" Kimber said. She pulled a camera out of her huge black satchel. "Go ahead and shoot me, be sure to get the marquee."

∽

"It's a beautiful color," Marguerite Gautier exclaims over the fancy dress cover of *Manon Lescaut.* "It must be a good story." Only after she's made certain fatal imitations does she discover the girl was unscrupulous and faithless, a liar and a cheat. Of course, like Garbo, *Camille* has little time to read. "How do you spell 'apology'?" Marguerite asks her maid. Garbo herself said she didn't talk grammar in any language and could never finish a book. But she did send a maid out to buy up all the movie magazines the day they appeared on the stands. If a given issue didn't include an article on her own career, Garbo, a famous tightwad, wasn't above returning it. And since she didn't grant interviews, it's tempting to speculate what she was looking for: a new angle, perhaps, something that would place the moonscape of her personality at a new remove, and finally show her what to do.

∽

The theater was the same tattered venue where I'd seen *Romeo and Juliet* with my entire ninth grade class. The red velvet drapes were torn and the gilt paint on the various golden scrolls was peeling off in strips. A deep smell of insecticide permeated the aisles. And even though the theater was practically empty, Kimber wanted to sit in the balcony. At the entrance of our box, I touched a curtain and some of its fuzz came off on my hand. Several chandeliers had been lowered to the floor in the boxes around us and covered with clear plastic drop cloths. They looked like wedding cakes covered in cobwebs, and I remembered that they'd been there when Kerry and I went to see *Rocky Horror Picture Show* a few months back. It looked like they weren't going to be replaced any time soon. I gripped onto the railing to make sure it was sturdy: that much had lasted, at least.

Kimber set up camp there: Coke to one side, soft black coat wrapped around her shoulders like a shawl, satchel resting under her feet. She grasped both arm rests and twisted her head back luxuriously against the back of her seat, so that her felt hat fell off, and she didn't even pick it up. Her hair was washed, for once, and it fell in pressed brown-red crinkles to her shoulders

"Well, I'm just as happy as an unborn child," she said. "Do you think he misses me yet?"

"Could be. It's seven fifteen."

"Let me see that picture again. What? The lighting's off. My cheek-bones are completely buried in fat."

∽

I'm surprised by the black and white, even though Kimber has warned me this would happen, and claims I'll forget about it by the end of the film. But the lack of color makes it hard to concentrate, since I'm so used to lamé, quiana and colored strobes of my own night life. I notice Garbo's hair is shaded in-between dark and light. I try to imagine its real color and realize, with a jolt, that it must be the same as mine, although I bet no one ever called her a dirty blonde.

෨ᴼ

About the time Marguerite and Armand escape into the country, we finish our sandwiches and Kimber starts passing me lozenges, which taste sweet and citrusy through the coating but then turn bitter as the baking soda my mom makes me use instead of toothpaste whenever we run out. I admit, I know they're not candy. So I just swallow them quickly, stop at three or four.

෨ᴼ

"How good the earth smells. Better than any perfume."

෨ᴼ

The sheep slump across the screen, loose inside their wool, the skirt of Marguerite's dress billows, the bees swarm. I see the camellias move open and closed: life, death, it's not so much to be afraid of. I can make the petals move any way I want. I practice peeling them back, bending them forward. The top of my head rises like the lopsided, homemade soufflé my mother made to celebrate her freedom. I can feel Kimber breathing next to me. I can smell her slight ammoniac odor and hear the obstructions in her nasal passages. It makes me wonder whether acting can really be that hard.

෨ᴼ

My father, sitting in a nearby bar booting up a recalcitrant machine, sees something unusual appear on the screen. A moving mouth, a bow, a pair of eyes. The Ms. Packman program has interfaced with the poker game again. "Get over here, you chippie," he says. "I've got a bone to pick with you."

෨ᴼ

"Damn it, Janet," we scream. I'm out of popcorn, and so I dip into Kerry's box, and come up with a handful of seeds, remember the rice at an aunt's wedding, and how she told us it was a cruel custom because when birds ate too much instant rice they exploded in air. But we all emptied out the blue net party favors anyway. Then I tasted one loose grain at the bottom, just to see. In the dark movie theatre, I drop the seeds onto the floor, which is so coated with debris that I think something may take root there and grow.

∾

At school, Aaron Morris is playing my part. He takes off his shoes to do it, blesses each loafer and tucks them into his gym bag. He spits on his forefinger and rubs his hands together like a melodrama villain, then covers his face to feel the eyelashes flicker against the pads of his palms. He's done this since he was five, whenever he wanted to get into character. It tickles, in the provocative way that sometimes, during sex, his hands become as sensitive as genitals, and he can't tell whether he's touching or being touched.

∾

But it's not Juliet, with her neck-high cleavage, that gets the boys all hot and bothered. It's Mercutio in tights, his little bag of marbles tied together with string and flapping dangerously close to the scabbard, close to the hero, who doesn't seem to notice a thing. Queen Mab will be all over them tonight, her maple syrup welling out of their woods. "Fag!" they yell. "Douche drain." "Cunt." It's a riot. No one can stop them, and even as I feel the warm tears rising high on the ridges of my cheekbones, like two perfect dots of rouge, I can't believe these are the people I'm supposed to be crying over.

∾

Armand throws the money onto her skirt. He's won it gambling, of course, won it from another of the barons who keep cropping up in Garbo's films. The poor hero's convinced she's dumped him for the cash. And now, just as Marguerite's character is turning inside out like a glove for him, he finally gives in, adopts the worldly view, and admits, without pity, that she's nothing but a whore.

∾

Beside me, Kimber's attention is waning. Her breath gets more clotted, until it's almost a snore. I'm afraid to look, to interrupt whatever's going on with her. She's been so excited about this, and now that we've reached the climax, she's finally gotten over her insomnia in a big way.

૭૦

We end, as we began, in an opera box in Paris. But this time Marguerite is gone, harvested by the disease which has been the only consistent love interest in her life. Even facing death, she looks fearlessly in the mirror, tucks a camellia in her sash for luck.

૭૦

I touch her shoulder, her coat collar, her coarse hair . There's a bit of foam on her lip, like the fine mustache off a Kahlou and cream. She mutters and lolls her head back in a way that frightens me. I don't feel too good either. I reach into my purse for the gold hotel matchbook my father gave me: his beeper number is scribbled inside.

VI. GARBO LAUGHS

"Remember when a siren was . . . a brunette and not an alarm?"
    Remember when your father walked into the lobby of the Bijou with his trench coat over his arm?

૭૦

At the hospital, he's all over my mother, asking why she didn't tell him about Kimber; I could be corrupted, her job could be threatened, we could be sued. His hair is blonder now, cut in leafy layers over his red ears and I wonder whether he's been using Sun-In too. He tells her how she's the irresponsible one, how he's been saving for my college tuition all the time she's been pissing my future away. She just sits tapping a rolled-up magazine against her crossed leg. Her mascara is smeared under one eye and her hair is as mismanaged as any soufflé.
    "Sandy," she says. "Could you go get us some coffee, dear?"
    But I am far too sleepy to move.

૭૦

"My face doesn't compose well," the Grand Duchess complains, before the Soviet envoy who will be *Ninotchka* takes over. "It's all highlights. I'm bored of this face." But when Garbo arrives on the set, she makes a pass at Ina Claire, whose role has been whittled to a cameo to accommodate the star. The Duchess turns her down, and Garbo retreats to the little boy's room. Later, Claire will report that the Divine left the toilet seat up.

∽

That night, after they pump Kimber's stomach and announce that she'll be OK, my father takes me home. He comes in, flips through the mail on the kitchen cabinet, unbuttoning his shirt with the other hand, and collapses on the sofa out on the sun porch. For a moment, I expect him to stumble over the back, then I remember where I am again.

"What about hitting the hay?" he says.

But I hear him flipping channels, shaking the ice in his glass, opening drawers and bumping into furniture deep into my sleep, while I dive into dream after dream, hold my breath, and come up for air again. My shoulders are sore. My belly is distended, pumped up, like a football or a bicycle tire.

It's an old movie, maybe Cary Grant, maybe Hitchcock, maybe Garbo. My mother's the surgeon and I'm the anesthesiologist. We wear black velvet masks with white strings to show our status. We have to operate on my sister's face. My mother holds the girl's head in her lap, while I assist. I see the sharp folds of flesh in the corners of her eyes, the gill-like quiver of her nostril. I press the sequined gas mask over her waxy lips. But the stuff isn't working, the girl stirs, my grip on her leg loosens, my mother's knife slips.

∽

Buljanoff, Iranoff, and Kopalski are your typical bunglers with a satirical twist: Muscovites who take too quickly to Paris. When seduced by capitalism in the form of Count Aigu, they lose interest in selling the Grand Duchess's jewels for the needs of the Russian people and Comrade Garbo is sent in to finish the job.

∽

In her hospital bed the next morning, Kimber sits up, asks for jalapeño jelly on rye toast, and makes a list of the elements repeated in Garbo's films:

stolen jewels
royalty
hotels
death
photographs
hats
Paris
staircases
champagne.

She tugs at the hospital bracelet on her wrist, the only thing that's changed since yesterday, and experiences a flicker of relief that she didn't choose that route. Her alimentary canal feels like snake skin, and tastes of brine and pickle juice. Her stomach lies coiled in a deep, muscular ache. She checks her cheekbones in her coffee spoon, then rings the bell again: she's going to need another take.

ꙮ

Why didn't they think of it before? In a tragedy, the beautiful woman with a foreign accent, no matter how sympathetic, must die. But comedy frees her up; as a Bolshevik she can be extravagant in her asceticism, and extravagance is plainly Garbo's only mode. Even her eccentricities: the thriftiness, the impatience with convention, the health food fetishes, are set into play. So it is only when she reaches her most serious character that Garbo is finally able make us laugh.

ꙮ

Before the final spate of movies, Greta packs her bags again. She's off to Sweden, then Italy, with Leopold Stokowski, the leonine conductor of the Philadelphia Orchestra. She brings: trousers, sandals, a simple swimsuit and enough jam to last for several weeks. Every morning at the Villa Cimbrone, she drags on her dressing gown and brings another jar down to breakfast. Afterwards the housekeeper washes them and lines them up on the casement, where Greta can see their clean edges cutting into the sun. Two, three, five days away from the business. She can't imagine any jewelry as beautiful as that. She and Stokowski lunch on beets and carrots; he teaches her yoga up on the battlements; they walk through the village examining the local produce. Every night, she retires with a box of salt and a bottle of olive oil. She doesn't think about it as love, only the air on her skin, the vegetable fibre yielding under sharp corrected canines, the gentle but astringent wind of his personality. She hasn't felt this calm since Stiller. When the press catches up to the couple, they hold Garbo under siege in the Villa Cimbrone for three weeks, until she gives up and makes a deal: a press conference in exchange for complete isolation.

The question is the usual one: When does she plan to marry?

Later, Greta goes to the kitchen, topless in her baggy shorts and big espadrilles, and packs up the empty jars, knowing they'll never keep their part of the bargain.

୧୭

He finds it in the kitchen pantry, alongside the oat flakes, the cans of tomato paste, the big tin of olive oil, the generic bags of flour, and the cute little jars of capers she must spill onto everything, now that she's off on her own, freed of meat, potatoes, calls to delay dinner every other night. It's the capers that make him furious, even before he gets to the real problem. They were like flies on his salad, his eggs, his spaghetti. Closer up, they looked like miniature sea urchins. And their slimy flavor of anchovy or tongue made it all too obvious that, despite his irregular lifestyle, it was his wife who had the exotic tastes.

୧୭

But all she was looking for, she told the press hounds, was a man who could show her beautiful things.

୧୭

Ninotchka wants the technical tour of Paris: the sewers, buses, and utilities. The Eiffel Tower is included only because of its reputation as an engineering feat. Count Aigu, unaccountably, knows nothing about it. He claims Parisians only go there for one reason—to jump off.

"How long does it take a man to land?"

"Now isn't that too bad—last time I jumped, I forgot to time it."

∞

"You've missed two rehearsals in a row," Mr. Morris told me on the phone. "You're developing some personal mannerisms that I don't particularly care for. You want to get your can-can back to work or should I go ahead and give away your role?"

"Kimber's the only one who knows my lines."

"Listen, I'm sorry about that. Maybe we took on a little too much there. Who knew she was really that gone? I promise, I'll take care of it, contact her parents, set something up for her. Now, tell me the truth, are you hungry enough to go through with this?"

"My father found your bag," I said, and hung up the phone.

∞

They're looking for a radio, some impersonal music to set off the champagne. But when the Count and Ninotchka stumble onto the hotel safe, they look into the empty box of the camera as if they've never seen the jewels before, as if this isn't what they've been haggling over the whole time.

"The czar sold ten thousand serfs in the market to buy these for his wife. They're the tears of all Russia."

And when Garbo says it, we believe it, we want some liquid misery of our own.

∞

"Epic," Kerry said. "So your old man is a player again."

∞

Kimber stands on the front porch with Sandy's mother. They stare at the shadow of the four o' clocks against the wall, the woman and girl in profile, just a silhouette between them.

"We don't have to go in if you don't want to. There's a matinee."

Kimber nods her fierce head.

Inside, Sandy presses a warm, yeasty cheek to the windowpane and watches them walk back to the car. She remembers her mother's story about sleeping with pennies in her cheeks, trying to make dimples. Now

Sandy spends her teenage years cultivating cheekbones. It's a wonder anyone ever makes it into film.

෨෨

"Don't ever ask me for a picture of myself. I couldn't bear the thought of being shut up in a drawer. I couldn't breathe. I couldn't stand it." But that's just what that pesky photographer Cecil Beaton does—hoards the famous profile his whole life, makes a reputation off it later.

෨෨

"Sometimes pictures or photographs are more like people than people themselves. Very seldom when I am walking along with Garbo am I able to see her." His favorite photo was taken in his own home, during one of the few periods when he managed to spirit her away from the possessive Schlee, whom he dubbed "the Russian sturgeon." In this one, Garbo's face is in the dark, her eyes barely visible. But the outline of her profile is lit with a thin, pencil-edged halo. Beaton, a technical genius, had used a simple heating element in a wall in his digs to achieve the effect.

෨෨

So it's a belly whopper, when it finally happens. At a stoplight, they run into a blond man in a black sports car, who keeps honking a musical horn that repeats the first bar of "The Entertainer" over and over. When they ignore him, he cuts them off at the intersection and gets out, empties a bag full of women's clothes and plastic implements onto the hood. Kimber feels the laughter tumble out of her sore throat, against her will, like coins from a slot machine.

VII. TWO-FACED WOMAN

The night of dress rehearsal, and Kerry and I are twisted together on the sofa trying to figure out how to lose our virginity. At least, I think that's what we're doing because we're both completely recumbent, our bodies touching all along their length, and this is the closest I can imagine to going all the way. He grabs onto my breasts like he's trying to pull himself up by them. As he snakes across my torso, I brush my hands over his naked back, feel the pimples on the skin, the sharp nuggets of his vertebrae. I smell my own sweat, which is sharp and cidery, all mixed up with his ginger and cologne.

On the floor beside us sits my present: a pair of burnt orange suede pumps, which, according to Kerry, will give me perfect poise and presentation, allowing me to walk all over the competition.

∾

"So you're stepping out in both directions?" Garbo said, when Beaton told her of his various affairs.

∾

In 1941, Hollywood had lost its European audience, due to the war, and MGM cast about for a way to give Garbo American appeal. They cut her hair, spruced up her wardrobe for a more cheerful outlook, and revived a domestic farce. In *Two-Faced Woman*, a long-suffering wife sets a trap for her straying husband. Using a ploy favored in Hollywood, she passes herself off as her own twin sister, and attempts to seduce him in disguise.

∾

There was a scraping of sliding doors, and Kimber's harsh voice slid like a putty knife between us: "Not to intrude, but don't you know that funny stuff saps all your energy for performance?"

Kerry propped himself up on his arms and stared.

Lying beneath him, I could see the line where his orange-toned suntan meet the fresh pink flesh of his neck.

"I didn't know you were so hot to cooperate, Ms. Mata Hari Movie Star."

I pushed Kerry to the side, and sat up to look at Kimber. She was wearing my velvet pants and one of my mother's scarves wrapped in a makeshift halter over her chest. Her skin was as rich and irregular as pulled taffy; there was a snail's trough over the appendix, a mole in her cleavage, a round white vaccination scar on the upper swell of shoulder. That was as much as I knew of her history, after six weeks of sleeping in the next bed.

"Not to worry. Gimme a ginger ale and a whiskey," I said. "And don't be stingy, baby."

∾

In screenings, the film was censored by the Roman Catholic Legion of Decency. The organization objected to the assumed adultery, even though it was only an optical illusion. So MGM revised the script to show that *the husband's onto Garbo's trick all along.* This, apparently, was more satisfactory. No one mentioned the immorality of the circumstances that led to her deception in the first place.

∽

Ever since that day when Kimber came home from the hospital and my mother took her to see *Manhattan*, they've been acting peculiar. They quote bits standing by the open refrigerator, making sandwiches and lemonade. "I finally had an orgasm, but I found out it was the wrong kind."

Kimber now only eats between meals, even though my mother takes special care to buy her favorite foods. She goes to school sporadically, but always manages to show up for rehearsal wearing some odd ensemble, her sallow skin marked with purple and mauve, her hair frizzed out to its limit. And, by some strange structural shift in house rules, she is allowed to wear our clothing without asking. Robes and sweaters accumulate over the backs of chairs. Shoes collect like fallen fruit on the floor. No one sweeps, and I start seeing tiny tumbleweeds of her long, red hair rolling around the hallway.

I hang around my mother's bedroom hoping for an explanation.

"It's not like you couldn't have called me," she says. "I was sitting here organizing my files the whole time. I don't know why you want to drag in the *gestapo*. You remember how much trouble we had with him."

"But how could you do it with Mr. Morris?"

"It never bothered you before," she said. "Or are you going to pretend you never noticed? You're no Sarah Bernhardt, you know."

∽

My last movie, like my first, is unwatchable. I disappear at both ends of the film career. Without the bad womens I hated so much, I become so to say unseeable. That's what I want after all. I am tired of trying to express myself. I pull the brim of my hat down when I catch eye of a camera. I step behind the gentleman friends. I have made enough faces.

∽

The effect, one critic quipped, was like watching Sarah Bernhardt get slapped with a pig's bladder.

∽

Neither of us slept the night before, but we didn't talk either. I lay in the dark and listened to her rough breath, like the sea in *Anna Christie* under a layer of tarp and burlap. I touched myself between the legs, as if I could unbutton myself from there, finding the thing that set me apart. But even though I shed my skin until I was raw, I never found the secret passageway into my own personality.

∽

Some roles considered for Garbo after *Two-Faced Woman* failed:

> *Marie Curie*
> *George Sand*
> *Sarah Bernhardt*
> *Desdemona*
> *Hamlet*
> *Dorian Gray.*

∽

In the bathroom of Mr. Morris's dramatic arts classroom, I critique my face one more time. A square open space with too many flats, not enough flow. Skin like onionskin paper, a single freckle blotting the freshly driven snow. Nose. Eyes. Broad bare expanse. Nose. Mouth. Nose. It's the bones that count, they say, and these were clearly inherited from my mother: I guess that's why Aaron likes them so much, he's jumped them often enough by now. I smear foundation over my forehead. I swear I'll never do this for them again. My skin bristles under the tangerine polyester pantsuit suggested in the script. I can't smooth my nipples down, no matter how many times I brush the front, and my neck is flushed with whisker burn and some kind of rash from the makeup. I know my father is sure to be there tonight; it's my fault, he'd never remember otherwise.

But now, he'll only be sitting around waiting to make a scene of his own.

∾

After her retirement, Garbo spent her days wandering around Manhattan, a hermit about town. Garbo sightings were reported like comet tails; she was spotted window-shopping in Times Square, fingering beets and carrots in the farmer's market, pricing baubles in an antique store. The screenwriter Mercedes de Acosta, a lifelong friend and one-time lover, worried about the deterioration of Garbo's mental state. Most especially, she worried about the pernicious influence of George Schlee, with his awful mixture of Slav, Brooklynese, and baby talk.

Garbo, for her part, distrusted the flamboyant Mercedes more and more as she aged. When questioned, she claimed the old queen brought her bad luck. At one point, Mercedes sent Greta to a chiropractor who "made her bones float about in her body" and distorted one side of her mouth.

∾

Watching from the wings, Kerry remembers his tongue in her mouth, the slug-like pressure of her lips. Sandy isn't the prettiest girl he's known; her breasts are too small, her hips are too wide, her looks wear thin after a few drinks. But he likes the wise way she pronounces dirty phrases. He likes the flutter inside her rib cage when he pumps her tit. On stage, Todd reaches for her elbow, Kerry gets a slide tromboner to the pelvis, and he likes that too.

∾

Marlene sits in the back of the house, avoiding recognition and laughing at the idea that she's become a stage mother. At thirty-six, she doesn't need the fuss of love. Her life has been a process of subtraction. First, the eye liner, then the girdle, then the bra, followed by the bows and frills she had favored as a young girl. After that, of course, the husband dropped off as a natural consequence. Now she's down to foundation and mascara, a pair of cotton underpants, a closet full of simple shirt dresses, and a secret lover with womanly hands.

But then there's the problem of daughters: as she pares down, they keep growing, multiplying, expanding. She made a concentrated effort to stop at one, but she's somehow ended up with two of them, one from the real marriage, one from the show. The whole thing makes her dizzy: no one should have to live through this twice. And when Sandy makes a suggestive move up there, Marlene squints into the light and sees her stretching out over the stage, a long line of paper dolls holding hands into perpetuity. What will she ever be able to tell them about how to keep their shadows under control?

∽

He'll bring a morals charge, that's what he'll do. The thought sends a current through his chest, his pectorals lighting up like winning numbers. He's sitting next to a gaggle of dyke-spinsters—Marly's buddies, who remember his wilder days and keep whispering among themselves, then ogling him through their cat-eye spectacles. Hey, hey, he wants to say, it's my daughter you're supposed to be watching up there. But he can hardly look either, when that thug puts his hand on the nutshell curve of the girl's lower back. All he can think of is Marly, Marly, you used to be that innocent for me.

∽

Just when everything was going so well, Aaron sees Kimber crawling onto stage, and remembers when he first saw her cringing on her front porch. The old tragic flaw. Catching up to him again. For the moment, the audience is distracted by the stage kiss, but that can't last for long, not with the priggish kids he's got doing his romancing up there. He signals to Kerry to go get her, but the boy seems hypnotized, staring at the mellow circle of light on the stage.

∽

I fall over the sofa, as expected, but when Todd gets up, it's really Kimber who reappears. We look at each other, sweating under the lights, the makeup globs melting fast as crayon on a hot day. She is Garbo, I think, her cheekbones gleaming like a pair of polished antlers on a trophy wall. I am Garbo, my big feet and shoulders shaking the scenery, my eyes dealing deuces, my X-ray skin recording the play of lust and sorrow in the crowd. What can I do but deliver the stage kiss, the way I've been taught? Her lips are cool. My tongue is raw. Her loose breasts nestle under my clavicle; her sour smell sifts up through my nose. And although Mr. Morris will never cast either of us again, I still take one last cue from him: I only hope we land without breaking any bones.

∽

I am not a normal man. I have a bad stomach, I don't go out in company, I can't drive, I never sleep at night. My only gift is to make films but I hate to be looked at. My only use is to make love, but I can't stand to be touched. Women are the only animals with naked faces, do you know? Women are sure some sad animals with their naked faces and their stupid love affairs. Never ask me about the movies. The bones are made to float about in my body, and I am not a normal man.

All Hallow's Leaves

y the time Danjamar gave in and visited the clothes cubby, his pants were up to his ankles, his waistband bit an ashy furrow into his chestnut skin, his three T-shirts pinned his shoulders together and showed off the fine Egyptian hieroglyphic of his ribs. Other folks' funk, just what he couldn't stand. Just what he'd been trying to get away from. He'd grown a full three inches since the day his mother left a mysterious note in his gym bag telling him to meet her at the McDonald's with any cash he'd accumulated from the day's aluminum can crop. If she'd just specified, he would've packed his whole drawer—the shiny orange and red running suit, the nylon gym shorts in green and yellow and purple, the six secret coded T-shirts and the leather basketball jacket in cardinal red and royal blue. His mouth watered thinking about the colors. She knew how much they meant to him, she could at least have given him a ten-minute warning so he could collect his property. But no, she had to go and do it on the sly, call Aunt Cel and get her to drive them all the way to Augusta for the Greyhound Bus Station. The way Mama carried on, you'd think it was the underground railroad.

Danjamar looked out the door again, just to make sure no one was watching. Miss Caitlin was filling out an *ex parte* in the office. Victoria was out to church with her mother. His sisters Sierra and Sienna were arguing over a bag of chips in the playroom. He could hear their skinny girl

116

voices chase each other around the block and through the trees, the way they did all the way from Georgia, in bus stations and convenience stores and homeless shelters in three states, while Mama filled out forms and made phone calls and split up microwave burritos four ways, all the time mouthing her Merits like it would give her some special secret powers if she just choked down enough smoke.

She said they were lucky to have got this far, to a river town on the Mississippi where he'd never think to show his pink and baldy head. Here, they watched the leaves turn from the gum wrapper green of late summer to reds and yellows and oranges like Danjamar had never seen on bark. Public services gave Sienna a pair of glasses, refilled Mama's prescription; they even paid for counseling services for the whole family. But Danjamar said he would just as soon sit it out, thanks. After all, he wasn't the one who'd been abused. And abused wasn't half the story when What's His Johnson got going.

No one was in the hall, no one was in the living room, no one was in the downstairs bathroom. Danjamar, who was used to listening from all those months with What's His J, wiped his hands on his back pockets and started through the first pile stacked up on an abandoned clothes dryer. He fingered a slimy blue dress, tossed through some baby clothes covered with pastel fuzzballs, rejected a girl's gray turtleneck sweater with an orangey stain down one sleeve.

The clothes cubby, that's just what they'd call it, trying to make it sound all cute and clean, like they did with everything here. "When you going to get busy in the clothes cubby, boy,?" Mama said to him every morning, pinching the tail of his T-shirt and lighting up a cigarette. "Look like you about to bust a move right through them drawers." But inside, it was just an old junk room, same as anywhere. Exposed pipes to the washer and dryer. A pink fiberglass furnace filter leaning up against the wall. An open drain in the floor. Bad as anyplace they'd ever lived, despite the bunk beds in the bedroom and the new dishwasher and the big screen TV. The mural in the front room showed smudgy pink ladies sitting in a forest by a muddy river of oil paint, one brown sister looking downstream and hugging her knees. But that didn't fool Danjamar any. He'd seen too much shit come down that river since he'd arrived.

He broke into the next pile: a pair of blue corduroy overalls, a faded red bathrobe, a dull gray and brown flannel shirt. No styling possible here.

What did they think, that just because he didn't have money, he was color blind and fashion damaged?

But what really got to him was the white people smell—their old vinegary pee stink, familiar from six months of living with Mama's last boyfriend. That's what was behind the sweet talk and the food stamps and the careful charts for chores and child care and Tuesday night "group," the place where the ladies cried and carried on about the cycle of violence and Mama had to hear everyone's story—the pregnant lady with the neatnik husband who tried to make her eat Drano every time he found a dustball, the recovering AA with the silver tooth, the grandmother with the biracial baby who'd been abused by relatives on both sides—over and over until she thought she'd rather be beat any day. Still, his friend Victoria was a complete white girl—no doubting that—with her long yellow hair and the five freckles over her nose. After school, she'd come home and lie on the sofa with a book: *Peaches Burns Student Nurse* or *Valerie in the Valley* or *The Secret of Love Cove*. She kept them all in a shoe box under her bed, reread them in a certain order like a sports schedule. One day, she informed Danjamar, she was going to have her own book hutch and then she'd never get anything out of order again. Her black patent leather backpack sat open next to her and she reached in for cherry cough drops and bubble gum lip gloss in between chapters, her little titties nipping at the thin sweater that she didn't need to get from the clothes cubby, since she had cousins in town who'd give her all the hand-me-downs she could ever use.

What would Victoria think when she saw him in some white boy's sloppy seconds?

He came across a stash of T-shirts in a cardboard box. They were the only respectable things in the whole cubby: yellow, red, orange, black, and blue. He flipped them open to read their messages: *Middlebury 10K, Beethoven Lights My Oven, Arms Are For Hugging Not Killing, My Husband Went All the Way to the Country Music Capitol and All I Got Was This T-shirt and the Blues.* Nothing he particularly wanted to proclaim. He finally chose a bright purple shirt with no words or letters, just a kind of hatchety design, a black ax with its double blade outlined in rainbow colors, each band another halo on the sharp profile of the weapon. Danjamar traced the logo with his fingers until he felt some power coming off it. He saw his runaway daddy throwing a dart; he tasted baked sweet potatoes with marshmallow topping; he felt the whole Georgia summer melt into a single day of purple shade.

It made him so hot he shucked off his tight basketball jersey right then and there. As he did, he smelled himself, a sweet mulchy musk that he didn't have to save up for, and that no one could copy or take away. When he re-emerged from the neck hole of the purple shirt, Victoria was already in the room,

"Oh, Mr. Mallomar," she called to him, after some kind of candy their mothers had eaten as little girls. "I'm looking for a costume for the Halloween party. You see anything good?" She was still in her church dress, a green flowered puff with the front laced up like a high-top and a fake slip hanging off the hem.

He shook his head, still pulling down the T-shirt. "Not hardly, girl. Unless you want to go as a bag lady."

"Maybe I'll go as a dope girlfriend, huh? Maybe I could pretend to be your lady."

She put her hand on his stomach and he felt his erection jump up, growing fast as Jack's beanstalk, tall as a tree, until he was just a plum hanging off its long purple trunk. So he reached over and kissed her cool, rubbery cheek, then moved on to her mouth, where her tongue was waiting for him, tasting of cough drops and bubble gum. He reached for her titties, but the lacing of her dress was too tight. He'd have to go in for a long shot up the skirt—fast now, while the new shirt was still working for him.

THE SIGN OF THE LABRYS

Later that day, he went by the office to get a voucher and Miss Caitlin asked him to sit down and help her with the Halloween decorations.

She was the kind of white lady you didn't judge by her looks. Her reddish brown hair grew in short clumps like a deer wallow in winter, she wore baggy T-shirts and cotton pants printed with smiley faces and peace signs, and her high freckled forehead always had a rolled-up bandanna pulled up around it like a headband. Sometimes, she wore little baby barrettes too, the kind Mama used to clamp together braids for Sierra & Sienna. When she talked, there was an echo in her mouth, as if she meant everything twice as seriously. When she moved her hands, the second and third fingers stuck together, so she looked like she was perpetually crossing her fingers, and she smelled of sheer bleach and sunshine, no juice to her at all.

"So what you doing these days, Danjamar?"

"What you mean?"

"Like, have you joined any cults or started any gangs? Anything that I should know about?"

"No ma'am. I'm trying to keep it to myself. I don't want any trouble."

"You're a good kid, Jamar. Would you hand me some more orange?"

He reached for the pack of construction paper, palming a handful of candy corn from an open bag along the way. His chest glowed in the mysterious purple shirt, and he felt his muscles ache with all the growing he'd been doing. The mealy candy seemed to feed the ache, and he grabbed another handful before he was done chewing the first.

"Ready for the Halloween party?" Miss Caitlin said, tracing out a pumpkin stencil. "Nothing scary, remember."

Just then, Mama came by the door, carrying Sierra in her hooded car coat. Sienna was walking along beside them, you could just see the topmost braid bouncing in its yellow clamp. Mama looked tired with her no makeup face and red Dove Bar sweatshirt, her long hair scraped out straight so the gray showed in ghostly streaks around her face.

"I'm just going to borrow this boy of yours," Miss Caitlin called out.

"Keep him long as you want. I got plenty more where he came from." But there was a sweetness under her voice like the sugar sludge at the bottom of a glass of iced tea, and he remembered how she had been before What's His J—sewing him a whole Halloween costume from scratch, playing poker with him on the back steps, cooking up gumbo on a long Saturday afternoon while he told her riddles and sang all the verses of a hundred bottles of beer. Now, she only talked about how nasty men was, how they thought they could get up in your face just because they been down in your drawers. Just last week, he heard her tell Miss Caitlin that she never wanted to be talking to one again.

Miss Caitlin nodded and pinched her lip.

Now, Danjamar wished she'd say she needed him right away and Miss Caitlin couldn't have him. He wished she'd notice his fine purple shirt, his long ribs, his expanding finger span.

"Jamar, you know about the facts of life, don't you?" Miss Caitlin asked.

"Yeah," he said. "You shoot your wad off and then you die."

"I mean, about boys and girls and boys on boys and girls on girls."

Danjamar looked out the window, to a house across the street where there was a blue plastic swing hanging from a tree. The grass was still green, but the tree had turned a tinny magenta and its fallen leaves spread out in a puddle of shadow around the seat of the swing.

"Because I just wondered if you knew. Well I only know because I'm a member."

She pulled a chain out of her polka-dotted blouse. On the end was a bright-colored charm that looked like a piece of candy or some kind of fishing fly.

"Know what it is?"

"Candy corn?" he said. Then he thought of the gem-colored pacifiers he'd seen hanging from the necks of the popular girls in his class. "Little nookie for when you get hungry on the sly?"

"Look at that shirt you've got on."

"This old thing?" He pushed his chest out until the pectorals showed under the loose cotton, nipples popping up like brass studs.

Then she held the necklace out against the purple ground and he saw the double blade times two, the ax head looking in both directions.

"It's a labrys. It means, you know, the ultimate chick flick, a girl-girl kind of scenario."

Danjamar thought of What's His J's magazines—the poses with one lady twisted into another, butt and boobie sprouting up in all directions. He pulled the shirt out straight and looked at it again, upside down this time.

"You?" he said.

"Well, Kay doesn't like us going around talking about our preferences. It can scare off the clientele. But I just thought you'd like to know. I mean I wouldn't want you to go around unaware."

"Unaware your underwear," he said. "You mean, you wouldn't even give a male-type individual any opportunity at booty?"

"Look," she said. "No offense, but it is your sex that's responsible for the Inquisition and the Holocaust and the Atomic Bomb, just to name a few highlights."

Danjamar felt his dick move against his leg. He didn't feel responsible. Then he remembered—smack that 'ho until she bleed—and he heard what she was saying. "So I guess you got a girlfriend, then."

Miss Caitlin jiggled the safety scissors, cutting a smiley face in the air, and sighed. "No one just now. We have to get you a costume, at least. Maybe you could go as a pirate."

"Maybe I could go as your Mama."

"You'll need a lot of hair spray for that one," Miss Caitlin said, and Danjamar felt suddenly dirty, like his chest was smeared in used beauty cream, some kind of numbing Noxema with toenail clippings and lady hairs thrown into the mix.

PANDEMONIUM

After that, Danjamar was more careful. But he couldn't even find any plain T-shirts; it was like people only gave away the fads and causes they'd outgrown. Finally, he located a deep spearmint shirt with a saying that appealed to him: "Keep the Dream Green." The letters were made up of vines and branches, and they floated above a green man with leaves for hair and beard. His chest was as broad as an action figure's and his skin was so dark that he could easily be African American, although Danjamar doubted that, what with the sharp nose and the library lady's lips. He remembered his Sunday school teacher saying they should love all people: black, white, yellow, and green. That was a good one, he thought, when the church shunned Mama for shacking up with What's His J and Danjamar's best friend Sy wouldn't even share a chocolate mint scoop in the Dairy Cream until his deacon daddy's stiff black back was turned.

For dinner, Mama brought out a bag of corn chips and poured canned chili on top. Danjamar didn't look up from the *Glamour* magazine he was studying for any incidental nudity until Sienna interrupted him by spinning her yellow plastic plate onto the "Dos and Don'ts" page and Sierra started crying in the middle of a mouthful. Then Mama lifted her sweatshirt right at the table and latched the baby on without missing a drag on her cigarette. Danjamar saw the dark rim of a nipple, like a coffee ring on a dirty counter. He remembered What's His J shouting that if she couldn't keep her shirt on, he was going to invite the whole neighborhood in for a pull.

"Aw Mama, can't you get out a blanket or something?" Danjamar said.

"What's the matter, boy, you too wise for the titty that feed you?"

The tinned chili turned sour and fatty in his mouth. But he was so hungry, always hungry, that he reached to the middle of the table and ladled more out of the saucepan.

Sierra beat her little fists against Mama's chest as she ate. She was a pretty thing, with her long eyelashes and candy-shaped mouth.

"That's the abuse," Mama said, holding one baby fist still. "They say she got to work it out, just like the rest of us."

Sienna dumped the ashtray into her plate and left the room. She looked like a mama already, at eight, with her glasses and her high tries at titties and her over-developed calves. When she came back, she was wearing a long skirt, a string of nutshell beads, and carrying a huge black purse like a briefcase. "Like my costume?" she said. "I'm gonna go as a principal."

Danjamar lifted his head from his plate. " Miss Caitlin say nothing scary. You better go back and try again, girl."

Sienna pulled out her lip at him and smirked. "Next year, we're going trick or treating at real houses, right Mama?"

Before she got an answer, Victoria came and sat down at the table with her bowl of stir-fry vegetables. Danjamar scooted his chair closer, set his magazine down, rubbed on her arm. "I'm gonna learn to cook and make me some stir-fry so we can eat healthy like Miss Victoria."

Victoria just pulled a cough drop out of her mouth and wrapped it in a napkin, which she sat carefully under the edge of her plate. She didn't edge away or move closer either, and Danjamar wondered if she even remembered that afternoon in the clothes cubby, that series of afternoons.

"Help yourself." Mama said. "You know where the kitchen is. Ain't no one stopping you from lifting a finger, just because you a man-in-training."

"Well," he said, licking the chili off his fingers, "I can see no one be appreciating me here. Think I'll just step out and shake a leg."

It was an elaborate process to sign out of the shelter, but they couldn't actually keep him from leaving. Outside, he looked up and down the street without a sidewalk and realized that he had no place to go. He wandered down the street to the local park, where there was a playground, a fitness trail, a picnic pavilion. He went past the port-a-potty and inhaled its chemical flush. He trudged down to the ditch and scared up a cat, fished a used blue condom out of the water with a stick, stomped an aluminum can with his heel and regretted that he hadn't brought his gym bag. It had just rained and the dark was just coming down, but he could still see the colors of the trees stretching out of the sunset—all burned in the same fire.

Hide it Under a Bushel-No. I'm gonna let it shine.

In just a few minutes, they'd be plain black and white and gray. It made Danjamar thirsty, to think of all that color swallowed up so fast. The chili backed up in his throat and he tasted its orangey shame for the second time that day.

According to What's His J, that's all the women wanted—to make a man hide his tail. "That's why a boy like you got to show his colors, Danger Man," he said. "Your baboon butt purple. Your blue ball blue. Pull out that thing and pee a fucking rainbow with it." This said examining Danjamar's fresh curved erection, which started out straight enough, then turned away from its target, something, in fact, a little like the letter J.

"Your Mama don't understand what motivates a man. She thinks she's got to put on a show. Ain't no show with me, Danger Man. Ain't no fucking fly girl extravaganza."

Danjamar let himself think around the shape of that; Mama had been after him since they left; she wanted to know the exact nature of his relationship to J. He didn't know if he should tell her; he didn't know what to tell her if he did. He hated the cross-eyed way the counselors looked at him, just trying to get him sorted out into a sheep or goat.

By now, he was crossing the bridge that led from one side of the park to the other. The damp boards were strewn with leaves of waxy yellow and woodsy maroon. On one of the rails, someone had draped a broken leash and it knocked against the cast iron with an irregular clang. The quarter moon hung overhead like a crooked pair of fangs.

How do they tell it's a man up there anyway, Danjamar wondered, and then, at the end of the bridge, he saw the figure of a person—someone bending over an outdoor grill. Danjamar's fists curled up inside his pockets and his penis shrank back into his package, his jaw ached with a metallic twang.

"Merry meet, brother," the man said, flooding Danjamar with a flashlight. He was wearing a dark cape with a pointed hood. Danjamar thought of the Klan legends, the beatings and brandings and lynchings, but no, the Klansmen always wore white, and there would be something over the face. This man's hood opened onto brown eyes, a big nose, an acne-scarred complexion, a dark and curly beard.

"Blessed be," he said. "What brings you out into our mother this night?"

"I'm just looking for cans," Danjamar said. "You seen any?"

"We've got a pretty good litter policy here. But it's a happy hunting ground for everyone, brother. The veil grows thin between the worlds." As he spoke, he fussed over the grill, which was covered with plant parts: flowers and fronds and roots.

"Yeah, well, I think I'll take a look around anyway."

"I see you're familiar with our organization. He pointed at Danjamar's chest, bumping him with the handle of the flashlight.

Danjamar looked down at his shirt, up at the stranger.

"We designed those for our Pagan Fest last summer. Sold over two hundred, then we had to run out and get more printed up. Since then, we've added several more ritual items to our catalogue. A night-sky cloak, a sage-scented athame, a solstice skirt, if you're interested. Did we get you on our mailing list?"

Danjamar wondered if the man had even noticed he was just a kid, and a black one at that.

"I don't think, I don't have a permanent address right now."

"I'm Shadow, my friend. Good to meet you."

"Danjamar."

"Danjamar. I think I know another Danjamar up in our Northwestern region. Lots of totem power there."

When he clutched Danjamar's fingers, the sleeve of his cloak fell back and Danjamar saw that the hand, the wrist, and the forearm were tattooed with fur marks, as if he was an animal under his clothing. How long would such a thing take—over how much of his body? Danjamar remembered the cigarette burns on his ankle, the fishing flies applied to his nipples, the beer tabs embedded in the flesh of his thigh.

"Are you about to make a sacrifice for real?" he asked Shadow.

"Just smoking herbs, my brother. In the light of the moon, on All Hallows' Eve. The real thing, you know, not the way the amateurs celebrate with their sweet little diabetes lollapalooza. Although, every year, you get those militant Christian groups protesting. A decade from now, we may have to take the whole thing underground again. Then we'll see who really gets the trick-or-treat."

"Shadow," Danjamar said, "I wonder if you'll do a conjure for me."

"And this would be who? Describe the fellow for me."

What's His J had few distinguishing traits—looked pretty much like any white man until you got up close and saw the nicks around the eyes, the lean yellow teeth dissolving into gum.

"He kind of favor the man in this picture," Danjamar said, stroking his chest counterclockwise—the gut and rib and tit and breastbone—all the stations of his memory.

"What's your poison, brother? Channeling, palm-reading, cards?"

"Just whatever you usually do, I guess."

Danjamar watched Shadow disappear into his cloak, where he started mumbling like a sampling d.j., droning on until the song broke off into two chains: a humming chant and a high nasal whistle. The hood vibrated and Shadow's shadow swayed between the trees. Danjamar stepped on it, for luck. He was holding it down, so the guy didn't get away from him, so the evidence didn't get dispersed—the way it had with Sierra and Sienna's medical exams. He remembered a cartoon about a wily coyote who carried holes around with him for trapping his prey. Then he saw J step out of the shadow and roll it up like a carpet, stuff it under his arm, taking the whole thing with him, so Danjamar could never look at it again.

Then another figure came over the bridge, with flashes of metal on breast and thigh.

"OK. I'm not asking what you're doing out here, folks, but it is after curfew for the little guy here. He's not bothering you, is he?" he said to the adult in the cape.

"No complaints, officer," Shadow answered, materializing out of his hood and winking at Danjamar. His voice went deeper, came up heavy with mystification.

"I see. Well, you just go on home, boy," the officer said, fingering his belt. Don't like to see the youth out agitating so close to trick or treat."

Danjamar wanted to say that he didn't have a home, that he was stuck in a women's shelter playing a mama's boy for Halloween.

"You can never be too careful about that pagan voguing," Shadow said. "The little spooks get my windshield every year." Then the officer walked on by and Shadow pressed Danjamar's head close to his chest and whispered: "Merry meet. Merry part. Merry meet again." The pits in his face were deep enough to puddle up with their own shadows and he smelled briny as tinned stew.

FUNDAMENT HOUSE

So it developed that the last thing in his natural life Danjamar wanted to do was attend the shelter Halloween party. He told Miss Caitlin he'd met some real kids on the outside was going to trick-or-treat with people his own age. She smiled sadly under her greasepaint freckles and red yarn wig; the Raggedy Ann costume was just a slight twist on her usual appearance; Danjamar could tell she had spent years trying to find a way to avoid trick-or-treating with people her own age.

"Well, you deserve a night out. But nothing scary," she said, tilting her head and twisting a swatch of yarn like it was her actual hair. "I hope you asked your mom."

Mama was still on the phone, trying to negotiate some public housing within walking distance of Sienna's school. They'd been at the shelter for three months now—half as long as they'd lived with J himself—and the counselors were beginning to hint at alternatives. Mama leaned against the kitchen counter, doodling numbers on a party invitation and trying to make the figures fit. One foot slipped in and out of her clear plastic jelly shoes. There was a snag down the leg of her red stretch pants, and a few spongy hairs stood up on her forehead. Every time she hung up the phone, she'd wipe them down, find a clean section of paper, and start again. Someone had lent Sierra a ballerina outfit, and she looked like a little cinnamon fairy picking her pink net butt in the picture window, silhouetted among the construction-paper pumpkins and black cats.

Victoria floated by in a Princess Leia suit—a paper crown and a plain white nightgown with a pop-top belt slung low on her hips. Unlike the actress she imitated, Victoria wore a training bra under her dress, and her panty line made a visible "V" over her rear. Danjamar closed his fists low in his pockets and nodded his head.

"Not even, Mr. Mallomar," she said.

He just turned away and shut himself in the clothes cubby. There must be something left here, something that would transform him into the boy he could walk away from. He tossed through *as is* pants and sweaters and T-shirts, all of them damaged in some obvious way. Stains and snags and missing buttons. Broken zippers, outdated slogans, concert tours that took place before Danjamar was even old enough to be aware of the constant shift of radio hits which formed the tectonic plates of his consciousness. He tipped over a big cardboard box and crawled inside, smelling the chalky sweetness of mothballs and baby shit. This was what he'd be reduced to if the shelter didn't work out; he'd be one of those hoboes with their own cardboard boxes out on the street. There were some, even in a town this small, setting up housekeeping downtown, their shopping carts parked in front of a church, their aluminum cans and beer bottles in order, blankets spread out on the steps every morning, playing guitar or harmonica in front of a Styrofoam cup full of change. There was a black man among them; Danjamar had memorized his ratty hair which looked permanently matted in shampoo, his broad nose, the blue striped cap probably out of a charity bin just like this one, advertising some team or product he'd never sampled. The one time Danjamar had dropped in a quarter he felt just as guilty as when he didn't stop. Who was his brother, anyway? His father left before he was six. His uncles stopped by with a chicken or a ham or b-ball but they never stayed long: one had joined the army, one had gone to jail for drug trafficking, one had run up North for a manufacture job. His mama's boyfriends came in drops and driblets, stayed to breakfast but not to dinner, kept their shoes on in the house. Only J had taken a real interest in him and look what happened there.

Danjamar punched the bottom of the box. He took a breath and did it again. The sound was louder than what you'd expect. Anyone came in and asked, he was boxing a box, beating the crap out of a side of cardboard. When Mama was out at work, J taught him the moves, wound up wrestling him to the bed, tickling him so hard he felt the misplaced handlebar of a cramp poke into his side and a spot of pee appear at the tip of his johnson. Eventually, Danjamar would end up face first on the mattress with J on top of him, weighing him down so every breath had to be squeezed out like a fart, telling Danjamar what he had to say to be released. Danjamar would refuse until J brought out the belt, the board, the spatula. Then, in a voice that carefully detoured all traffic signals and stop signs of emotion, he asked J to do whatever was necessary to make a man out of a pitiful backwoods bedwetter like himself.

One day, someone came to the door, a white voice with little bells, some kind of feeble jewelry. Danjamar heard What's His J answer the door, listened to the woman's story about needing a boy to help with her yard work. I thought I heard a little one here, she said. J just laughed. What you need to come way out here just to find someone to fix your fanny for free?

"If you must know, I'm offering five dollars," she said, and J slammed the door without comment.

Later, some police showed up on the front porch. They sipped on jelly jars of iced tea and sawed away in the rusted glider, making a noise like a guttural jazz solo while J instructed Danjamar to strip right there—shirt, pants, socks. The head officer stopped him before he got to his underpants. A skinny one, ain't he? Look like some kind of half-harvested coon carcass to me. They mentioned the child services office. J mentioned his employer, Mr. Ames, who owned the feed store and the Wal-Mart in town. They mentioned a follow-up visit, stood and set their jelly jars down on the moving glider. When one slid off onto the porch, spraying glass across the boards, Danjamar picked up a piece and pressed it into his hand, just to see how far he could get without calling out. It was halfway up his arm before J came back from the police car and yanked him back into the house. "Lucky your color hides so many flesh wounds," he said. "Otherwise, I don't know how you'd make it, kid."

In the cubby, in the shelter, in a cardboard box in an anonymous river town on the Mississippi, Danjamar contemplated what he had to do to get out of his own funk. He crawled out of the box, peeled off his baggy jeans, his handed-down green shirt, his inside-out underwear. The room was cold; it smelled of pickles and rotting potatoes, all the things that get put away in the fall. Danjamar wanted to be put away too—to fold his shadow and shove it back in the box. The door handle jiggled and he grabbed the first thing available: a long stray T-shirt, so black he pretended that the intruder wouldn't see him in the dark.

"Hey, it's a little Jesoid," a man's voice said.

Danjamar couldn't believe he'd gotten so careless—no one ever snuck up on him at home. "Who are you? Did Miss Caitlin let you in?"

"Relax, Jebediah. I'm here for the bash. And hey, I won't even ask what you're doing in here without your pants."

He was tall with shiny brown hair and brown eyes, a brightly colored cap with bells and tails and tassels hanging down into his eyes. "I'm War- ren. I'm a jester—go ahead and say it—I'm a fool. And you are, you're a missionary, right?"

Danjamar clicked his tongue in surprise before he looked down, once again, pulled his shirt away from his chest, and read its message: Complete darkness, out of which sprouted the wild yellow eyes of a beast. "Keep Watch," the writing said. "For Ye Know Not the Day Nor the Hour When the Son of Man Cometh."

"Yeah, just for the night," Danjamar said, pulling on his pants. "If you can excuse me, man, I got to go out and find my people."

On the way, he passed a whole parade of adults dressed in full Hal- loween regalia—two tall witches, a sailor, a pussycat, a Darth Vador, and a cheerleader intermingled with little kids in rag and tail ends of costumes. Mama sat on the couch in her red stretch pants and Dove Bar sweatshirt, her head resting on one hand, eyes closed. Asleep, in full headache, or just resting up for the next phone call?

He slipped in next to her and kissed the soft cheek that smelled of cigarettes and corn chips and the gardenia hand lotion that came in big bottles from the drugstore down the block—he'd broken into his cash jar to buy one for her birthday. He waved his hand over her eyes.

"You in there, Mama?" he said.

"I'm working on it, boy."

As they talked, Miss Caitlin led the parade of children and volun- teers around the living room, through the office, into the kitchen, and back again. It made Danjamar dizzy, just thinking how little room there was to move. Sierra was near the head of the line, in the arms of the pussycat, trying to pull out its whiskers. Sienna trailed along near the end, constantly turning around to adjust the tail of her skirt. At the entrance to the kitchen, Victoria stood leaning into the door frame and parcelling out the candy one piece at a time, her hip conked out and one yellow coil of hair collapsed into a pigtail and nosing into the candy bucket.

"I was just speculating about if I was to go out. I mean, I'm not going to get me another note that says leave all your possessions and follow me to the next state, am I?"

Mama cut her eyes at him, looked mad, then strained, then sorry. "Did you really want me to leave you with that hound? Don't you think no better of yourself than that?"

Danjamar looked down at his chest again. He wasn't sure what to think.

"You plan to tell your mama what he done with you?"

"Ain't no kind of thing to tell your mama about."

"Every morning, I pray God let me forgive him. And then every night I look at my babies. Sierra, she can't even talk yet. Sienna, she can't do right in school, have all them nightmares, chew her fingers till they bloody. You won't hardly look at me. Can't have a conversation to save your soul. And then I know I have to stay away from down there because I'll kill him if I ever see him again. I shoulda killed him if I had to do it with my bare teeth. What I need to know is, whose side you on, boy?"

Danjamar grit his molars. He rubbed at his chest and felt the next message melt into his lungs.

"Danjamar, the counselors they say we gotta communicate. They say get in there with your sorrow and kick it around. Pick it up. Get a good whiff of it. Then you can put it away in your pack and go on."

"I'm going, I'm going," he said. "I can't take no more of this shit."

The wind outside raised his hair, his courage, his nipples; he felt it slide under his shirt like a cold white hand and ruffle the thin fabric until the garment rippled up and down his back. The air was filled with the smells of fall: burnt leaves, melting marshmallow, paint and gas fumes. Danjamar picked up his pace, ran past the church, past the park where he saw a couple of people in robes like Shadow's setting up in the picnic pavilion. He ran up the street and into the little downtown, where there was a coffee shop, a comic book store, a video arcade. When he stopped for breath, he heard someone behind him. A teenage boy, about sixteen, riding a skateboard that scrabbled over the rough brick street. His pale ghostly hair floated out around him. His skinny knee stuck out of a hole in his jeans. Before Danjamar could think, the boy had jumped off, popped the skateboard up with a loud crack, and caught it in his hands like a missile. For half a second, he thought the kid was going to throw it at him.

"Hey, Mojo. We're out looking for people for our haunted house. You know, other kids who heed the call."

Danjamar looked more closely at the boy. His plaid shirt opened onto a black T-shirt with a 3-D image of a heavily muscled savior carrying a cross. "Bench Press This," it said.

Danjamar flexed his fingers in his pocket.

"Yeah, I see you're saved too, bro. We don't believe in Halloween, but, you know, we like to do something. So we put together this incredibly wicked haunted house. I mean, we got devils, we got metal, we got hell fire."

"I don't know," Danjamar said.

"Hey, we're not prejudiced, man. It's true we don't have too many of your people but that's only because they've got their own religion. Like, they crossed over with the sons of Ham. So what's your name, bro?"

"Danjamar."

"Then we'll call you Daniel—like Daniel in the lion's den. I'm Samson and my pal here is Goliath." He cradled the skateboard and bounced it up and down in his arms, emphasizing its weight.

"But didn't Goliath get beat over the head?"

"I'm down with that," Sam said. "I just like the name."

He led Danjamar up the steps of the same church where the bums congregated for their sessions. One was still there, crouched in his cardboard, playing a penny whistle. Danjamar gave him a quarter as he passed. His fingers were sweating on the metal, he could hear his own eyelashes click as he blinked. At the church door, Sam chained his skateboard to the railing and wiped his feet. Danjamar looked at the marquee—"For the wages of sin is death. Come visit our haunted house and check out your paycheck."

The dim vestibule was filled with teenagers laughing and talking, wearing drab colors over their pale skins. A pretty blonde girl stood in a long gray sweatshirt, her hands tucked up inside the sleeves so they resembled stumps. A redheaded boy slouched against the bulletin board in a camouflage jacket; a voluptuous brunette pulled at the broken strap of her overalls; a whole crew of loners lounged around the registry in loose black jeans. Their clothes seemed to drip off them like candle wax. Rips, shreds, tears and safety pins. Muddy hiking boots. Sloppy hats and stringy hair. The colors of fall gone to seed. This must be where all those damaged goods were coming from, Danjamar thought, standing in a corner and scratching at his teeth.

"The tour is almost ready to begin," Sam said, and someone flicked a lighter. Another one went up, then a third. The lights grew even dimmer, and a shout crossed the room: "Haunted House. Haunted House. Haunted House." All around them, flames flared in little groups of two and three. Someone cut a fart and its fumes fanned out, making Danjamar think of the tuna casserole he'd had for dinner.

"Who's ready to see hell?" a male voice bellowed, ending in a long trombone slide. "Who's ready to battle Satan?"

A dozen shouts erupted and teased out another round of "Haunted House."

Then a single female voice floated into the crowd and everyone was still. It sang of a rich man kneeling in the pit of Hades and asking Lazarus for a glass of water. The man's brow radiated liquid lead. His kneecaps turned to coal. His tongue petrified in his mouth, and his head rattled like a dried-out gourd.

Danjamar thought of the rich voices in his church back home, the thick batter of sound. This voice was just a trickle in comparison, and yet everyone held completely still as it skanked and slithered through the room.

The roil of people straightened out into a line and proceeded down the stairs. At the bottom of the stairwell, the same male voice instructed them to place a hand on the shoulder of the person in front of them—railroad style—and close their eyes. Sam pushed Danjamar into the line behind a girl in a short horseshoe haircut and a tobacco-colored halter. Danjamar didn't know where to put his hand. The whole back was there in the open, exposing its damp moles and naked pink curves. He closed his eyes and found a spot. Even before he touched down to it, he could feel the heat moving up, smell the dank sweat commingled with burnt orange perfume.

The line began to move.

Danjamar felt the skin sweat underneath him, so much sweat that his hand kept slipping out of position. The line moved in a hobbling hop, like the members were chained together leg to leg. He passed through a doorway and into a cooler space, where there was howling and groaning all around him.

"Open your eyes and behold your sin," the announcer said.

Danjamar stood in front of a cubicle with two boys sitting at a table, a bottle between them. Its crayoned label showed a skull and crossbones.

The boys spoke in exaggerated drawls and sprawls, and he wondered why everyone tended to sound more southern when drunk.

"Just having some fun," one was saying, when the stereo system kicked in and a wall of flames shot up in front of the cubicle. On closer inspection, it was a kind of hose laid along the floor which shot up flames like a sprinkler. Danjamar wanted to bend down to get a better look, but he couldn't get down that far without breaking up the whole procession.

Then, once again, the male voice commanded them to close their eyes and move on. Each time he stopped in front of a new cubicle, Danjamar expected something more dazzling—but it was just a series of skits in boxes, all of which ended the same way, with a spritz of hell fire and a blast of heavy metal. Behind him, Samson was chanting the Lord's Prayer to a reggae rhythm. Danjamar looked across the room at the kids who were just entering. He didn't know why he even bothered to open and shut his eyes. What he'd seen would blow this little white boy's hell to ashes.

The smell, though—now that was overpowering. The sweat of fifty white kids mixed with whatever chemicals it took to light their Halloween hell fires. That and the noise of at least three separate metal tunes playing in stereo.

The fire door at the back of the church was open. He could see someone smoking under the neon EXIT sign.

"One thing you got to decide, Danger Man. Are you the fucker or are you the fuckee? These girls, they don't got a choice. They're nothing but holes. But you a man. You got the equipment, both ways."

Suddenly Danjamar was very thirsty, his throat backed up with chili and tuna and hamburger meat from days and days of shelter dinners.

Outside the fire door, the man gestured to him, signaling "Come here," or "Go away." He wore a loose white shirt with quarter-size nipples showing underneath. He'd grown reddish sideburns and a mealy yellowing beard. Danjamar saw the long hawk nose, its pores and blackheads, its deviated septum, in microscopic detail, even though the door was at an odd angle from him and maybe twenty feet away. Josiah. Jebediah. Jacob. Jesus. James. He opened his eyes and closed them, listened for their click. But whether he looked or not, the man was still there, opening and closing his hand.

Danjamar's gut clenched in rhythm, first a butterfly, then a bass, and then a hot and wrenching fist.

Come here. Shit on the newspaper. Ream out your sister. Give us a smile.

He felt Sam pinching his waist behind him. He gripped onto the shoulder of the girl in front. Her meat was tightly packed under the sweat-slick skin and he grabbed as much as he could handle, grit his teeth, and pulled. The filmy halter came away in his hand, the color of a faded leaf wasting away at the base of a sycamore tree. He pressed it close to his face. He smelled the funk and junk and unidentifiable fluids, found the message printed deep inside the cleavage, where the label protruded out of a band in a curled white tongue and never ceased to proclaim.

Goddess Love

*A*ll that year, our toilet was broken. You had to kneel down to adjust the water pressure and the men at our various parties went out to pee in the backyard instead. I never went back there myself because the landlord rarely got around to mowing and I didn't want to know anyway. I imagined: wild mint and stinkweed, box elder bugs and raccoons, a couple pairs of bikini underwear Sonia had spread out over a bush to dry, and a naked female figure stretching her arms up toward the collapsed clothesline—the Goddess in her domestic guise. Sonia had been courting Her ever since the second abortion and the attendant short course in matriarchal religions. When in doubt, my new housemate consulted a series of colorful paperbacks, a herbal reme-dy recipe book, and a round deck of soft focus, water color tarot cards for guidance and instruction. And after I moved into the back bedroom with the warped wooden floor and the smell of insecticide and ginger root in the corners, I was expected to do the same.

Back then, Sonia was married to someone in another state and I was practically a virgin. She told me stories about men with independent businesses and illegitimate children who bought her gifts of edible underwear and Kama Sutra coffee table editions. I could only remem-ber a bottle of sweet white wine with my boyfriend of six years, a dis-posable sponge with a red stain in the middle, like a broken jelly donut, the Moody Blues on a jerryrigged stereo. Sonia was just three years older than me, but she seemed to belong to a completely different gen-eration.

I watched her sitting at the kitchen table in her white nightgown and vintage mohair sweater, looking over a cookbook and testing the texture of the herbs between her thumb and forefinger. Then she'd lift up the pestle and start grinding again, without even shifting her gaze. Her long brown hair wasn't curly or straight; it turned in different directions like the fringe on a worn leather jacket, and she had a habit of lifting strands of it to her face, scanning for split ends. Her eyes were long, her hips were broad, her face flushed easily with anger or red wine—sometimes I couldn't tell which until it was too late.

"I'm trying to figure out, did you do the dealer guy before or after you found the Goddess?"

She gave me a patient look and blew her hair out of her eyes. "You know, Lori, you're obsessed with cause and effect. I've always had a sense of goddess energy underlying my relationships. Remember, we've got the power to give birth. So when they act out like that they're just trying to make up for their inherent biological inadequacy."

"Hmm, spooky."

"I'm almost ready for the eggs."

"I just wonder if it has anything to do with the boots. They say guys really like boots. It makes them think you'll be willing to do it standing up."

"You should get out and meet someone," she told me. "The road of excess leads to the temple of the oversoul."

I nodded and plied at the edge of my hand-loomed place mat with an extra quarter left over from my half of the laundry. My boyfriend hoped I'd be faithful while he was gone for job training in Maryland, but he wasn't going to be leading me down any roads of excess. I'd learned that much, anyway. So when he got the assignment and had to stop split-ting rent, I checked around and finally ended up in Sonia's house on Jewel Avenue on the recommendation of my best friend Camy, who'd known her since the tenth grade.

"No ponies there," Camy said. "And she's a little bit of a chippie. But she can dole out some excellent *dhal*."

Camy lived in a big house with four other people in their twenties. They shared a microwave, a prize-winning street sign from a local barbe-cue, and a pottery vase full of change at the front door. But they tried to avoid actually meeting in person. When I went over, we'd go into her bedroom, shut the door, take off our shoes, and dance to Lou Reed until the floor shook, her Evangelical Korean housemate slammed the wall with his Bible dictionary, and we collapsed sweating onto her futon and tried to think of songs about masturbation:

"*Turning Japanese,*" she said.

"*Pictures of Lily.*"

"*And She Was.*"

"No fair—that's more a spiritual-type quest motif."

"You've been living with the high priestess of porn for how long now, and you still haven't figured that one out?"

"She's OK." I said. "Anyway, she's your friend."

"She's my ex-dealer's ex-squeeze. And she's all yours now."

Camy butted her shoulder against mine, and I went for her ankle. She had on gray stretch pants with construction workers printed on them, a flannel shirt open over a blue tank top, unshaved armpits, high-topped tennis shoes. She was beautiful in a feral kind of way: her cheekbones branched out with all the force of antlers and her breasts stood out the size and shape of turtle shells. But she claimed that men liked my type better: flyaway angel hair, long legs, small tits.

"You know, you could be in a painting," she said. "Dutch realism, Italian Renaissance, French rococo. What am I though? Nothing. A cheap Italian fuck flick. Or maybe some damn Cubist whore."

"Come on. How do you think of these things?"

Camy threw her leg over mine. "I just close my eyes, clench a few muscles and place an order. Now, you try."

I plumped the pillow underneath me and leaned back against the wall. I could smell Camy's hair gel and the essence of clove she'd picked up at the head shop that afternoon. I could hear her housemate's computer keys clattering in the next room. But all I could see was Sonia standing over the kitchen sink, peeling an avocado half in a single motion, her robe slipping off one shoulder, her face glossy with some herb she'd just inhaled, and her mind sloping off into a vaster astral plane.

"How can you do it alone?" I said, and Camy got up to put on another tape.

By mid-September, I had it down to a drill. I'd set my clock radio and try to beat the second hand to the very top of the third minute. I'm a three-minute egg," I thought. "I'm whipped into peaks." If I timed it just right, the music would burst in on my surprise party, froth into the moment, bring me out on the other side. If it was a bad day, I'd get the d.j. plugging zit cream or making spanking jokes about his sidekick. This put me off my mark, set me to thinking about my future, how I'd quit my job at the record store, go back to school to learn electronics, and travel around the country as some know-it-all sound man for a trash thrash band. Sonia said I thought like a man, anyway. Plug and socket. Cause and consequence. Bump and grind. I pushed my breasts up over the top of my torn-up T-shirt and contemplated their shape. Maybe Sonia was right.

But sometimes, I'd be interrupted even before this point. The doorbell would ring and it'd be some guy with a leer and a six-pack, or Sonia's husband would phone in from his excavation site in New Mexico and say where's Lady Lucky? I played with the pegs on the cork bulletin board, mumbled something about the co-op, or if it was too late for that, the movies. I never could get used to lying.

Sonia came home and said I was a puritan, a legalist, and a positivist.

"You think like a man," she told me again, pulling long stalks of bok choy out of a grocery bag. So maybe she had been at the co-op after all. They were dark green fading into bulbs of white at the ends, and I imagined that she was going to plant them in the back yard and raise up a whole army of dealers to defend her cause.

"What do you mean, just because I think?"

"There you go. Do you really believe Ty wants to know who I'm with? Is that what you think he's asking? And even if he was, do you think he has the right to know where I am every blessed millisecond?"

"Well, I don't know your relationship."

"That's right. Now, let's get these groceries put away so we can clear the table and do our moon charts."

"How's Gary?" I said.

"Angry, as usual. He can't come to terms with the Neptune deal. You know, his father was a Marine. When was your last period?"

"What? What are you, a doctor now?"

"So I know what number to start you on."

"I don't know," I said. "Why would I remember something like that?"

"The Wednesday Gary brought over the mushrooms. That was your period because you said you were cramping in stereo."

"You're not keeping track of this, are you?"

"Well, Lori, I can't believe you're not. You're so out of touch with the Goddess."

This Goddess was the third person in our house, the figure who was always slithering between us and causing little patches of spiritual friction, like glitter on sandpaper. She scattered sesame seeds on the kitchen floor, left open bottles of red wine out on the counter, gutted candles and reshuffled tarot cards. She turned the heat up too high in the middle of the night, so that the furnace heaved in heavy sighs that made us twist the covers in our sleep and dream of burial at sea, then wake up to long bilious arguments over the heating bill.

By now, the Goddess showed up in every conversation, and I kept hearing something different about her. She had three faces, for example. The virgin, the mother, and the crone. Nothing at all about a whore, the aspect amateurs liked to go on about. No woman was a whore, if she truly respected herself and kept the doors of her senses open. At the very most, she'd be a sacred prostitute. The Goddess saw to that. The Goddess saw through everything. She swept away lies like cobwebs. She demolished arguments with a swish of her hips. She smothered all objections under the weight of her huge tits. She was an excellent cook. She pre-existed God, had no use for monogamy, and didn't care for my taste in rock'n' roll.

So I just stayed in my room reading magazines, listening to tapes, and perfecting my technique. Occasionally, I heard Sonia and Gary through the wall: a steady hum with bright medallions of vocalization. I went to my stereo and turned the music down, not up. I even thought of taping them. I was becoming a connoisseur of sound.

My boyfriend wrote me long letters illustrated with hallucinatory doodles and coffee stains. He was working hard, he didn't much like Easterners, he missed my pearly teeth and gritty conversation. He'd grown up reading too much sci-fi/fantasy fiction, he'd never be able to help me become a woman, and there wasn't much I could do about it now. I missed him too, in the dark, lizardy space above my spine, and I knew I'd never find anyone as perfect as him, as straight and sweet-smelling as a birch switch with the bark peeled off. Something you carry around through the whole afternoon on a great snipe hike in childhood then can't bear to toss back into the woods.

In October, Sonia threw a party to celebrate All Hallows' Eve. She fixed huge tubs of humus and *baba ganouj,* made party tapes of eerie Irish folk music, set broomsticks and painted gourds out over the house. I was supposed to clean the bathroom. I swabbed the fixtures down, made a few swipes at the grimy porcelain island under the toilet, burned some opium incense on the rim of the sink, then called it a day. Everyone would go outside anyway.

I mostly concentrated on my costume: a punk Tinkerbell, with short boots, green tights, and a painter's cap with exotic earrings dangling from the bill. I had to get the tunic from a theater store in town. Sonia just threw on a black robe at the last minute. Her cleavage sliced up out of the bodice. Her hair expanded with electricity, and her body masses made shiny patches in the worn thrift-store velvet.

"Look, we're going as good and evil," I said.

Her face flushed to the color of the paprika she was sprinkling on a margarine tub full of humus. "You know I don't believe in those distinctions."

Camy came as Venus in Furs, and had to strip down as the night went on. We ignored Sonia's friends playing spades and rolling weed in the kitchen. They were behind the times, hippie wanna-bes who couldn't get over the stash in their big brothers' closets. We ate chocolate bars and candy corn out of a paper bag instead, snubbing all drugs that came with men attached. We drank three beers each and switched to water after eleven. Then we turned the stereo up to nine, took off our shoes, and switched Sonia's tapes for ours.

The floor shook. The stereo skipped. Camy's upper body vibrated like a raw filet of chicken breast. I felt a run spring open over the left cheek of my tights. Sweat tickled in my cleavage. Gradually, my brain fluid stopped sloshing around and gently soaked into the distant crannies of my physical equipment. I felt it glimmer over my throat, shimmy down my shoulders with individual shivers of feedback, saturate my thighs. I'm not thinking of Sonia anymore, I thought.

At some point, it hurts more to stop dancing than it does to go on throwing your weight around. We'd reached this level when she came in and turned the music off.

"It's an old house, girls," she said. "You don't want to raise the spirits."

My lungs were too raspy to breathe; I rested my hands on my thighs in a runner's pose, panting; Camy's garter had fallen down. A bunch of guys were staring at us and nodding. "What's the matter?" Camy yelled. "Haven't you ever seen a woman move before?"

"Probably not," I said. "Judging from their reputations."

But then the slow music was on and one of them pulled me away, while someone else globbed onto Camy. Mine was tall, with a broadcloth shirt, the sleeves rolled up over his long blonde forearms. He didn't smell like a hippie.

"Cute costume," he said, rubbing a fake green leaf from the tunic against my shoulder.

"You too. What are you supposed to be, a young Republican?"

"OK, I admit, I crashed. But at least I brought my own beer. Good stuff, too. Not this Nazi Coors swill."

"Then why are you drinking it?"

He blushed, and I felt the room curve in around us: my cheekbones ached from the smile I wanted to give him.

"Let's go out on the porch," he said.

The wooden slats were cold on my bare feet in their skimpy stirrup straps. We slumped down against the wall of the house and he pushed at the broken porch swing with his knee. Up close, I could tell he was too good-looking for me.

"Your music's better anyway," he told me.

"Yeah?"

"Definitely a few notches left of the dial." His head bobbed a little as he talked, as if he was trying to look serious. He was actually that awful thing: a handsome guy. The kind I'd always avoided. Lucky for me, the effect was marred by a pale mask of honey-colored freckles, a thin upper lip, and odd dented ears pressed close to his head. He snuck a sideways look at me to see how I was taking it. Who was I kidding? The man was completely beautiful.

"Well, we aim to satisfy," I said. "Folk come slumming from far and wide."

"Is that what you think I'm doing?"

"Want another beer?"

"Give me your hat," he said.

"The whole thing's coming apart. See this earring? My boyfriend gave it to me in 1979, and I still haven't figured out how to work the clasp."

"Let's see, it's gold, not brass, isn't it? That's a really fine metal, but it's delicate, I've got to tell you—extremely malleable shit."

He leaned down to kiss me, my hat still in his hand, and my lips blurred into his. I curled my legs in toward him. He was working his finger between my stirrup strap and the sole of my foot when Gary came out of the house and banged his hip flask on the screen door.

"Hell, I'll piss in the front yard then," he said. "Oh, sorry. Lori, is that you? Don't look, darlin. It'll just ruin you for other men."

"I'm doing fine, thanks."

"Hey, go around the side, dude. We're involved out here."

"Easy, Scooter. I'm just taking a pee. Watch out for the poontang, huh? We don't have enough to go around."

"Fuck off and go play with your hose," I yelled out into the dark yard.

He stumbled away and the guy on the porch wedged his hand between my knees. "Cold, man."

"Look, what's your name?"

"Bill."

"Bill, this is a weird time for me."

"The witching hour," he said.

In the morning, my throat was rough and dry as a rice cracker, and I felt air pockets popping in my head. My hair smelled like burnt popcorn on my pillow. When I stood up, my compass spun out of control, and I had to lie back down again: I'd only had four beers.

At the refrigerator, Gary was dipping a pretzel in the leftover *baba ganouj.*

"You look like you treed a power line," he said.

"I'm just getting juice. I'm not awake yet. Don't talk to me."

"I'd feel sick too if I spent all night slurping up some yuppie scum."

"Look, I'm not in the mood."

"Neither's your friend in there. Better watch out, Lula."

Later, Camy called and said she'd fallen in lust. "A big gooey pile of it. He's just some dumb fuck barfly with Donna Summer flashbacks, but he's one fantastic lay."

The floor was sticky under my feet. I sat down at the kitchen table, pushed away a mayonnaise lid filled with cigarette butts, and ran my finger through the crust on top of the dried-out bean curd. "So what makes a good lay?" I said.

"Manual dexterity plus some sort of basic personal insecurity. This one's a dental student."

"No kidding."

"On sabbatical."

"You're sleeping with a dentist."

"Gotta do it with somebody. How can you do it alone?"

"Manual dexterity," I said. "Personal insecurity."

"Come on, you're not going to meet your soul mate. They're guys, Lori. They travel in packs. They bond over alternators. They get a mystical experience when they scratch their balls."

"Do you think I act like a guy?"

"Well, you sure as hell don't dance like one."

At two o'clock, Sonia came out of her room holding an alpaca jacket closed over her blue gauze nightgown. She looked around the living-room, retrieved a gourd that had rolled into the fake fireplace, then started picking up around me. I didn't move. She finally came over and handed me a mop.

"We've got the dry rot," she said. "Careful where you put this thing."

"Have a good time?"

"Not as good as some people." She touched her forehead then picked up a dishcloth and started slapping at the counter.

"Hey, I was sober."

"Maybe that's the problem," she said. "Western systems of rationalization. Self-consciousness. Denial."

The phone rang again, and it was for me.

"Lori, it's Bill. From last night. I was wondering if I could come over and borrow your party tape."

I looked at Sonia making her slow rounds of the kitchen, leaning over the sink to palpate the tomatoes ripening on the windowsill. Her hair looped over her shoulder, and the long uneven piece at the front slipped down, dripped into the pile of dirty dishes soaking in the wash basin. She didn't lose a beat, just ran the slick strand through her fingers, working the water in, as if she was experimenting with some kind of dye.

"So, are you having a party now?"

"That depends," he said.

She finally looked my way, her hair still in her hand. The sleepy wax-paper expression was peeling off her face. Underneath, some new enthusiasm was forming; she looked as if she'd just had a facial.

"Boy at 6 o'clock." I said

"Look," She pointed out the window. "It's starting to snow." The first day of November, and already flakes were falling onto the weeds in the backyard. Someone had tied a pink feather boa on the clothesline, and it was twining and untwining in the wind, like some obscene exotic bird sprawling over our yard. Or the famous goddess making her appearance at last. I rested the mop handle against my leg. I looked for a sign. Beer cans glinted in the bushes. Orange napkins blew from one shrub to another. There was a cuff of icicles hanging from the leak in the drainpipe, and when Sonia let her jacket slip open around her shoulders, I saw the battery of love marks lingering on her neck. He had an overbite, whoever it was.

By the time Bill got there, we'd brought our house back to its usual condition of low-level sloth. He tracked mud onto the kitchen floor, and stood there melting while Sonia made the tea.

I leaned against the counter and closed the tape case on my index finger.

"How'd you hear about the party?" Sonia said.

"Oh, the word gets around."

"What's the word?" I asked.

Sonia handed him a cup and rubbed her hands over her arms. "You know, we're a private home here. Not just another stop on the party curcuit."

I pinched my finger, hard. I was afraid I'd have to take a powder before Sonia ever got around to leaving us alone.

And as it turned out, I was right. After Bill gave up and went home, we boiled more hot water and moved into Sonia's room, where she spread her gown out under her on the futon and I sat on the rag rug. Her walls were covered with earth-tone weavings and bright crayon-colored tapestries; dried flowers suicided down from the rim of her bureau; and even the bedspread shone with tiny chips of mirror sewn into the design, making me wonder if Gary ever got nicked and whether he was the type to really mind. I sat with one ankle touching the futon and my hands around my knees. I wished she'd let us turn up the heat.

"Want me to read your tarot?" she said.

"I'm the captain of my fate. I'm not going to lob off the responsibility onto a deck of cards."

"It's not like that, Lori. How many times do I have to tell you, it's just a meditative device?"

"And a rubber's just for the prevention of disease," I said.

She pulled her gown down over her stocking feet. "I don't know why you've got so much negative energy. I'm the one covering for you. I'm the one who should be mad."

A bath bead popped in my stomach. A gush of liquid smoke spread out over my chest: she was going to tell me what she thought of me. This was the moment I dreaded worse than anything, when another woman started detailing all my intimate flaws: the nail-biting, the sloppy house-keeping, the stains on my underwear, the personal dirtiness hidden under a veneer of clear-skinned cynicism. It was excruciating, like being poked to death with hairpins. I took another sip of tea.

"When you moved in here I thought it would be progressive. I thought we'd form a mini co-op. Make things together. Keep house. Worship the Goddess." She paused, narrowed her hazel eyes, twisted the swizzle stick, and released a long strand of honey into her tea. It whipped its tail in slow motion like a lazy sperm in a sex-ed film, then dissolved into a thinner and thinner stream. Her hand slid into the safe space where her gown dipped between her knees. "I even thought we'd have an affair."

I saw my leg shaking before I felt it. I crossed my arms over my chest and my nipples poked into my wrists, aching as if they'd been through a pencil sharpener.

"Want a sweater?" Sonia said, and I shook my head. "I just didn't know you'd be so immature, so invested in Western norms of behavior. I asked my psychic about it, and she said that you were still resentful because I adopted you in a previous life. It was in pioneer times. Your parents died of influenza, and I took you in."

"Pioneer times? Couldn't I at least get to live in Atlantis or something?"

"I've got it on tape, if you don't believe me. Anyway, you felt like there was no way you could pay me back, so you're still upset about it. And I realize that if we ever get involved, you'll become so obsessed that I wouldn't be able to handle it. So it's all for the best, really."

"Oh, good," I said. "So we don't have to talk about it now."

"Well, obviously we have to talk about it. We can't just let it fester like an amputated limb."

When I stopped shaking, I picked up the phone in the kitchen and dialed the number Bill had given me. Four rings and a roommate later, I was asking him out to hear a band, claiming that I had passes from my job, even though they hadn't given me any perks in weeks.

"Squid Orchid" I said, shuffling through the paper. "It's sort of like metal through windowpane."

"I'm there. Why didn't you tell me before?"

"Stage fright. Performance anxiety."

I went into my room and put on as many layers as I could think of: lace underwear, maroon tights, sleeveless T-shirt, silk blouse, velvet jacket, Army coat. It was still snowing. When I got to the club, he was standing under the awning with flakes on the shoulders of a baby blue jacket, pockets in all the right places. He leaned down and his breath tickled in my ear, a nerve curled up in my neck and made me lean away from him.

"I knew you'd call back," he whispered.

Inside, the floor throbbed under our feet and it was too loud to talk. The band had a female vocalist in a net dress and leopard skin tights. Her voice ripped into the high notes, then dragged them down through the harmony like ladders of runs in a pair of long-legged nylons. The bass guitarist picked at my entrails. We sat near the dance floor, I paid for every other drink, and he reached down and rubbed my boot under the table. We only made it through one set.

At his apartment, he told me he'd suspended disbelief long enough, he kept thinking I'd come up with another excuse, but now I'd gone too far, I had to sleep with him, I was obligated.

"I don't mind," I said. "As long as it's just physical."

He unfastened my boots and we stayed in bed through the rest of the snowstorm. When I looked up, he pointed to my watch on top of his speaker.

"I see what you're up to," he said. "You're going to go home and tell your girlfriend how long I lasted."

"How long is it?"

"Don't stop the clock yet," he said, and moved into me again.

The next morning, he brought me orange sections and sausage links on a plate. They required a subtle variation in molar pressure: the orange membrane gave just before the rubbery casings. I tried to keep them in balance. But when I bit into the links, they sprayed a thick savory grease over the citrus and the combination stayed in my mind. The salt and the sweet. The fat and the lean. The thick and the sharp. I wondered what Sonia would make of this particular offering. Was it a tribute to my inherent female power or just a little flourish of chivalry to convince me that I wasn't giving it up for free? My skin was sensitive, burnished by Bill's whiskers to a sandstorm patina. I pictured the fat clay figures in Sonia's book, the fertility fetishes her husband was digging up in New Mexico. Who's the Goddess now? I thought.

The sex wasn't easy for me. I had to close my eyes and force myself at the last minute. My diaphragm got stuck several times. Once or twice, my body just wouldn't open. But usually, I would walk home in my miniskirt, raw and dripping, to lie on my bed and close caption what we'd just done. I walked up the cracked cement steps and into the chilly house, hoping Sonia would still be in her bedroom napping or meditating or performing strange rituals with yoghurt and sage. Once I was safe in my room, the clock unwound through whole afternoons. Bill was rough enough to make a better teacher than my boyfriend. He pushed me into the positions he wanted, made jokes during key transitions. But he always stopped when I said. And after the friction of the initial entry, the orgasms dropped away from me like scattering tea leaves.

"Why do you put your leg like that?" I said.

"Why, is it OK?"

"No, I just like to know all the technical points."

"What, so you can show your boyfriend how? Sorry kids, don't try this at home."

At Jewel Avenue, we made lentil soup, listened to Gregorian chants sung by a women's choir, and hoped our attraction would blossom into friendship. Sonia, dressed in a red satin smoking jacket, asked if I'd like her to throw my *I Ching* while I made another pot of tea for her bladder reaction to the lotus position the night before. Bill called, told me about the erotic preferences of the three top lyricists in the business while Sonia waited at the kitchen table with apricot crisp and the utilities bills. The season was veering toward the dead center of winter. Our plumbing problems had gotten even worse.

"So, cut me some slack. So I'm giving it a try," I said.

"Conserving energy?"

"This Goddess scam. I'm laying myself open to the eternal feminine."

"You're getting screwed. You're letting him have it on his own terms."

"Why, because he doesn't come over to meet the family?"

"Please. A guy who respects the Goddess in you doesn't talk about bagging women. That's patriarchal dog shit."

Bag. I told myself it had something to do with sleeping bags. Bag. Hag. Fag. Drag.

"Sometimes, sex is just boring," Bill said, leaning back against the headboard, while I sawed away on top of him. "You've got to accept it."

"You want me to stop?"

"Wait, no, it'll pick up in a minute."

"I'll bet," I said.

"You want me to move the mirror over here?"

"You want to check your hair?" I said.

We did move the mirror sometimes, and I saw my body scissor into his. We were almost the same color, the pale gleam of the crust on homemade bread. I couldn't tell whose limb was which. The winter sunshine fell on his plaid flannel sheets, and everything smelled of brine shrimp, like science experiments back in school. I picked a hair off the pillow. Bill lifted his arm up to switch over the tape. His armpit was blond too.

"Well, you're the only chick I know who wants to do it to thrash. It must be some bo-ho deal."

I laughed and bit his shoulder.

"Hey, don't get cocky. You've still got plenty to learn."

☙

"So what does the boyfriend know?" Camy asked me, when I got back from a weekend in Maryland and we were on our bimonthly expedition to the Salvation Army.

"He knows there's something he doesn't know about."

"And?" she said, fingering the satin tape running down the side of a pair of tuxedo pants.

"And he doesn't want to find out."

"So Sonia's right—they don't really give a shit as long as their status doesn't suffer."

"I'm beginning to explore that possibility," I said. The shopping was sparse this week. I saw a pink taffeta '50s party dress that could easily be cut up for a blouse to go with my black miniskirt, but at $15, it was still too steep.

"Mine's just getting possessive. He wants to know my work phone. Isn't that cute?"

"Clean your mouth out yet?"

"Don't get me started. He's expanding his repertoire. Last night we did it with implements."

"And how was that?"

"Cold. Then scary. Then sort of mechanical. At least there's no drill involved." She threw a sequin bra top in my direction. "What do you think? OK, OK, just because I have a jones for novacaine, it doesn't mean I'm in love."

Out on the sidewalk, we made a sharp left and almost bumped into one another, then steered past the drugstore, the grocery store, the head shop. In the plate glass windows, I could see how good we looked together, our matching matchstick legs and high-top tennis shoes, hands jammed into the pockets of boxy black jackets. Then I noticed Bill in the parking lot of the convenience store, hanging up a phone. His hip angled out of the phone cubicle first, as if he was making a basketball move. I passed behind Camy.

"Hey," he said.

"Hey," I answered, resisting temptation.

"Hey Lori, you left your K-Y jelly over at my house," he called as he sprinted away across the parking lot. "And I was just wondering whether you wanted it back."

By December, I was only home every other night; the rest of the time, I was at Bill's. Sonia answered the phone for me, got in a fight with Gary over his alcohol consumption, learned t'ai chi to calm her soul. I sat watching her practice: she'd explained that this was an art of nonviolence and psychic well-being, but when I saw her taking the moves, I knew something more had to be involved. In her bare feet and white Turkish towel outfit, she looked like she was swimming in air. Blue tendons flexed in the webbing of the foot nearest me. The world was thicker to her, I thought. With Sonia, it was all thick and physical, an oil painting you could hardly move through. Her feet seemed to stick in the goo of life. Her wrists turned against the tide of dust motes. Her hips deflected blows.

I had to be at work by two.

And Sonia wasn't talking.

"If I wait for a man to respect my feminine principle, I'll have to be celibate for the rest of my life," I said.

She sailed her arm toward me, in what looked like a New Wave dance move. "That's not so bad. Look at the great mystics. It's not like you have to give up the flesh. But you don't have to gorge yourself on it either. That's not the point. That's the problem with Christianity. It's so dependent on outmoded dichotomies."

"I don't want to be a mystic. I don't want to see the Goddess. You're the one who told me to go out and get laid in the first place. Now you want me to stifle my sex drive like some repressive male regime?"

"All right, all right," she said. "Why don't you ask him over for dinner? I'm making Indian on Friday."

That night after work, I looked at the chart Sonia had made for me and realized my period was late. I jostled my breasts. I palpated my abdomen feeling for water weight. I sniffed under my arms. I filled up my diaphragm at the sink and checked for leaks. Then I called Camy.

"I'm used to having sex alone," I said. "I can handle that. Now I might be two people having multiple orgasms with more than one partner. It's getting too complicated. I can't even do the math."

"What does Bill say?"

"Are you kidding?"

"Sorry. What are you going to do?"

"That's why I'm calling you."

"I say we go out dancing. Maybe you can shake the stuff out of you."

It wasn't Bill I was afraid to tell: I could pretty much lipsync his response without asking. But what about Sonia? Would she suggest we stay together, build a cradle out of driftwood, buy a food processor for organic baby food, consult a midwife, commission a birth chart, and raise our child in the sweet, prehistorical decay of matriarchy on Jewel Avenue? I shivered, thinking about that night in her room. My nipples drew out as stiff and hard as thimbles. Some Tinkerbell I made.

Of course, it would be a girl. Smarter than Sonia, warmer than Camy, more feminine than me. A redhead with cowlicks, dimples, freckles, nerve. Someone to make up for the fights and yeast infections, the aloof or abusive boyfriends, the suspicious Pap smears, the superstitious doctors, the abortions and contortions that we'd gone through trying to make women of ourselves. I tried to materialize her and when I did, she mutated into a sci-fi box elder bug and flew away home.

Two days later, and nothing was working. I'd taken hot baths, applied cold compresses, done all the calisthenics I could remember from high school gym, drunk laxatives, straight whiskey, and herbal teas. I called Camy every few hours.

"Why me? Sonia's the one with the broad hips and the maternal urges. I don't even own a bra."

"You don't have to," Camy said. "Think of *National Geographic.*"

"Great."

"I'm not helping, am I?"

"Hold on. I think I'm having morning sickness. No, sorry, it was only a burp."

Bill didn't even notice anything was strange.

"Roll over and I'll take you round the world," he said.

"Do I look bloated to you?"

"You look oversexed, same as usual."

"I don't want to right now."

"You always want to, babe."

"Yuck, don't call me that."

He pushed me over onto the pillow and I felt his chapped fingers on my hip.

"You're thinking of the serious boyfriend now, aren't you?"

"Not exactly."

He began to open me like the halves of a melon. I could picture my insides yielding, swelling to a bluish purple mass, with a little Brussels sprout clinging to my lining.

"Yeah, you say it's just physical, but you don't really mean it. You're holding out for the L-word."

I gave a little groan, just to get him going.

"You want me to look at your face when we screw. That's what you all want, isn't it? A dick and a diamond and a missionary lay."

"I want you to do it as hard as you can," I said. "I want you to fuck my brains out."

"You got it, babe."

I thought the pressure would help. But I was just more depressed, lying there sore and heavy watching him get dressed for work. He ducked down and whipped his undershirt over his neck; he snapped the waistband of his briefs. His neck muscles flinched as he went through his closet, and I knew he'd wanted to hurt me. His limbs were still shivering from it. In dress clothes, he looked younger, a boy turned out for his first job interview: the punk cut transformed into a head full of cowlicks, the long legs skinny and coltish under unaccustomed creases. I felt pitiful for choosing someone like that to bully me. But it was exactly what I'd wanted. That was the point of the exercise, like leg lifts for the thighs. Now I was the one to blame for the overdeveloped, steroid-stunned nature of our friendship.

It was the first time I didn't orgasm. So there was no need to lie around recuperating as usual. When I heard the door click shut, I stood up and looked around for my knapsack and I saw a typed letter lying on the desk. I was very strict about these things: don't look in medicine cabinets, don't listen to his half of the phone call, don't open the address book. I even turned away when he used the personal code on his bank card. But the letter was sitting there in the open, fair game, next to his slick metal pot pipe, like something out of a James Bond film, his Frisbee, his jock itch spray. It was almost like he wanted me to look. I read the address of the slick men's magazine that's usually tucked behind the *Time* slot in the convenience store. I glanced at two more words, *I'll give myself two words,* I thought, *just two words to go on, like a party game.*

The words were "boho" and "back door." The sentence was longer than his spoken variety. It rolled out on a raft of female flesh, its billows humping up between clauses, crashing over the boundaries of moral order, individual identities, and punctuation marks. I'd been transformed, multiplied into several women, all of them generally fitting my physical and socio-economic description. It was like Sonia's goddess: three heads, six breasts, twenty-one openings. I couldn't escape her, no matter how far away I went for gratification. I looked in the mirror, which we had out, propped up on a chair. I was already looking puffy in the belly, a discreet bulge over a tan mat of pubic hair. A flush branched out across my breasts. My aureoles had spread like ink stains.

I squatted down, clenched my fists between my thighs, and started to move.

In the kitchen on Friday, Sonia's curry cut through the smells of pesticide and decay. We'd been cooking all afternoon: ginger, garlic, pepper, cilantro, basil, lemongrass, cumin. A jar of tahini butter lay open on the counter. A cookie sheet of *nan* sat cooling on the stove. I'd cut my fingers twice, chopping vegetables, and the smells were so hot they infiltrated the nicks, giving me a preview of the evening's possibilities.

Sonia stood over the stove in her slit and patched jean skirt, red tights, and embroidered Chinese slippers. Her hair was pulled up into a loose bun and bisected with chopsticks; her face flushed somewhere between naughty and nice. She dipped a wooden spoon into a brown mass alive with potatoes and chicken parts and peas, and another attack of curry racked the room. Then she licked the spoon and let it drip back into the stew while my stomach flopped over like a raw wad of useless dough.

"Blessed be," she said. "That'll stir up the juices. Give it a try."

"No, I'm not feeling so super, OK?"

"What's the matter? Another hangover? Drinking up with the boys again?"

I shook my head and thought about spilling it. The guys were out back comparing irrigation techniques, maybe picking up a few tricks off the dentist, while Camy stomped around the living room lining up tunes.

"What goes with the Indian? Reggae? Dylan? Ska?"

"You're the expert," I called out to her. "What goes with novocaine: house, Euro-thrash, Duran Duran?"

Then I picked up a spatula and started scraping unleavened bread off the cookie sheet, stopping to adjust the bra I'd found in the bottom of my clothesbin and strapped into action, even though it hadn't fit since junior high. It kept riding up under my pink lace thrift store formal, getting in the way of the virginal line.

"Easy, Lori. Why don't you set the table, and put a gourd by each place, will you? I want to celebrate the harvest."

"What's to celebrate?" I said.

Sonia turned from the stove, her head canted up a notch like some impassioned Indian princess from one of her past lives. "Try the earth. The air, the fire, the water. The Goddess in all her forms. Or haven't you picked up on that yet? I guess you're too busy with your little dyke fling."

I made a mental note to clock Camy's position; she'd be up to "P" by now: Petty, Pogues, Police, Pretenders, Prince, Psychedelic Furs. But after that, she'd be able to pretty much wing her way through the rest of the alphabet. I imagined her reaching for the Lou Reed at the back of the fourth peach crate, her hair a black and purple haze, forearms showing through her ripped sleeves, coat tail hiked up and the heart-shaped curve of her ass all plumped out in stretch gortex, resting on an Army boot.

"You know," Sonia said, "It's getting just a little embarrassing, the way you're all over each other like yin and yang every time I entertain. Not that I think it's immoral or anything. But I figured you'd be through that tomboy phase by now."

I felt a stitch give inside me, the lining ripped out of my wind sock for a change. "Yeah, I guess you got over it real fast when I turned you down." I threw the spatula across the kitchen, knocking one chopstick out of her hair, so that she stood looking at me lopsided, half feral, half tame. Her collarbone surfaced; the tendons in her neck purled. I could see the cabernet mask forming over her cheeks. But it was too late for me to pull out now. "I don't know what you want from me. God knows I'm trying to get laid the right way. Now that you've wasted your own body you have to go after mine. I suppose you won't be satisfied 'til I wind up barefoot and pregnant, all spaced out and herbal as you."

I turned my face to avoid her hand, her several hands, that seemed to reproduce themselves as they lashed out at me. You could unleash your inhibitions. You could flirt with a woman. You could fuck with a man. You could give it and take it, play a little dirty, get knocked up along the way. But nothing ever seemed to be enough to please that fat, ratty whore hag nesting in the back of the brain. I couldn't dodge it anymore. I gave in and let her hit me—only by that time, she'd lost the rage.

"Just remember, sister," Sonia said, turning back to the stove. "You missed your chance. Now it's your fantasy, not mine."

And then I recognized the warm paste between my legs, the spicy smell that wasn't curry: I'd fallen off the roof again, braved the odds, taken my chances, and landed safely one more time.

Of course, maybe she calculated wrong, maybe there was never a fetus wrapped like lentil burger in a cabbage leaf, maybe it wasn't possible to live with another woman, maybe it was all in my mind.

After I felt the loose change start seeping through my bikini under-pants, I went into the backyard and sat on the porch, bleeding a tie-dye pattern onto my party dress. I had to stitch the lace back together every damn time I wore it and I had no plans to put the thing on ever again. The weather was warmer now. A strong wind shook sense into the bushes, made the drainpipes clatter against the walls of the house. I smelled the curry on my fingers. I felt a tic along my jawbone, like the sweet glitch in guitar music that tells you this is it: real, live, unsynthe-sized. I heard a key change in the house behind me. I saw a white flash in the yard. Maybe there was still a chance for Her and me. Next time, I'd be ready.

Galpal's Cribnotes to Pregnancy

alfway through life's Stairmaster routine, we must've grown bored of our perfect figures, our low or high-powered careers with their prestige perks or cute accessories, two-hour lunches, five-alarm orgasms, and three-night stands. Because we all wound up pregnant within six months of one another. Ten little galpals, knocked up all in a row. Ten little galpals, how do your knockers grow? Beady snagged her investment banker; Agnes landed the barracuda who'd been keeping her on the line since the last recession; Allison gave up dating musicians for the greater good of the gene pool. Sarah, who'd been married since well before her first leg wax, took her husband on a Caribbean cruise and pumped up the inflatable bikini bra top. Ramona lost at Russian roulette with a sheepskin condom and a reversible vasectomy. Brooke and Nina gave into peer pressure. Heather and Elise fell afoul of hormones. And me, just say I realized that I wasn't going to be a B-movie babette forever and launched myself into the next phase of hooterdom with as much panache as I could muster.

What we learned almost immediately is that husbands are a necessary accessory to motherhood—none of us is the type to do without. But when it comes to support, what you really need is a good nursing bra and a choice selection of galpals on your automatic dial. Husbands have limited sympathy for aching nipples and swollen ankles—in fact, if you have swelling in any area whatsoever and you'd like to maintain an active sex life into your third trimester, I wouldn't point it out. Husbands have a limited vocabulary of soothing phrases and helping verbs. What they like best, when you complain, is to go out and buy something truly worthless at the hardware store. Go ahead, let him assemble that three-tier entertainment center or industrial swing set. It will give you a little private time to call up your favorite galpal and indulge in some heavy-belly-aching on the phone.

It came to me at Lamaze class, as I looked through a forest of swollen ankles, full body pillows, and varicose veins. A med student to my left. An attorney to my right. On the ceiling, a pastel poster of the female anatomy—colors not a one of us would be caught dead in. On the floor, a footing chart from the ballroom dance course that met the hour before. Behind my head, my husband's indigestion gurgled in a white noise of general anxiety. In front of me, the instructor slid into a pelvic tilt with well-oiled ease, leering like a dominatrix in her leopard skin leotard. There was no way out—that's the thing about pregnancy. So who do you choose to get you through? My husband's leg began to jiggle, like it does when he's about to reach the far side of his attention span and pull out the cell phone. My back and bladder met in a tango of desperation. Then a tube of fluorescent lighting bent toward me, buckling back and forth until I saw it detach from its setting and land like a halo on Ramona's frizzy auburn head as she rushed through the door in her faux fur, fifteen minutes late as usual.

Ramona is my idol; she can reach orgasm in under three minutes, whether the guy's cooperating or not. She can plan a dinner party with the leftovers in your refrigerator and make a hairdo out of spit. When she got pregnant by a visiting client from Budapest, she called in every boyfriend on her rolodex and interviewed them for fatherhood, dangling her real estate and stock options in front of their aquiline and Roman noses. Then she chose the only one she hadn't slept with, thinking at least he'd never feel like he'd been deceived. Now he comes home early every Friday to take little Raymond to play group—so you go figure it out.

"Not the pelvic thrust again," Ramona whispered in my ear, "That sleaze would do it with every one of our husbands, if she had the chance. Hell, she'd do it with a ginseng root. The only thing natural about her is her b.o., which smells suspiciously like sulphur, if you ask me."

She's right, you know. If I'm going to trust anyone, it's not the Lamaze lizard and it's not the man who fathered my firstborn, no matter how sweet he looks at 3 A.M. chugging Maalox in his boxers and shouting cut the theatrics, you bastard, at the bassinet. For one hundred per cent loyalty, it's Ramona and the gals like her who make the final cut. These notes are cribbed from their pregnancies and dedicated right back at you.

Because maybe you're not lucky enough to have an Agnes or a Ramona in your life. So, galpals far and wide, here's the program. No lectures, no science, no family values or feminist rap. Just a straight-up cheat sheet from some gals who're in a position to know.

Month One: Conception. And they wonder why girls have math anxiety. All that counting backwards and forwards makes a galpal dizzy. I don't know about you, but all the figures I've ever known go out of my head when I'm about to ovulate. For you teenagers out there with regular 28-day cycles, it's not necessarily a problem. But after a decade or two of hard dating and heavy pill use, your guess is as good as mine. Certain granola sources will suggest that you learn to recognize your time of month by smell, testing your love nest with a finger like a lucky cake batter. But we're going to go out on a limb here and recommend you just give in and buy a kit. Although one galpal we know swears by cold medication to speed the process along.

Once you're sure you're cooking, it's a question of getting the H-man to comply. Now we realize you've never had trouble with him in this area before, but trust me, once you call game time, the best of them will choke, stall, and time-out you to death, or menopause, whichever comes first. Consider Nina, who hadn't initiated foreplay in years, her guy was so overeager. When her number came up, she just plunked it open on the computer console and said hey babe, I'm ready for your investment. Well, once her lawfully wedded learned that something was required of him, he suddenly developed a keen interest in star gazing and internet smut.

"You think you're doing the nasty and then it's shop class or something," he told her. "All this emphasis on constructive fun. Anyway, it's the ultimate end of your personal ambitions. Like, give it up for the next generation, if you want to enter your genetic code here."

She finally got him, months later, when he came home trashed on smart drugs and forgot to check his calendar watch.

"Not smart enough," she said, and went out to charge her maternity wardrobe.

Then there's always the matter of confirming your suspicions. Sarah was so sure she went through three pregnancy kits before she got a positive. Meanwhile, she dogged her husband, her brother-in-law, the mailman and the dog, asking everyone she came across, is it pink or is it blue? Ramona skipped a meeting to run out to the drugstore for a reliable peestick and bumped into her boss in the family planning aisle. Needless to say, it wasn't an appropriate moment to discuss maternity leave. And I looked up from a half eaten jar of peanut butter to realize I hadn't had PMS in five weeks and wasn't faking it anymore when laughing at my husband's jokes.

Keep in mind, this is the easy part. From here on in, you'll need a guide.

Month Two: Morning Sickness, let's face it, is a euphemism. Call it noontime nausea, call it afternoon indigestion, call the six-week flu. The only difference is when you disentangle yourself from a hot embrace with your toilet, you don't feel any relief, and you know you'll be back and dialing your dinner up again before the next meal. If your poison is something as avoidable as pizza or caviar, so much the better. But for some galpals, the offending flavor is Evian, whole wheat bread or air. It can even be something inedible, like your favorite television program or perfume. Every time Beady turned to the home shopping network, she'd get a tremor of nausea, starting with a little fizzle of gas under her breastbone, nothing more than a champagne *frisson,* and accelerating to a true rotgut burr in the bowels. At first, she thought it was just shame, since she'd always prided herself on her great taste in department store markdowns and designer fire sales. But with morning sickness, let's just say she wasn't getting out much, and she had to feed her addiction with whatever was readily available twenty feet or less from the throne. One day, Ramona was over, and the two of them were munching pastel wedding mints and cackling over a silk cami, mimicking the saleswoman in more and more exaggerated lisps and purrs, until they reached for their cell phones simultaneously and threw up wedding confetti all over the green velvet chaise lounge.

"No more," Ramona told me. "That's positively the last time I let her tempt me. From now on in it's water biscuits and public TV for me."

Still, morning sickness is the first real indication of the discomforts of pregnancy, and once you cross the great river of ralph, you won't be coming back any time soon. Look at it this way, it prepares you for the indigestion which will be your constant companion all through your perilous journey. Or look at it again, this isn't even close to the worst that you could do.

Month Three: Appetites return, and I mean all of them, with interest. One day, Galpal Allison was at the Whole Foods with her sister, when the check-out girl asked her, she said: "What do you crave?"

World peace—personal domination—a night with Kurt Cobain in an opium parlor in Amsterdam in the hereafter. The checker looked like Madonna with a nose ring and a few extra pounds. She was trying to be friendly.

"For me, it was sour balls. That and burritos with little candy sprinkles. I had to eat them every day, in this certain preestablished order, then wash it all down with chocolate soda. Either that or I couldn't sleep. So, what about you? What do you crave?"

Allison couldn't even begin to tell her. The things she'd put her husband through, he'd never look at her the same way again.

But at least he cooperated, girls. A husband's erotic response to pregnancy is something like his reaction to lesbian sex. It's a stop or it's a go, and there's not much fudging in between. If your guy's a positive, work in the whoopee now while you can, because once the baby's born, you may never get lucky again. But if he's like my sweet no-extra-meat man, just buy a spousal equivalent attachment for your electric massager and stock up on the mud pie ice cream.

Month Four: Skin Discoloration. It happens to the best of us, the blondes, the brunettes, the redheads, natural and otherwise. An amber mask of freckles for pale Ramona. A spray of lavender pimples for Sarah. Pearly stretch marks like love decals on Brooke and Allison. A long line of kohl down Heather's belly to match the buttons going down her back.

Melanin the likes of which us white girls have never seen.

Or—as my loved one asked me—is that your neck that's spreading or is it your moles?

Forget makeup. Forget a flattering haircut. Forget forgiving underwear.

Remember to take photos at ten paces and keep your compact mirror in your bag, where it belongs.

Month Five: Quickening. They don't mean your tennis game, either, or your wits. As the baby moves more, you move slower, and less. Now something's definitely happening down there, though it may be difficult at first to distinguish between life and indigestion. By now, your jeans don't fit, but your sweatpants still do. Your belly is roughly the size it would be if you'd let yourself completely go—but then, you're still recognizable. Your breasts are the ones you dreamed of at thirteen, that means a B for a pixie like Ramona and a lucky D for me. You've reached the apex of pregnancy. Go out with your galpal and drink a sloppy mixed drink—just one now, for the road.

Also, it's not bad to have solid evidence after all these months of special pleading. Every time Elise felt a leap, she'd reach for her husband's paw and apply pressure firmly. But the little bugger—you can be sure he was a boy—ducked and dodged down to the bottom of the uterus, only bobbing up again when the coast was clear, in the locker room, say, or at the mall. At this point in our pregnancies, Ramona got her kicks by challenging me to kick counts in the health club pool with the embarrassed teenage life guard for a referee, his left hand over his whistle and the thick blonde fingers of his right lodged in her baby fat. She seemed to be enjoying herself, offering up her little fanny pack of pudge while I was suffering the sorrows of the damned, letting a hard body prod me in that condition.

Month Six: Braxton-Hicks. Yes, month six and you're still nesting. We were too. Then Agnes calls from the spa, she says she's going into labor, can we meet her at the hospital? As it turns out, these are what they call practice contractions, Braxton-Hicks, Ramona says knowingly, like it's a designer no one else has heard of. Don't worry—it's late for miscarriage and early for premature labor.

"Since when do you savvy all the jargon?" Agnes says, and then

Ramona makes a mysterious face and comes out with her story about a teenage pregnancy, a miscarriage in her twenties, an emergency D & C.

Agnes raises what's left of her plucked eyebrow; Heather straightens her little purse strap and pulls at her lip.

Watching Ramona rope off a section of her hair, the way she does when she wants to be emphatic. I feel the jarring start at the top of my uterus and shimmy down along the sides. It's a sensation too experimental for pain, but it reminds me of what I'm going to suffer. I'm carrying all my emotional baggage right out in front, carrying high and wide and pigeon-toed. Meanwhile Ramona's barely showing; it makes a galpal wonder what else she's keeping to herself.

Month Seven: Swelling. The true lower hell of pregnancy. Of course, there's the obvious punch bowl belly. But no one tells you about the fingers like sausage rolls, the doughy ankles, the water chestnut cheeks, the bulbous aching breasts. Sarah's husband had a bet that she could make it to 180—his old wrestling weight. But at least she was spared the indignity of outweighing her mate. I wasn't so lucky, I had to give up wearing the breadwinner's trophy shirts and pass them down to Ramona, who'd accessorize with huge Andalusian scarves and shell necklaces while I tagged along in the pastel parachute sack of the week.

Here's the moment for your Lamaze class, if you're so inclined, although we all agree that a really good massage session is a better use of your time. In our section, we learned a whole car pool of terms: *Braxton-Hicks, episiotomy, effacement.* We went through the motions of natural childbirth, but if you looked closely, you could see that people were barely moving their lips or hips. Our favorite word was *epidural*; we couldn't get through a breathing exercise without cracking up.

"Pant and blow," Ramona said. "It sounds like a porno technique."

"Come over here and try it," my husband suggested, and my focal point leapt right off the wall.

Month Eight: Lightening. Three weeks later, my baby almost dropped when I heard the news: Ramona was contacting the daughter she'd given up for adoption, at this late date. It seems that passing through the process again brought up all kinds of stray emotions. Of course, this is a time in your pregnancy when you will feel desperate, you will be tempted to make irrational decisions like changing your therapist or cutting your hair. Anything to make you feel lighter, to make you believe that you won't be in this state forever, or until your laugh lines melt into your family jowls. This is an impulse you must—I repeat, must—firmly resist. It's true Allison bought a Ferrari and Nina moved in with her mother-in-law. I even called up a former fan or two, just to get in some flirtation before I was completely through. But I knew Ramona had gone too far when I walked into her condo and found her sitting in an empty bathtub in her electric curlers and maternity camisole, a box of red hots in the soap tray in front of her, a shoe box of old papers and photographs in the memory of her lap.

"Shit," she said, "They make us abandon our children, they make us forsake our ideals, they make us shag our girlfriends and shoot our youth."

I knelt on the tiles and pulled a dismembered baby picture out of her hand. "Just who do you have in mind?" I said, and then a trap door opened in my uterus and I felt the bastard slip.

Month Nine: Delivery. It's the story everyone wants to tell: Elise's water breaking in the post office, Nina's two hours of pushing, Agnes with her last-minute caesarian, Brooke's bum epidural, Sarah's scare with neonatal distress. So try to pay attention, no matter how it hurts, gals, because you'll want to remember the gory details for baby books and cocktail parties later on. Either that or just hand over your diary to the couch coach let him take the notes for a change.

As it turned out, Ramona started in her sleep, kicked off by an imaginary orgasm. Then the real horror show began. Twenty hours of labor and she wouldn't even discuss pain management. Nurses and interns filed in and out rolling their eyes. Shifts changed and doctor's orders shifted. The poor designated H-man stood by the window, his Lakers T-shirt tie-dyed in his own sweat and a cup of ice melting in his hand. We called around and organized a round robin to keep a constant vigil in the hospital room.

"This time," Ramona said, her face paler than the pillow and her hair climbing the empty I.V. pole, "I want to really feel it when I'm getting screwed." She didn't breathe so much as hiss.

In the next six hours, she cursed us comprehensively. At four centimeters, she called Sarah a coward for marrying the first man who'd take her orders and give her head. At five centimeters, she predicted that Allison would wind up a bitter old nymphomaniac, sucking off faux garage bands in their panelled suburban basements. At five and a half, she questioned Beady's taste in home furnishings and Elise's taste in men. At five and three quarters, she claimed Agnes had had so many abortions her parts were perforated like a Ritz cracker and here she was, still laying on the cheese. Six, seven, and eight revealed, in that order, Brooke's thick ankles, Heather's bulimia, Nina's shady business deals. "And you," she said to me, just before she was completely effaced, "Just how long are you willing to live in a state of pure contempt?"

When there was nothing left to say, she finally opened her legs and pushed. We held our breath through the forever between each long hyphenated grunt—no one had to teach us how to do that. Then little Raymond was born, fierce and skinny and purple, patches of auburn hair on his arms and head, and tiny sideburns stretching practically down to his chin.

Six days later, when it was my turn, I wasn't having any of the nonsense. I got them to strip me right then and there and paint up my spine for the epidural. As the anesthesiologist slipped in the needle, I gripped onto my husband's chest hair and pulled. He gave off a sweet smell— candy corn over sulphur—so strong that I gagged with a distant memory of morning swill. "Listen," I said. If we ever do this again, big fellow, you're going to have to skip the cologne."

Month Ten: Letdown Afterwards, you come out on the other side of the world. You're bleeding, leaking, sagging and stinking. Your uterus hangs there like an empty windsock; people keep sauntering into your hospital room to give it another good poke. If you didn't know before that you're an animal, you'll know it now.

Three to five days after delivery, your milk comes in. That's roughly the period for postpartum depression, or baby blues, as they call it in the funny papers. The term for both is letdown, gals. When your breasts harden up like silicone implants and your baby cries an endless high-pitched busy signal because it can't get a hold on the poor crimped nipple, let the sperm donor do something useful, send him out for a pump and then stand under the showerhead massaging those hooters until they give, until they drip, until they weep for everything they've been through and everything that's bound to occur to them.

Once the baby's at the breast again, you'll have time to reflect. She clings to you like a galpal. Whatever happens, she's the one you'll have to protect.

Evacuation Route

argie was one of the lucky ones who had regular orgasms, and with her own husband, at that. Every time she closed her eyes, tensed her thigh muscles, and jumped over the gate, there'd be something else to meet her:

A pinwheel
A jeep with 4-wheel drive
A relish tray spinning on a lazy Susan
A paint box filled with nothing but different versions of the color blue.

Jay got to the point where he'd ask, leaning back on his elbow and stroking her long, odalisque's stomach with the same gesture he used to dip his hand into the wooded stream that divided their property from the Norris'.

"Well, what'd you see this time, Pook?"

He was keeping a list, hidden in an old dented beer keg left over from Margie's unsuccessful days of home brewing and stored at the back of the toolshed. Margie bragged to me about it later on. She was scarcely literate herself, though no one could find her lacking in intelligence. She just preferred to use a middle man—or in my case—woman, that's all.

So when she asked me to relay her life experience in the enclosed volume, there was considerable labor involved. Margie wasn't an easy subject. She backtracked, she digressed, she grandstanded; she bragged and haggled and exaggerated in operatic style. She had no concept of the demands of formal prose. Her own father, the mayor of Kerbeyville for twenty-four years, had never written down a single one of his speeches. But no one in town could forget his Kudzu Conspiracy against the Confederacy Theory, or his protest when they brought in the nuclear power plant from up North and sat it down right next to the Trent Powell National Park. Signs appeared on every curve of the winding road that vamped its unsteady way, spilling Spanish Moss at every opportunity, through Kerbeyville: Evacuation Route.

"That's about right," Mayor Kemp countered. "That's what Sherman said too. Isn't anyone else tired of being the large intestine of the Union Blue?"

Apparently not, because, by the time Margie started getting restless, most of the 2,000 members of the incorporated township were employed by the Southern Lights Nuclear Power Plant, and the Spanish Moss had grown to embrace it too. Residents even began to attribute the peculiar beauty and fertility of the local women to the fumes and radiation emanating from the eerie white tower, its shape as lovely and elaborate as a great aunt's antique perfume atomizer on the horizon. Kerbeyville girls had a certain mango lustre to their skin, a hue easily distinguished from the sunburn and acne bread pudding of outlying regions, and their hair, in fine ponytails, if blonde, in heavy buns and braids and sailor's love knots, if brunette, gleamed with otherworldly highlights, as if they had universal access to some well-tended chlorine pool. Although, in fact, the closest municipal facility was over fifty miles' distance. Kerbeyville women were even riper, if possible. The average family size was verging on six, at last census. But Margie, with ten living descendants at the age of thirty-eight, was the most prolific of citizens.

This, in itself, does not account for her visions. But, as Margie confided, over *uva ursa* herb tea in my Arizona town house, the hallucinations began with her first pregnancy and increased in frequency with every parturition. Pleasure, like labor, requires muscle tone. Visions aren't for the narrow-hipped, as I've learned in the twenty years it's taken me to accommodate, assimilate, sort, describe, and publish the series of extrasensory visitations I received at the lip of my thirtieth birthday, not in childbirth, I remind you, but at the height of a rare and extreme incident of toxic shock syndrome.

Margie wasn't particularly sympathetic when she first heard about my case, standing in her living-room folding clothes, the ten different sizes of 100% cotton underwear, exclusive of decoration, with racing stripes and superheroes and lace, the sunsuits and bodysuits and team T-shirts, the horrible orgy of socks. The oldest daughter had forgotten her chores again, to go down to the creek with her best friend—who knew what they did down there—but Margie had been visualizing condom wrappers, acorn caps, and tiny twigs stuck in the sweet skin of her teenage daughter's back and buttocks, the dainty white loaves that should be covered, at all times, by at least a swimsuit.

Margie wasn't ready to be a grandmother yet, she thought, as she fingered the green prewashed silk blouse she'd bought herself the last time she and Jay had taken off for a weekend in New Orleans, and she'd seen recurrent flashes of rain forest, as if she was flipping through a photo album too quickly to identify location or plant species. She arranged the blouse on the back of the sofa and looked across the room. The television was on, and a woman with oddly cut hair, girlish on one side, womanly on the other, and a fierce orange suit, crossed her legs and propped a black and yellow book up on her exposed knee.

"I see," she said. "Can you explain your title, 'Celebration'?"

The camera panned to the author on the other side of the coffee table, a chrome plane that had no clothes folded on top of it, no pop cans or art projects or coffee rings—just two ceramic cups sitting in awful certainty.

When the lens centered on the long nose, the cheek pouches, the turquoise beachcomber's eyes caught in a fishnet of wrinkles, something shifted in Margie's gut. It was a falling sensation, like the onset of ovulation. She touched the back of the sofa, then rummaged her other hand up under her patchwork appliqued sweatshirt. Her stomach was warm and lumpy. Not again, she thought.

I was in my outer-directed mode that day, made up in the studio, so that I was actually visible. Part of my theory is that we disappear, for all practical purposes, as we age. First our secondary sex characteristics, breast and buttocks, diminish into obscurity, then the contours of our faces melt away. Finally, the legs lose their clay palpability, and we're just stranded up here floating in air. Our eyes tend to linger to the end, however, trick mirrors haunting even the youngest and most scornful of men: do we see them, do we see them, and don't we want to stay?

I flicked the microphone fastened to my silver squash blossom neck-lace and addressed the young woman's aggressive knee, though I was fair-ly sure she would not be able to comprehend my philosophy: "Celebra-tion has a riotous meaning in our culture. When we think about celebrating, we're likely to imagine someone drinking or drugging or womanizing themselves into insensibility. But when I use the word I mean something else: the satisfaction of the inner festival that comes with celibacy."

There was a collective shiver in the studio audience, and the inter-viewer recrossed her legs, so that her pelvis downshifted at an uncom-fortable angle, one hip barely touching the mod mauve chair. Damn, when will they get these television personalities to read? Of course, there's not much time left for that sort of thing between the workouts, the face lifts, the wardrobe-fittings and manicures. I know because I've researched the operation, and this woman's schedule would make a mystic's regimen look like slothful ease.

At home, Margie clicked her tongue. She knew the word from her Catholic upbringing. But she'd never heard a secular woman talking about it so happily on television before, and wasn't sure whether she approved. Celibacy. It did sound beautiful, the way the woman with the cracked pepper voice said it, like a girl's name, or a Christmas basket wrapped in cellophane.

Margie decided she was tired. She walked around the sofa, pushed aside the bicycle helmet that had passed from son to son and had now settled on the unathletic third, and sat down for maybe the second time that day. Her legs ached like a frayed fan belt. Maybe she should give in and hire a maid for a couple of days a week, as Jay had suggested. They could certainly afford it, with his salary from Southern Lights and the investments she'd inherited from her father. But it didn't suit her to have a stranger handling her laundry or giving her girls ideas.

By this time, I was just reaching the first major refutation of my argu-ment, the amazing historical sleight-of-hand by which woman's sexuali-ty is freed from its chains to a single man's erotic foibles only to become the great undifferentiated energy source for the infrastructure of late cap-italism. The interviewer's violent blue eye started twitching. Contact trou-ble. I was about to be interrupted again.

"I'm sure our viewers will want to see how you work that out in your book. But for now, we need to take a commercial break. Stay with us, folks. We're here interviewing Julie Norwood, the infamous bad boy of the feminist movement, about her new book *Celebration,* and her return to traditional values."

Margie was fairly sure she'd never heard of me, and now she knew why. I was a feminist, a person with bad apple breath and a rough complexion left over from a bumpy adolescence, someone who didn't like weddings or baby showers, lace bras or party shoes, and wanted to make sure no one else had a good time either.

However, her reaction couldn't have been worse than mine when I heard that interviewer deliver her smug little sound bites, tight and artificial as the two-bit tucks of her ass. Which, incidentally, wagged at me with impunity while she turned away to get wardrobe's help with the contact.

I didn't get a chance to protest until we were back on the air and she was beaming the replacement at me—one green eye, and one blue.

"Julie, I think I speak for the rest of the nation when I express my curiosity about this change in your position. Can you tell us a little about the personal experiences that led you to your current views?"

"Well, Vicki, I feel that I will only disappoint the nation's curiosity. I didn't OD on heroin or Valium, attend the Betty Ford Clinic, have a breast implant go bad on me, or catch my husband in a compromising position in the hot tub with my gay hairdresser. I didn't forget about the snooze button on my biological alarm clock or get a wake-up call from my latent lesbian tendencies. I just made a thorough study of the circumstances of women's lives, material and spiritual, and arrived at my conclusions."

Vicki's face fell open, so I could finally see the woman behind the screen image: an Iowa farm girl who loved her Daddy, loved her own strong legs, loved winning blue ribbons so much she just couldn't stop, and ran right into the Moloch's mouth of the patriarchy, or the New York Media Establishment. She wrinkled her forehead and turned to the Teleprompter.

"Isn't it true that you say you had a vision, or some sort of conversion experience?"

I flexed my fingers and gathered my voice up into the old lady hush I reserve for these occasions.

"When I was younger, I was a feminist guerilla," I said. "I laid every figurehead I came across. I took my shirt off at protest rallies. I worked on the editorial staff of *Ball* magazine. I cock-teased rock stars until they gave E.R.A. and pro-choice endorsements. I played Hamlet in the nude in a Shakespeare In the Park production, where they made Ophelia pull the rue and rosemary out of his pubic hairs, so that he was just about bald by the time of the cast party, when we finally consummated. I wrote a book called *Drag Queens and Dust Bunnies,* which, for those of you who are more recent on the scene, revolutionized Western thought on the subject of women, consumption, and production. Am I finished yet? Am I running out of time?"

Vicki nodded, and I went on.

At Margie's, a middle daughter charged into the living room, followed by a younger son. She had a baseball, he had a bat, and they were both smeared with dirt, and engrossed in argument.

"No yodeling in the house, you yahoos," Margie said. "Go ask Jeff to umpire. My story's just getting to the good part."

Donna tossed the ball back to her brother, barely missing the clay angel one of her sisters had just brought home from Sunday school. "Yeah, is this the one where you can't figure out which of these old ladies is that bitchy model's mother?"

"No, doll, this is a talky show. You don't watch this one."

"Oh. Jeff said it's out. But it didn't even touch the catalpa tree."

"Then I guess you've got to choke up and play it over."

"Play it over? Play it over? Red rover, red rover, make Donna eat clover. They never play over in the pros." Randy collapsed onto the clean clothes, disgusted with the girls' rules he always had to go by at home. A disgust which I predict will root in him, and flower seasonally, with every disappointment, reminding him of the pale showy flowers of the catalpa, their cloying smell like stewing apples, and the white flurry of sisters standing between him and the great game of hardball that he wants to join as soon as possible but which gets farther and farther away as he grows.

The next night, when Jay came in from his Rotary Club meeting and rotated Margie around the covers, over, under, loop-the-loop, she didn't feel what she usually felt. The pleasure teased at her skin, like needles of lukewarm water when too many family members had taken their showers before her. She didn't even want to be reminded of the steam. But when her husband clenched underneath her and squinted his long, blue eyes as if he was sighting pigeons in the sun, she skidded into the place where the orgasm was supposed to happen, a swan's neck dip in the road. But there was nothing there. Just a layer of sweat, grit in her eye, a handful of gravel tossed toward her pelvis. Nothing.

Jay reached up and rubbed her back. "How are you doing there? You look like you want to join the circus."

"Well, hey to you too, partner." she said. "I didn't think you were ever going to notice."

"So what've I been doing here? Watching the NFL?"

"You might as well. Maybe I want to know what happened at your hot dog meeting. Maybe I want to tell you which one of your kids cracked my corn today. But you'd rather just rearrange my bones."

Jay ran his hands down her arms. "Such pretty bones, though. They can't wait to get hold of them at that field museum in New Orleans."

"Jay, did you ever hear of a woman just getting tired of that?"

"What?"

"That sweet talky taffy you always come out with."

"You're not wanting to start a business again, are you? Remember what happened with the beer."

"That was only because of the water. Blame it on your damn Yankee spook house. Anyway, that's not what I meant."

"You want me to help more with the chores, right? Tell you what, I'll take off work early Friday and clean out the garage."

"Forget it, soldier," Margie said, and threw her leg back to twist off him, a gesture that's grown familiar through generations of gymnasts on the uneven parallel bars. But it still thrills me, every time I imagine the dismount. The weight shifting from one arm to the other. The jiggle of the bar or bed beneath her. The moment of suspension before the fall.

"Well, what new and exciting miracle of love did you see tonight?" he finally asked.

Margie claims that this was the first time she ever lied to him, at least about something so important. She straightened out her breasts and stalled for time. Then she just had to settle for the first thing that landed. "A monster dust bunny," she said. "Rolling around the floor like a big old tumbleweed."

In the following weeks, Margie told more lies than she can remember. She lied about the heavy flat package that arrived from New Orleans. She lied about the long-distance phone calls to New York and Arizona. But worst of all were the things she didn't know how to lie about, the visions that had escaped the bedroom and tumbled around the house at random, with radioactive ease. The glowing azalea in her baby's ear when she went to apply the Q-tip. The lumps of raw hamburger that kept showing up in the carpet sweepings, in the folds of the morning paper, on her plate. The squash blossom necklace in the silverware drawer. The ring of fire that settled periodically around the catalpa tree, and the tiny wax faces melting in the upper blooms.

She left before any of the children woke, before she had to encounter Jay again, or feel the lip of the day curve over her head, encasing her in its relentless samba rhythm. But before she went, she set life in motion one more time. She threw out the coffee grounds, started a new pot, swept up the cracker crumbs from the kitchen floor, and packed lunches for all the children, even though she'd assigned away this responsibility long ago.

In each, she included a party napkin with a note written in red ink: "Ignore Billy Hinton. Gap teeth will make you a model one day. See you in the magazines—Mom." "Put one over third plate for me. Sometimes girls' rules get you furthest. Remember your Mama." "Dr. Martin will fit you with a diaphragm whenever you're ready. The more rubber the better, as far as I'm concerned. Don't start 'til you're ready. Don't let him stop 'til you're through. Best wishes, Margie." For the baby, who couldn't read yet, she just left a box of animal crackers taped to picture of a woman in a red car, her vehicle trailing shoes and tin cans and streamers like a bridal getaway. In one corner was a family group, a critical mass seeking balance, the shortest child standing in front and waving a racing flag in his brief arms.

As she stuffed her suitcase into the back seat, she imagined each child sent off into the world, opening his or her soft brown lunch sack like a fortune cookie, a destiny wrapped in their mother's flesh. The morning was cool and damp, making her feel like a girl sent off by her own mother, draped in the blue travelling cloak she'd bought especially for the trip, along with one of the safari-type pants outfits she thought she'd need for Arizona. She drove by the power plant, smug and soft-core behind its veil of morning mist, and winced as she passed each marker on the evacuation route. She thought of her father buried in the local cemetery between markers three and four, the strange entailments and entitlements of his political life sprouting in colorful mutations from his ears, beard, and fingertips. How could she have lived for so long in a place where she was constantly reminded that she'd have to leave, and probably under disagreeable, if not completely fatal, circumstances?

As she drove straight down the gullet of the Mississippi, she thought of all the times she'd driven that direction with Jay, his hand on the inner curve of her thigh, and Margie convinced she was moving closer to something: the land getting flatter, rolling out like the thinnest possible pie crust, while the air turned wet and groggy, and the sky washed through every shade of salt water taffy, its clouds pulled into pearly stretch marks by the gulls. Then she understood why the sailors used to think they could drop off the edge of the earth; she even sympathized with them some. But she was more impatient than that now. This was like reaching down a child's throat for the offending chicken bone. It was an emergency, and she wouldn't stop until she got there, wouldn't stop until she found me and shook me and made me see:

watch on a windowsill

a pile of red wood chips

a half-open catalpa blossom in a painted china saucer

a row of irradiated daughters awaiting her return.